# PERSPECTIVE
# OF
# MATTER

## David C. Fletcher

A Wise Grey Owl Publication

First Published in Great Britain by Wise Grey Owl Limited 2009

Copyright © 2009 David Charles Fletcher

1

This book is copyright under the Berne Convention. All rights reserved. No part of this publication may be reproduced, stored in a retrieval system, or transmitted in any form or by any means without the prior permission of D C Fletcher, nor by otherwise circulated in any form of binding or cover other than that in which it is published and without a similar condition being imposed on the subsequent purchaser.

ISBN 978-0-9561574-1-6

All characters, with the exception of Einstein, Podolsky, Rosen, Dirac and Chandler whose characters are not elaborated, are fictitious and any resemblance to real persons, alive or dead, is purely coincidental. The names, incidents, dialogue and opinions expressed are products of the author's imagination and are not to be construed as real. Nothing is intended to be interpreted as expressing or representing the views of any institution, company, government, university or academy.

Published by Wise Grey Owl Limited

www.wisegreyowl.co.uk

Farthings, Main Street, Staveley, Knaresborough,

North Yorkshire, HG5 9LD

Publish@wisegreyowl.co.uk

# PERSPECTIVE OF MATTER

*For Helen*

# Author's note

I would like to express my thanks to my lovely wife and all my loyal friends who have read the numerous drafts and patiently told me what they think.

I would also like to thank you for buying my book. I hope you find it entertaining and although it has been created out of my imagination, I have tried to make the science and the story as plausible as possible. I apologise in advance to any purist, who may find some of my theory is at variance with accepted knowledge. In the last analysis the book is a novel. All of the protagonists are made up, but I cannot say the same for all of the science. It is amazing what happens when you fiddle with the velocity of gravity. Who knows perhaps you can!

# Contents

Part One        Yakawa
Part Two        Crystals at Dawn
Part Three      Rocking the World

# Part One

# Yakawa

# Yi

# Cheng He

'Hello little brother,' said Jiao, looking out over the prow of the ship, 'Isn't it peaceful?'

Zihao stood next to her quietly. He never had much to say. She knew that behind his silence was an intelligence that was much more advanced than his years. But he was still a child and she loved him deeply. Zihao was four years younger than Jiao and half a foot smaller. He was the eldest male child of Laing T'ing-nan, the head of the Academy of Guangzhou and as such, much would rest on Zihao's young shoulders. Zihao was recalling his unhappiness as his father and tearful mother waved the siblings off at the quay. Zihao could not understand why his parents wanted him to go to Beijing. He was too young to understand the sadness they also felt. Zihao could only see things from a child's perspective. But his father knew it was imperative to obey the Emperor.

Jiao knew that Zihao was as frightened as she was. At the end of their journey, both of them would start new lives. Zihao and Jiao had little understanding of what lay before them, but it was important that they followed their father's wishes. Jiao wanted to comfort her little brother but he was learning to be a man. There were too many eyes on the ship and it would not be seemly to cuddle him.

Even though he was only eight years of age, Zihao had been told that his destiny was in the Emperor's service. This meant he must be properly educated. In Beijing, Zihao would be prepared for entrance to the Han-Lin Academy, the greatest place of learning in the world. He slipped his hand into Jiao's. He was pleased his big sister was with him.

She felt a tiny tremble in his childlike fingers. She squeezed his hand to reassure him and wondered what her new husband would be like. They both looked out towards the direction that held their future.

Chang T'ien-pe'i was the master of the Cheng He. He watched the two children from the stern deck. They looked too young to understand the risks of a long sea journey. Chang was thinking back twenty four hours ago, reflecting on his conversation with their father. Laing T'ing-nan was a very important mandarin in Guangzhou and Chang was greatly honored to have been asked to carry Laing's two children to Beijing. But he did not understand why they could not travel over land.

'I do not wish to sound impertinent, your Excellency,' Chang had asked earlier, 'but I would like permission to ask a question.'

Chang was aware that to challenge a mandarin of Laing T'ing-nan's rank could be unwise, so he had chosen his words carefully.

'Yes, go ahead,' replied Laing T'ing-nan.

'There are barbarians and pirates who operate in the China sea,' said Chang, cautiously. 'The journey to Beijing would be safer over land.'

'I am aware of this,' replied Laing, not unkindly. 'But the over-land journey will take nearly a quarter-year. Jiao must meet her new husband before he takes his new post in the West. The sea voyage can be done in less than thirty-five days. You should arrive ten days before he departs for his new assignment.'

'I understand Excellency,' said Chang.

'I hear you have a son,' said Laing.

'Yes Excellency.'

'So you understand how important it is to me that my children are safe,' said Laing, empathetically.

'Yes, Excellency I do understand. A father's love is strong. My son Lei, is fourteen years of age; one year older than your daughter. He is learning discipline from my crew. One day he will serve the Emperor valiantly.'

'Chang, you are a good father and an excellent sailor. I trust you to look after my legacy,' Laing said dismissing him.

That was before they had put to sea. Chang was proud to be held in such regard. Chang's thoughts returned to the present. He must give the children some guidance about ships. He did not want either of them to fall over board. No time for lessons now though; he was busy piloting his ship out of the river. Chang needed to be close to the rudder. There must be no mistakes. The river could be dangerous. He was not going to allow his ship to run aground on this falling tide, especially not with such an important cargo on board. He was not happy that his two charges were so exposed at the prow of the ship. He would leave them alone for the moment and then bring them aft before the ship entered the open sea. He carried a heavy responsibility ferrying the two of them to Beijing. Their father had put much trust in him. Chang must not, he dare not breach that trust. His thoughts went back to navigation.

Chang's ship was a three-masted Jung-Gorl, or river ship. They had cast off from Guangzhou at the Hour of the Hare. Chang had caught the tide exactly as planned. He hoped he had judged it right. Chang was pleased about his crew's efficiency. They had organized the loading well. There had been only a small load to take on board. Most of the holds were already full with products from the barbarians. These were taken on board earlier, in Macao. He knew that many other captains would also take on opium, an odious substance. He abhorred such immoral profiteering and he would not do this. He had seen the effect on the people of Kwangtung Provence. He was sometimes ashamed of the greed of his fellow merchants. It may make him poorer, but he would not have this filth on his ship. He wondered why the Emperor let it happen. He wondered whether it was indeed what the Emperor wanted, or was it simply to line the pockets of corrupt officials. Chang immediately erased the thought from his mind; even thinking such thoughts was dishonorable. Chang's mind switched back to when the two siblings came on board his ship. He had off loaded some of the cargo in Guangzhou and taken on gold bullion for the onward journey to Beijing. He was curious about the other small wooden box that he was given by one of the Governor's servants. It was to be delivered to the Han-Lin Academy. The box was made of ebony and had a stout lock. He had been told it was a precious stone from a comet, but he could not see how they would know. There had been barbarians' stories last year about a sighting of a bright light in the sky of the southern seas. It was probably just gossip. Barbarian sailors were not honourable and it was impossible to believe anything they said. He felt a steady breeze from the land. The Cheng He would make good headway, helped by the currents of river water returning to the sea.

****

Walt Jefferson was still furious. He was on the quarterdeck of 'Perseverance' waiting for the junk to come out of the Pearl River estuary. Perseverance was standing about two leagues east of Hong Kong, a desolate, deserted island at the mouth of the Pearl River. He expected the junk to take a Northerly heading towards Peking as soon as it arrived at the open sea. He needed to intercept the Chinaman before he tacked because the junk could sail closer to the wind than Perseverance. Although it was unlikely, he did not want to be outrun. Jefferson had been at sea for most of his life. He had seen real action against beasts much more dangerous than this junk. In the Anglo American war he had been part of a gun crew aboard the USS Constitution. He would never forget the elation when the masts of HMS Guerriere crashed to her decks. By God we whopped their goddamn arrogant asses, he thought. In the twelve years since then, he had lost none of his pride. He was now the master of his own merchantman and no Chinaman was going to swindle him out of his fortune. He had off loaded his cargo of cotton and opium in Macao. He did not like dealing with opium, but thanks to the English, it was a profitable trade. He had taken on silk for the next leg of the voyage. It was a better cargo. As was normal he had been working through Portuguese agents and the bargain they had struck included a payment of silver. With all the loading complete the Chinaman had paid only half, saying this was what had been agreed. By the time Jefferson had paid for the silk, he was out of pocket and furious. In the middle of all the negotiation with the agent, he saw a Chinese junk heading up river to Canton. Jefferson did not go into the interior to intercept him because he knew the Chinese authorities would try to impound his ship. Let them try, he thought. But it was not the Chinese navy he was worried about. He did not want to give any Navy a reason to accuse him of breaking treaties. George's Navy frigates were patrolling these waters. He had a grudge with them; they behaved like they owned the world. His thoughts returned to the Chinese junk.

'Look alive there,' he shouted, directing his voice to the top of the mast. 'Keep your eyes peeled to the West.'

'Aye, Cap'n,' came the reply.

Perseverance was a one hundred foot racer class brig. She had ten guns and as the name suggested, she was fast. He knew that Chinese junks were deceptively seaworthy, with shallow draughts designed specifically for these waters. Even so, Jefferson was very confident he could chase one down if he needed to. Besides it would probably never come to that.

****

Chang could see the swell increase as they were about to enter the ocean. He decided it was time to bring his two young guests aft. As they came from such a high-ranking family, he knew it would not be appropriate for him to shout an order to them. So he ordered one of his second in command to have them escorted from their present position. The officer looked around his crew and shouted to Lei, the captain's son.

'Take our guests to their cabin and ensure they are protected until we are safely at sea.'

'Yes, Sir,' came Lei's reply.

Lei was an enthusiastic apprentice officer who was keen to pull his weight. Even though he was the most junior of the ship's officers, the crew knew and liked Lei. He performed his duties diligently and without complaint. His superiors did not discriminate in his favour; in fact his workload was disproportionately tough. He was the Captain's son and this meant he must do his share of the work and more. His father had insisted on this; otherwise how would he learn good discipline? The duty he had just been assigned was unusually light. He made his way towards the bow, where the mandarin's children were standing.

'Pardon my intrusion,' Lei said addressing them together, 'but I must ask you to come back with me to the forecastle.'

'Why?' Zihao asked, a little too arrogantly for an eight year old child.

Lei was surprised by being questioned about the captain's orders. However he knew these were not ordinary children and he must play a long with them.

'Because it may be dangerous here as we enter the swell of the open sea,' he replied, politely.

'Of course,' said Jiao, diplomatically, 'it is for our safety Zihao. We must do as we are asked.'

Jiao glanced up at Lei but shyly avoided eye contact. Lei too averted his eyes from hers.

Lei escorted them to their position further aft and stood a few feet away from so that he could discreetly offer protection to them whilst they were leaving the estuary.

Chang, the captain, was standing on the deck above them. He glanced down to make sure the mandarin's children were safe. He refocused his eyes on the horizon before him. Chang could see the change in colour of the water before him as the river emptied into the ocean. As he strained his eyes he thought he could see two masts directly on the Cheng He's course. Chang moved to a higher position and put a glass to his eye. Yes he was right. A barbarian was waiting just outside the estuary. It seemed to be the American ship that had been unloading cargo in Macao. Why was she waiting there he wondered? He knew there had been some disagreements with the barbarians, but could not believe that they would be stupid enough to blockade Guangzhou.

Chang saw a flash from Perseverance, followed by a bang. The first shot then splashed behind the Cheng He. The barbarian was firing at them! Was that a warning shot, or were the barbarians attempting to sink his ship? Chang quickly considered his options. He could try to out-sail them. He could return to Guangzhou. No he would not run! He would prepare to fight. He ordered his crew to prepare for battle.

Chang ordered his son to take his passengers to safety and guard them in their cabin. Lei asked his charges, in a manner that left no option for disagreement, to go below with him. Jiao and Zihao followed Lei obediently to their cabin below deck. Chang was impressed by the way his son had exercised his authority.

Chang steered to port so that he could use the shallow waters near the island to his advantage. He knew the ships of the barbarians were designed for deeper seas. Chang was now sailing closer to the wind and therefore had lost some headway, but he felt this was his best option. As the Cheng He set its new course, Chang ordered his crew to fire. All their shots fell short. As he soon found out, Cheng He's cannons did not have the range of his opponent's. There were more distant flashes. A cannon ball whistled through the rigging of his ship. One shot hit the fore gaff rig, showering the crew with splinters and bringing down the foresail. Another split the main mast, a section of which came crashing like a battering ram towards the deck below. Below, Jiao, Zihao and Lei heard a deafening bang as part of the mast came crashing though the deck above them. A massive timber had now become wedged against the door imprisoning the three of them in the cabin. Splinters of wood were scattered like deadly arrows all around the cabin. One of these had pierced Zihao's thigh and blood was oozing out of the wound. Jiao screamed for help. No one came. She pulled at the splinter. Zihao bit back a scream. The splinter came free. Now blood was pumping out of Zihao's wound. Lei jumped towards Zihao and applied pressure to stem the bleeding. He shouted to Jiao to tear up bedclothes. Jiao and Lei bound the wound. Zihao had fainted. Lei felt his pulse; he was alive. There was a huge bang as a cannon ball blasted its way through the hull into the cabin. More debris and splintered wood filled the air. Water was flooding through the hole left by the iron ball. The ball continued on its trajectory and collided with the remains of the ships mast. The ship was listing. Lei saw daylight through an opening in the timbers above them. The impact of the cannon ball had shifted the remains of the mast. Lei realised they must get out of the cabin before they drowned. He ordered Jiao through first. He pushed her towards the hole in the deck above. Jiao struggled through the opening. She turned back to help Zihao, who had regained consciousness, through the opening. Lei was lifting him from below. Zihao was free. The ship's list increased. The mast moved and blocked Lei's escape. Water was filling the compartment below. Jiao heard his last words.

'Father help me!' pleaded Lei, as he sank beneath the water. But his father could not hear.

As she cradled her brother in her arms, Jiao felt helpless. She looked around her. One of Chang officers was pinned to the deck screaming; his leg appeared to have been severed. The ship was listing to starboard, so the gun ports on the offensive side were pointing into the water. The Cheng He could not return fire. A cannon had rolled back over one of the gun crews and one sailor was pinned, his pelvis crushed; his blood oozing through the gunwales. His shipmates were trying to free him. There was chaos all about her. Chang was giving orders to his crew to cut away the rigging and get the mast overboard.

Jaio looked down at her little brother. At first she saw him cough then there was the blood around his lips. It was then that she saw the wound in his back. A plaintive cry was buried beneath the ambient noise. It was the sound of a young girl wailing in grief.

As Jefferson boarded the stricken ship he and his crew were well armed. He had no sympathy for these people; they had tried to swindle him. The Chinese crew were soon subjugated. The Master of the junk held Jefferson's eye with revulsion and hatred. But the junk's crew was under armed guard and he was no threat. As Jefferson looked around, he realised he had gone too far. As one of Jefferson's crew was a Cantonese speaker he asked him to translate Jefferson's words for the benefit of his crew.

'By God, we are not pirates,' he said, 'We are only retrieving that which belongs to us. We traded with you fair and square.'

He paused waiting for the translator to catch up, 'You must learn that we will be paid what is rightfully ours.'

Whilst he was making his speech his crew had returned with four strong boxes.

He went on, 'To evidence that we are no Goddam pirates; I will take only two of the boxes. That will cover your debt to me.'

Jefferson waited for the translation to finish.

The junk's Master fixed Jefferson in the eye. He spoke softly. Jefferson did not understand but the malice was clear. There was no need for translation. Jefferson and his crew retired to their longboats and rowed back to Perseverance, leaving Chang and his men to sort out the havoc.

The Captain had his duties to perform. He must get the mandarin's daughter and what remained of his crew home. Chang was an experienced sailor and he knew his ship well. Even though the Cheng He was holed below the water line, he was confident she would not sink. The ship was built with watertight compartments and would remain buoyant. With skill he could get her on an even keel. He made the orders to shift the cargo and ballast to compensate for the list. This should be enough to make the ship seaworthy. As the ship started to right herself, water began to drain from the main deck through the scuppers. She was low in the water but his plan was working. Chang's thoughts moved to his passengers. He looked around and saw Jaio and her brother near where the mainmast had skewered the deck. At least they are safe, he thought. Lei has done well. Chang felt a sense of pride; a physical sensation in his throat and in his stomach.

With difficulty Chang made his way across the debris. He needed to reassign his son to other duties. He found Zihao cradled in his sister's arms. She was quietly sobbing; her dress and hands were covered in blood. There was a dreadful wound in the younger child's back and leg. A sense of panic hit him as he looked around for his son. Then he saw Lei's white face looking up from the flooded compartment below. Desperately, Chang reached through the small opening in the deck. I can save him; I can get him out, he thought. He could not move the timbers that obstructed his son's escape; they were too heavy. But it was too late. His son was not moving, just floating. Lei looked at his father through wide lifeless eyes, his mouth open as he had made his last cry for help. A tear rolled down Chang's cheek as panic turned to grief. His only son and Jaio's brother were dead. Together, they wept.

# Two

# The Interview

Paul arrived at the train station early and he was queuing for a ticket. If he had known about the interview a week earlier, he could have bought the ticket at half price. On the positive side, the late invitation had given him only one day of pre-interview nerves. He did not feel confident about this application. He knew he was qualified on paper, but he expected there were others with better CVs. Paul's train of thought was temporarily broken when the queue moved a couple of steps forward. He briefly looked around to see how the other queues were moving. He noticed two men walking towards the ticket machine queues. He had recognised one of them. Oh damn, he thought. It's Nikolas. Nikolas had been Paul's laboratory partner when they did their first degrees. Paul and Nikolas would not have been paired if they had known each other before they arrived at university. They were like chalk and cheese. Their approach to problems, their attitudes to other people and most other choices one makes in life, were poles apart. Paul felt that Nikolas was completely self-obsessed. Paul knew that Nikolas thought he was naïve, someone to exploit. They were not exactly kindred spirits. Fortunately in the later years of their studies they had been allowed to choose their own lab partners. Paul's reverie was broken; Nikolas had seen him. Oh shit, he thought. Nikolas was walking towards him with his friend in tow. Why would he do want to join me? Paul wondered. Perhaps he's a reformed character. Then Paul realised that he was nearly at the head of the queue. Then he understood.

'Thanks for keeping our place for us Paul,' said Nikolas in a loud voice.

'I didn't,' said Paul.

'You like you're little joke don't you?' said Nikolas, totally unabashed.

Paul knew it was no good. He was remembering how manipulative Nikolas could be. Paul ignored him and addressed Nikolas's companion.

'Hi I'm Paul, we haven't met,' he said, holding out his hand.

It was typical of Nikolas not to introduce his friend.

'Phil,' he said, offering Paul a limp handshake.

'Are you two travelling together?' Paul asked, addressing Phil.

He knew Nikolas liked to have a hanger-on around him, usually a person who was susceptible to Nikolas's didactic style. No one could accuse Nikolas of being stupid, on the contrary he was not.

'Oh we're not travelling together,' said Nikolas; not giving Phil the chance to answer, 'I'm going for a job interview. Phil's just off to look at the big city. He gave me a lift to the station.'

That figures, thought Paul. Phil nodded.

The phrase "job interview" gave Paul a sense of foreboding.

'It's a foregone conclusion though,' said Nikolas. 'The job's mine.'

Whilst Nikolas was speaking the couple behind them moved to another queue.

'Where are you going?' asked Nikolas, rather bluntly.

'Same as you Nikolas,' Paul replied,' I've got an interview for a research assistant's job.'

'Not at the Centre for Astrobiology and Genetics?' Nikolas snorted.

'Yep that's the one.'

As they were having this conversation a middle-aged gentleman joined the queue. The lady in front of them was taking her ticket from the machine.

'You don't think you'll get it do you?' asked Nikolas in a condescending tone.

'I applied because the work looked really interesting but I think they'll want a theoretical guy. You're probably better qualified,' replied Paul, not sure why he was being nice to Nikolas and unsure why he felt embarrassed about the application. Nikolas sometimes had this effect on him. He changed the subject and addressing Phil asked, 'What are your plans when you get to the City?'

Phil was gazing around the concourse and not really paying attention.

'He's on another planet. You'll get no sense out of him' said Nikolas, then continuing with the original subject, 'Anyway, if they've got any sense the job will be mine.'

The middle-aged man behind them moved to the next queue.

'You're probably right,' Paul responded, feeling it was better to concede the point, rather than start an argument.

Paul had got to the head of the queue. He took out a credit card and bought his ticket. He then said his good-byes politely and headed for the platform. Paul walked towards the middle of the train so that he could be sure to be somewhere else if 'the odd couple' approached him again. Although he did not think they would want to join him on the train, Paul did not like the idea of spending two hours cornered by Nikolas. Nikolas would have nothing to gain this time, like a place in a queue. They would probably sit somewhere else. Paul saw Nikolas and Phil walking along the platform as the train drew in. Phil waved. Paul nodded. Paul headed for a carriage that was almost full and took an empty seat in a block of four. The other seats were taken. He heard Nikolas and Phil making their way through the carriage. As they came past, they acknowledged each other but to Paul's relief Nikolas and Phil continued to the next carriage.

Paul pulled out a book and tried to read it. He was finding it difficult to concentrate. Usually, he liked travelling by train because it was an opportunity to observe or reflect; to observe the scenery, the people and if the carriage was quiet, he could collect his thoughts. He had much to think about. Paul's conversation with Nikolas had certainly annoyed him and despite or because of, Paul's self-control, the adrenalin had not dissipated. He was irritated that he had backed away from an honest confrontation with Nikolas. If he had taken him on, Paul knew he would have come out worse. Nikolas had a gift for intelligent, caustic rhetoric. Nikolas used it to belittle and bully the unwary protagonists. In the past Paul had thought Nikolas would end up as a politician or a religious guru. Paul had many skills but he was no match for Nikolas in the use of invective. He had been there; this was not a good use of his energies. Paul decided he must put Nikolas to the back of his mind. Nikolas's appearance was not the primary reason for his agitation. Paul had been a research assistant with his current team for nearly three years and now the money had run out, he would lose his job. He was frustrated, that he, and the team, were addressing some of the biggest questions that mankind could think of, but society did not think it was important enough to fund it. Paul was starting to wonder if he was in the wrong business. His confidence was at an all-time low. Then, why was he going to this interview? The job advertisement had asked for candidates with "strong influencing skills"; what the hell did that mean? To cap it all, it was in a multidisciplinary group where individual perspectives would be completely different. He would probably spend his time arguing about semantics! Paul was not sure he could get his head round such vague concepts. At least maths and science were predictable. Paul could argue a scientific point with the best of them, but would he be able to hold is own in an environment where everybody had their own rules? He thought about his encounter with Nikolas and was disheartened. Paul found he was still angry, but he had controlled it. That did not mean he was beaten. It was at that moment Paul decided he wanted the job. The only way he could beat people like Nikolas was to prove that he was more valuable than a devious, eloquent debater with excellent interview skills. Rant over; Paul was going to be the physics research assistant at the Centre for Astrobiology and Genetics. If not, he would give it a bloody good try.

****

A few days later a letter dropped on the doormat of Paul's flat. He recognised the postmark. It was the same as the invitation to the interview he had received a week earlier. The letter inside the envelope seemed to be thin. Ah well, he thought, it was worth a try. He felt the interview had gone badly. He was forced to think on his feet too much. He thought he had not answered anything with sufficient confidence. Mind you, he had had other interviews that had gone well and had been unsuccessful every time. He should be getting used to it by now. There are too many people chasing too few jobs he thought. His friends told him to keep going and he would come though in the end. It is a matter of statistics. If you keep going, sooner or later you will get the role you want.

Paul took the unopened envelope into the kitchen area and put the kettle on. He made himself a cup of coffee. Whilst he drank he continued to look at the letter. I wonder what it says, he thought.

'Oh bugger,' he said out loud. 'It's got to be done.'

He tore the envelope open and read the contents.

'Bloody hell!' said Paul, 'I'd better find somewhere to live.'

# Three

## Too Much DNA

Paul threw his leather jacket over the back of the chair and sat down. He had had his new job for a week and was still confused. Why did he feel so much out of his depth? As much as he disliked that pratt Nikolas, at least he would have understood this morning's briefing. He wondered if Nikolas had been successful at the interview, would he have fitted in any better? Probably not, the team was too strong. He looked around him. Everyone seemed to have their heads down, working on their bit of the project. They seemed to know what they were doing, even the graduate students. The skills here were quite mixed. There were astrobiologists, biochemists, geneticists (a word he could hardly pronounce let alone understand), computer scientists, and mathematicians. He was the only physicist. Their raison d'etre was to research the possibility of extra-terrestrial life. The team seemed friendly, but they did not yet know what he did not know. He was going to have to learn fast. It was a multi-disciplinary team and he was the team's physicist. Physics is a vast subject and Paul felt ill equipped to handle all the topics that they had associated with his discipline. He knew enough to nod in the right places, but he thought they might expect more.

It was not like Paul to be so negative, but this challenge seemed huge. The team, like most research teams, was as large as funding would allow. Hence they were a small, tight unit. Paul was used to working with other people. This was different. He was used to clambering over the servo systems of massive radio telescopes and being surrounded by lots of people with slightly different perspectives of the same subject. He used to share a beer with colleagues who talked the same language. He was no longer in his comfort zone. It was like his first day at school, lost in the playground.

Paul realised, before he had applied for the job, that being part of a multi-disciplinary team would give him new challenges. He was intrigued by the discovery of DNA on the Starburst mission. They had found organic molecules on earlier missions, but never DNA. It may only have come from bacteria, but it was a huge surprise. The news certainly hit the headlines with a bang. It usually took the press years to catch up and then only after their science journalists had scanned Nature or Science for a few well-informed snippets. They wrote headlines like 'Intelligent life in space proven' and 'We are not alone'. Had Paul too been carried away by the sensationalist idea of extraterrestrial life? He knew that the bacteria around his bath were not particularly well educated, but it was life and they had found some in space! He hoped that the popular press did not completely distort his judgement. Even so, he felt less knowledgeable than he should and it was clear from today's briefing that the different disciplines did not all talk the same language; yet another barrier to conquer! He wanted desperately to represent his subject professionally and accurately. He wanted to make a real scientific contribution. His knowledge of plasmas, atomic and nuclear physics should be valuable. He just did not yet know how to apply it. He supposed on day one everybody had the same fears. Maybe he could solicit some help from his old friends.

Feeling more positive Paul switched into action mode. Right, he thought, a march of 1000 miles …. He reached over to take the first step. He lifted a book from the shelf in front of him. It was a weighty tome appropriately entitled 'GRAVITY'. He had read it before; perhaps it would go in this time? If nothing else reading this will help with my biceps he thought. He glanced up to see a woman taking off her white lab coat and hanging it on a rack by the door. Paul had met Claire for the first time at the departmental briefing. She was about five and a half feet tall, slim, with curves in the right places. She wore blue jeans, the standard apparel for university research teams. This morning she had on a light blue top with a modestly cut neckline in a square. She had bright intelligent eyes that seemed to sparkle whenever she was interested in something and especially when she smiled. Her smile was warm and open. Claire had light brown hair tied back in a neat bundle at the back of her head. A couple of wayward strands however had broken ranks and were expressing their individuality by falling down the sides of her face. Strangely this did not look untidy. Her green eyes had a colour depth that seemed impossible to him. Her eyelashes were naturally long and she wore no sign of makeup. Her only concession to vanity was two studs, one in each earlobe. Paul didn't remember everybody at the briefing but he remembered Claire. He smiled, nodded and dropped his eyes back to his book. 'Must concentrate!' he chastised himself.

'Hi Paul,' she said walking over to him, smiling. 'That looks weighty'.

Normally he would have been annoyed by the interruption; given that he was starting a paragraph entitled "The Non-singularity of Gravitational Radius" but a conversation with a very pretty biochemist seemed extremely appealing.

'Hi Claire', Paul said, pretending to drag his thoughts from black holes. 'How's things?'

'Fine thanks,' Claire replied. 'Has anyone showed you around the laboratory yet?'

'No they haven't. I'd be really interested though if you're offering,' he said looking as lost as he felt.

'It would be a pleasure,' she said, smiling warmly. 'Just give me a few minutes and I'll come back and pick you up.'

There's that smile again he thought. Careful Paul you could get lost in there.

A few minutes later Claire came back with a white coat.

'This one is for you,' she said handing him the garment.

He thanked her and put the coat on. Claire put hers on also. Even in a white coat she looked wonderful, thought Paul. Paul followed Claire to a pair of double doors. There was a sign on the wall.

It read 'Extraction and Purification.'

'Sounds painful,' he said.

She smiled but said nothing.

He followed her through the two double doors into a laboratory. He had a strange feeling in his ears as he went through, like he was descending in an aeroplane. There were eight to ten benches with sinks set into them. At one of the benches, a PhD student, Mike, was working with a rack of tiny plastic test tubes. He was wearing gloves, his hair was covered and he was wearing a white mask. There was quite a lot of expensive looking equipment in the room. He could identify weighing balances, a centrifuge and sterilising equipment. There was a large refrigerator in one corner labelled 'incoming' and in another corner a large glass box, open at the front with big ventilation tubes plumbed into it. There were a number of locked cabinets containing labelled bottles of chemicals. It was a similar to the 'wet' lab that he had used when he studied chemistry. This lab however was spotless. The floors, the walls the benches were immaculate.

'Good morning, Mike,' she called out. 'I hope we're not disturbing you.'

'No problem.' Mike replied.

Looking at Paul she continued, 'This is where we prepare and store the samples.'

'Extraction and Purification?' said Paul, demonstrating he could read but little else.

'Yes,' said Claire, privately amused that he was trying to impress her. 'Mike is extracting a sample from the X/2009/D2 (Yakawa) Comet. That fridge contains vials of incoming samples,' she said. 'At every stage we separate the incoming products from the output products.'

'Why?' asked Paul, he always felt the simple questions were the best. Or was that because he was simple? He wasn't sure.

'To avoid cross contamination,' replied Claire. 'We have a place for outgoing samples over there,' she said, pointing to another fridge standing at the opposite side of the room.

'I think this is the cleanest laboratory I have ever seen,' Paul remarked, genuinely quite impressed.

'Well thank you kind sir,' Claire responded using the mock Elizabethan phrase with a smile. 'We keep everything scrupulously clean to avoid contamination.'

'Is that a big issue; contamination I mean?' asked Paul, wanting to ask intelligent questions, but not really knowing where to start.

'Yes it is,' she said, smiling and making eye contact. 'For two main reasons, we get samples from anything that is suspected to have come from space. Any organic material may be dangerous to terrestrial life. For example a virus is often just a short length of DNA or RNA that injects itself into an animal's cell. Who knows what extra terrestrial DNA might do? So we're very careful.'

'And the second reason?' asked Paul, to demonstrate he was being as attentive as he truly was.

'Our little blue planet, Earth is teaming with life. This means there are bits of DNA everywhere, pollen in the air, food on the ground, all over the human body and many more sources. Some of the samples that we analyse in these labs are tiny, just a few molecules. It doesn't take much accidental exposure to completely corrupt our results. So the air in this room is thoroughly filtered and we keep all the work areas very clean.'

'But you and I have just walked in here, could we be carrying contamination?' asked Paul.

'Yes we could, but we take precautions. Did you notice the special double doors when you and came into the room?'

He nodded with an air of sagacity, but feeling more like an obedient puppy.

'It's a low-pressure air lock. It has slightly lower pressure than outside, which is lower pressure than in here.'

'You mean I've been vacuum cleaned?' asked Paul.

'Yes,' she replied, 'You've been dusted down and you're now a very clean boy.'

'And much the better for it!' he grinned, still feeling like a puppy.

She smiled back and continued, 'Most of the really sensitive work is done in laminar flow cupboard over there. She pointed to the glass box in the corner. We give it a thirty minute blast of strong ultra violet light at the beginning of each preparation, to destroy any contamination that may have been left over from the previous experiment. I'm still not happy though. I think we should have complete clean room conditions, but that is too costly for us poor academics.'

Claire led Paul towards a second room, past a sign that said 'PCR laboratory'.

'This is our PCR laboratory where we amplify the DNA,' said Claire.

She led him though the first set of double doors. Claire paused in the air lock and looked though the windows of the second set of doors without opening them. She looked into the PCR laboratory. Aware of the air flowing around him, Paul thought he would be a very clean boy if he stopped here much longer. Clearly she was not going to take him into the lab and respecting Claire's wishes, Paul stood next to her as she looked in. Paul became conscious that he should be looking in also, so he peered through his window. The laboratory looked much the same as the last one except some areas had been partitioned.

'Usually we receive very small samples of DNA, so we use this laboratory to make multiple copies of the original.'

'This is what you mean by 'amplification',' Paul asked.

'Yes,' said Claire, 'but if we get contamination in here, it will be amplified also. That is why we segregate the lab.'

'These partitioned areas are to prevent the outputs of one area, contaminating a different part of the process.' said Paul feeling he was beginning to get the hang of this biochemistry stuff.

'That's right,' said Claire, pleased her student was paying attention. 'Let's go to the sequencing area.'

They approached a room marked 'Electrophoresis'. He was relieved that Claire did not stop. By itself the word sounded long and complicated. He was not sure he would be able to absorb what it meant! He did not dare ask Claire, because he was sure she would tell him.

They came to another room that said 'NMR and Mass Spectroscopy'. He hoped she would stop there because this was a subject he knew something about. She continued down the corridor.

They stopped outside a door marked 'Sequencer'.

'How much do you know about DNA structure?' Claire asked.

'Well I know that the DNA molecule has a double helix structure supported by a sugar phosphate backbone. The backbone is made up of sections that are joined together with a repeating linkage. In each of these sections you find one of four different bases: adenosine, guanine, cytosine and thymine, A,G,C and T for short. As you move along the molecule these form a code. This code is read by living cells to produce the bits and pieces that are the building materials for all living things.'

He thought he'd better stop there, as he'd only read half of 'Genetics for Dummies' last night and he was not sure how good his memory was.

'I'm impressed,' said Claire.

I'm going to read more. He thought, quite pleased with himself.

She continued, 'Amongst other things, an organism's cell uses DNA to produce proteins. DNA is like a cooking recipe. It uses a special code.'

'Like a secret coded recipe for a spy,' Paul letting the analogy take hold of him.

'If you like,' replied Claire 'The code word uses three of the four bases. That is A, G, C and T. Each code specifies an ingredient to be added to the recipe.'

'So by using different code words arranged in different orders, you get different proteins,' surprised at what he had just said and determined to keep up.

'Yes and by putting groups of code words together gives a recipe for a protein. This recipe is called "a gene".'

'Each gene, being a recipe for a protein?' he asked rhetorically. It would take him some time to get away from the idea of spies who cook.

'Yes. Can we talk about genes now instead of recipes?' said Claire, wishing she'd never brought cooking into it. 'Let's go in.'

Claire then led him into the Sequencing room. It had a large cabinet in it with the words '3130x/Genetic Analyser' written on the side.

'Don't tell me Claire. Let me guess. This where you analyse genes,' Paul said grinning, forgetting there was a sign on the wall outside as well.

'How did you know?' she asked amused, glancing at the trademark. 'This is one of the machines we use to decode the DNA.'

'So you break the A, G, C, T code with this?' Paul asked, hoping it was an intelligent question.

'Yes' Claire replied, 'This is one of the ways of doing it. It is also on of our more expensive gadgets and it's quite expensive to run.'

They had now gone full circle and come back to the team room.

'I hope you enjoyed the tour. If you want any help just shout. My desk is just there,' said Claire pointing to a desk diagonally opposite Paul's.

'I really enjoyed it thanks,' Paul replied. 'I've learnt a lot about biochemistry as well. If I can ever return the favour you can shout at me. Sorry for me.'

She laughed at his error.

He laughed also.

****

Dieter had asked Paul to pop into his office when he was free. Because of the guided tour, it had completely slipped Paul's mind. He knocked on Dieter's door and walked in. Dieter was on the phone, but he smiled at Paul signalling him to sit down. Paul had enquired about Dieter's background before Paul had applied for his new role. Dieter had an excellent reputation for experimental science. He was educated in Germany and had a doctorate from Gottingen, where he did research into genetics. His publication list was as long as Paul's arm. When Paul had first met Dieter, he had instantly taken a liking to him. However he would not like to get on the wrong side of Dieter, as his reputation for perfection went before him. Dieter was the main reason Paul had joined the team. Dieter was putting his phone in its cradle.

'Hello Paul,' said Dieter, 'how are you settling in?'

'If I'm honest, I've got a lot to learn,' said Paul, 'but I'm sure it'll come.'

'It's only your first day Paul,' he replied. 'You don't really know the team yet.'

'Claire was kind enough to give me a tour of the labs,' said Paul. 'I was impressed.'

'She is very professional,' said Dieter. 'We are very lucky to have her on the team.'

Paul knew Dieter would not say this lightly. Praise from Dieter was praise indeed.

'Dieter,' said Paul, changing the subject. 'I need to get my teeth into something. Can you give me a steer on how I can make the best contribution?'

Dieter thought for a second or two. He opened one of his desk draws and drew out a document.

'I have heard on the grape vine, that there are some anomalies concerning the orbit of the Yakawa comet around the solar system. It's not my field but I have an article here that explains it.'

He handed Paul the paper.

Dieter continued, 'I guess Claire told you that we are analysing DNA extracted from the tails of that comet.'

'Yes' Paul replied.

Dieter explained, 'To find DNA on a comet is remarkable. Then to find the same comet is doing weird movements in space is either a coincidence or a related phenomenon. I'd like you to investigate. Read the paper, you'll see what I mean.'

Paul, pleased with a tangible problem to solve, thanked Dieter and left.

Paul was back at his desk reading the article when Claire came into the room. He looked up and smiled. She nodded and smiled back. Claire sat down and started to key data into her computer. She occasionally glanced up to see what Paul was doing. He was absorbed in his journal. She did not want to be intrusive, she just found him interesting. He had a nice sense of humour and could laugh at himself, without too much self-abasement. He seemed slightly vulnerable in these surroundings. She wondered if he was always like that.

Paul's mobile rang. He answered it.

'Hello Prama how are you?' Paul said into the phone.

Claire looked back at the columns of numbers in front of her. She was trying to tune out of Paul's conversation. It was difficult. Paul was quiet for a moment listening to the person at the other end of the line.

'It's not another of your crazy ideas is it?' Paul asked, not critically but with a smile in his voice.

He waited for the reply.

'Oh, I'm completely out of my depth,' Paul answering a question, his voice humorous, but with a tinge of fact, 'but you know me. It's always like that.'

Claire did not want to pry. She stood up and put her lab coat back on. She headed back to the Sequencing machine.

*****

Half an hour later Claire had returned. She thought she would ask for that favour Paul had offered.

'I wondered if you could help' said Claire, 'I've got an anomaly in some data. How good is your knowledge of molecular biophysics?'

If Paul's knowledge had been non-existent, he would have lied.

'I did some work looking at organic molecules in vacuum some years ago, but I'm a bit rusty.'

Well, he'd tried his best.

'Great, that may be relevant' said Claire.

Wow, thought Paul.

'Do you remember the DNA sample that was collected from the Yakawa Comet mission?' Claire asked him putting on her most professional voice.

She didn't wait for a reply, but he nodded anyway.

Claire continued, 'We have been asked to analyse some samples that were collected by the probe. We've amplified one of them and I've just produced the first DNA code sequence.'

'Great,' he said. He wasn't sure why but it seemed appropriate.

'The results don't make sense.'

'Why not?' Paul asked, desperately trying to remember the discussion they had had about A G C Ts and sequencing.

'The DNA is not old enough,' Claire replied.

'How do you work that out then?' asked Paul, putting on his best 'little boy lost' expression.

She smiled her warm smile and looked down to collect her thoughts.

'The output from the sequencer looks like this.'

She put a sheet of paper on Paul's desk in front of him. At the top was a graph with rows of peaks in four different colours. Beneath each peak were block capital letters. He had noticed only four letters were used, A, G, C and T.

'The AGCTs refer to the four bases of the DNA code?' he asked, hoping it was not too obvious.

'Yes,' Claire replied. 'This is a set of results from one gene extracted from the Yakawa comet sample earlier.'

'Oh yes 'gene' meaning "spy's coded recipe",' he asked cheerily.

Claire looked at him sternly, wondering if he was doing this to tease her or was he really that stupid?

'Ok from now on I will say "genes make proteins",' Paul said, suitably chastised. He may be stupid but he knew when he was in trouble.

'If we start reading the code here,' Claire moved a little closer to pick up a pencil on Paul's desk and drew a vertical line between two of the letters. 'We can read off the code that specifies one of the genes.'

Paul was having some difficulty with his brain and his breathing. She was very close and he liked it. It did not help his concentration at all.

Claire stood back a little and continued, 'We only have small fragments of DNA from the space agency. So we probably have incomplete strands of DNA. We can only amplify and copy what we have. So there will be many genes missing from our results. Also you would expect this DNA to be very old.'

'Why?' Paul asked, getting his brain back in gear.

'It came from space, there's no living thing around it for miles except on Earth.' said Claire, answering his question.

'So it must have been travelling for years to get there. Ok I understand.'

Paul was on safer ground with non-biological stuff.

'Analysis of old DNA presents some challenges,' continued Claire. 'After a few days, most of the soft material around the DNA would have decayed due to the action of bacteria, the atmosphere and other chemicals. After a few months, sometimes years, the DNA itself would normally show decay. Obviously this depends on the environment it is in. If it is in a protected environment like a fridge, bone or amber, it can last longer.'

'Oh yes I remember that film about pre-historic animals,' said Paul.

'Science fiction, but yes,' Claire went on. 'After thousands of years, the codes or bases can become corrupted.'

'What even when protected in bone?' he asked.

'Yes even then. For example when old DNA from woolly mammoth bones was analysed some years ago, some of the Ts had decayed and become Cs. This can be very confusing,' she said.

'So given we are looking at extra terrestrial DNA from the tail of a comet, the samples should be thousands, if not millions, of years old. This means the sample should have many of errors in it,' said Paul, remembering his conversation with Dieter, now completely engaged.

'Exactly,' she said emphatically, 'before getting the samples I was told that they came from the Yakawa Comet's tail. I am not sure how nice that environment is but I suspect it is a very hostile place.'

She stopped. She seemed to be waiting for a response from him.

It was strange, Paul had listened to every word and he thought he'd kept up well. But now he was lost. He had to come clean.

'Sorry Claire, I'm being slow. What is it you're asking me?'

'Well, this DNA has travelled half way across our galaxy. As you put it earlier; a journey over thousands or maybe millions of years. There is evidence of soft tissue around it. It is pristine. It looks as though it is only a few days old,' she paused.' Can you think of how that could be possible?'

'Oh,' Paul said. 'I see.'

# Four

# Gravity

Claire was going over the same explanation with Anil as she had earlier during Paul's tour. She had a great deal of time for Anil. He had worked hard to get here. Originally from northern India, Anil's grandparents had followed European investment into central Africa. His family had had a good life until social upheaval and political power struggles made his father, then sixteen, a refugee. Separated from his family, his father had been put on an aeroplane and was deported here. He did not know why, but his father ultimately ended up in a detention centre. Anil's parents' first language was French. Anil knew how difficult it had been for both his parents. They had come to a foreign land without a bean to their name. They used their intellect and determination to make something of themselves. His father, who knew no English, taught himself the language by watching television in the Harmondsworth immigration centre. This was where he met Anil's mother. After getting married they had one child, Anil. The family battled on together. Anil's father became a lawyer. His mother studied to be a doctor. Anil was the bright offspring of two able people. There was an immeasurable bond between the members of this small family. Anil left university with a first class honours degree in maths. His parents were immensely proud of their son. He took a job as an actuary in an insurance company. This did not challenge him. Determined to stand on his own two feet, he worked for a few years to collect enough money so that he could extend his education. As it turned out, he got funding anyway so he resigned from his job joined the team as a PhD student. Anil had inherited his parent's self-sufficiency, intelligence and tenacity. In addition he had curiosity.

Claire was finding the conversation with Anil a great deal more straightforward than it had been with Paul. But somehow it was less fun. She was felt that was a strange thought. Why had that gone through her mind? Anil was repeating something back for confirmation.

'I understand,' Anil was saying, 'so every gene we find is likely to correspond to a protein that can be found in the host creature.' He caught on very quickly.

'That's correct,' said Claire. 'Each creature is made of combinations of proteins. This means that each species has a specific combination of genes. Put all these genes together and you have a complete picture of the animal.'

'In that case,' said Anil. 'We can identify what animal owned our sample by matching our data to a sequence done earlier. It's like looking up our sample's DNA code in a reference book'

'Yes, except the amount of information involved is huge,' Claire explained. 'Over the years, biologists and biochemists have analysed many standard species like mice, bacteria, fruit flies, humans and many others. Sequences like the AGCTs on this paper,' she said pointing to the sheet she had shown Paul, 'are held in large databases. If we input this information into a search computer, we can look for a closest match in these databases. We'll then find out if anyone has seen that sequence before. I'd like you to run those searches for me.'

She continued, 'If the organism has not already been sequenced, you can find species close to it and work out how they are connected though evolution.'

'Ok,' said Anil. 'It sounds like a challenge I'll enjoy.'

****

All the team was together under the impressive title of the Centre for Astrobiology and Genetics. Dieter, the centre-head, was chairing the meeting of four PhD students and Post doctorate researchers (Zihang, Paul and Claire).

Zihang had just finished explaining his mathematical analysis that would point to the most likely place for the team to find life. It was full of complex equations and clever algebra. His model contained a huge volume of data on known stars, spectrum analysis and records of previous phenomena that could be connected with extra terrestrial life. Paul thought that this sounded like a lifetime's work. Zihang was still in the process of building his model, so there was some way to go before he could report back any conclusions.

Claire then went over the details of her experimental work she explained the problem about the missing mutations in her results. But she thought this could have been a 'statistical blip'. The problem may only appear in the analysis of the first gene in the first sample. She was reluctant to come to any conclusions until she had sequenced more genes in more samples. This was a lot of work. Anil was doing a great job with the data analysis. Anil grinned proudly. Claire said she would appreciate some help to build the various chemical mixes and perform the PCR temperature cycling.

It sounded like cookery to Paul. He had heard Claire mention 'PCR' yesterday. It was such a day-to-day expression to her, so he thought he'd let it pass and look it up in his handy book on genetics. He was now kicking himself for being so stupid and not asking about a key bit of 'DNA-speak'. He resolved that in future he would ask.

Claire had moved on to explain that she was still puzzled about why the DNA had lied about its age. Although she would like to get the other work done in parallel, she felt this problem must be resolved urgently. Paul had given her some ideas on why the sample was so pristine. She felt these ideas should be followed up. Dieter had agreed to allocate Mike (one of the PhD students) to help Claire with re-sequencing the remaining DNA strands. This would confirm or challenge Claire's earlier findings.

'Ok Paul can you give us your perspective,' said Dieter.

Paul awoke from his musings. He drew a deep breath. He was not sure why he was so self-conscious but he didn't want to say something stupid or use language that was too esoteric. Paul was aware that some people thought he was facetious. He had to try to contribute sensibly.

He started, 'There seem to be four main possibilities concerning Claire's problem. Option one: the original samples were contaminated either en-route to our labs or in our labs.'

He saw Claire wince – another relationship blown.

Paul ploughed on, 'The second possibility is that the DNA has been held for millions of years in some kind of protected environment; a shielded, frozen vacuum bubble for example.'

He paused for the thought to sink in. There were no comments so he carried on.

'Thirdly the DNA did not come from the comet at all. And four, the weird one, the DNA has been in wrapped up in a different time frame.'

Paul paused again, to check everybody was awake. They seemed to be so he described his opinion of each option.

Paul continued, 'Claire tells me that contamination is one of the most common problems when sequencing DNA. This is particularly true if human DNA is involved. We have been told that the sample can be traced back through all the steps that led to it arriving here. The trace goes all the way back to when it was extracted from the Comet. We have been assured that it has been held in conditions better than any 'clean room' you would find in a semiconductor company.'

He had never been in a computer company's 'clean room' but he knew that they had a reputation for not being too dirty.

He went on, 'Claire tells me that there is a chance that in or en-route to our labs, a stray human or other organism's cell may have dropped into the sample. If this is the case then we may find a match with one of the most common pollutants. The sequences don't appear to have any human genes in them. Claire has asked Anil to check the databases of all standard species we have on record. If we find a match, it does not mean that the sample has been contaminated. It could be that the species identified is somewhere out there. However depending on the complexity of the gene, the probability of this is much smaller.'

'Why would the complexity of the species matter?' asked Anil.

Paul responded, 'Claire may correct me but I understand that in space, we are most likely to find only the most primitive forms of life; these could be single cell organisms or viruses. If we find anything more complex, then it is likely to have come from a completely different evolutionary history. So if it is related to terrestrial life, the most recent evolutionary connection would be at least hundreds of millions of years ago.'

Claire thought that was close enough. She nodded; Paul was pleased, both with the confirmation and the eye contact.

'We should be able to quantify this probability when we have the results from your matching software,' Paul said, looking at Anil.

Then looking at Claire, 'If you like, I could I work with Claire to do the mathematics.' His voice pitched slightly higher at the end of the sentence, as in a request.

Paul wondered at this point whether his mentioning of possible 'contamination' in her laboratory meant that he was in Claire's bad books. She must understand that the option had to be considered so that it could be eliminated. Paul thought he could do this by helping with the mathematics. It was not really his field but all scientists work with probabilities and he liked the idea of working with Claire. He hoped she would like it too. Claire nodded thoughtfully, agreeing to the idea. As Dieter was the boss, the question should have been pitched at him. Dieter hadn't disagreed, so Paul assumed Dieter's acquiescence.

Paul continued, a little unsteadily, 'If we eliminate contamination then we have the three remaining possibilities. I do not know whether or not DNA and surrounding tissue could survive for long in a comet's tail. Near the sun, in the solar wind, a comet's tail is in what is called a 'plasma' state. I have done work with plasmas but not with comets. I know a man who has. He is an expert in this area. I'd like your agreement to tell him about our problem so I can discuss our ideas with him.'

This time he was looking directly at Dieter. Dieter was pondering.

Paul thought he needed to be more persuasive, 'If we do this, my friend will give us some idea of what it would be like to live in the tail of a comet. He will help us understand whether our sample could have been protected inside our friendly Yakawa; in the tail or anywhere nearby.'

Paul paused for Dieter's agreement. Dieter nodded.

Paul continued, 'My third possibility is that the sample did not come from the comet's tail at all, but was simply floating there in space as the comet, and the probe passed by. I have thought about this option a lot. I wondered about the odds of a probe from Earth happening to be in the right place at the right time to pick up a few molecules of DNA in the vacuum of space just after a comet flew past. It seemed unlikely. In fact about as probable a large hadron collider creating a weird particle or black hole that is big enough to suck the Earth into its void.'

He waited for this to sink in.

Then Paul carried on, 'Anyway, I've worked it out. It's a 10-18 probability or to put it another way; less than 1 chance in a billion, billion.'

'Not a dead cert then?' said Dieter, amused.

'I wouldn't bet on it,' Paul went on, 'Finally the 'far out' one. We all know it is an experimental fact that no object can travel faster than the velocity of light. If an object travels at speeds approaching the velocity of light or it passes near a massive object, it will experience different clock speeds to us, the observer. It is possible that we think our DNA sample has been travelling for millions of years, but it thinks it's only a few days.'

Anil was starting to frown so Paul looked at him and asked, 'Got a question Anil?'

Anil was very bright, but was sometimes too reserved to volunteer concerns.

Anil paused as he structured the question in his head, 'I understand you are talking about relativity, but surely we know how fast the comet was going, because we could see it and we have visited it.'

He paused again, being careful to avoid misunderstanding, 'When I say 'we' I don't mean 'us' in this room; you understand?'

Anil went on, 'This speed must be far less than the velocity of light. Surely there is no way time will be affected significantly?'

Paul was really pleased that Anil was working on the analysis. He was a good contributor.

Paul responded, 'You are right'.

Anil looked relieved

'But,'

Anil looked concerned,

Paul continued, 'We do not know the comet's history beyond five years ago. There is evidence thats its orbit around the sun is not what it should be. This could be due to some unexplained mass somewhere. It is possible that it decelerated or was affected by a large mass. Has anybody any ideas about how to look back into its history?'

'Look back over the space it came from,' said Anil tentatively.

'Yes,' said Paul.

Anil looked relieved again.

Paul went on, 'We need to get some star maps, find ourselves a big telescope and look back into space. Of course someone may already have looked so we'll need to talk to them. We have two threads of research…Sounds like fun… Any volunteers?'

Anil volunteered. Dieter agreed, hoping it would not cost too much. Claire smiled. Maybe he hadn't blown his chances after all.

\*\*\*\*

Paul and Claire were walking back to their desks. He had been looking for something witty to say when Anil interrupted.

'Excuse me Paul.'

Paul turned and Anil was just behind them looking a little lost. Claire carried on walking saying she would see them in the office. They nodded.

'A problem?' Paul enquired.

'I need some guidance,' said Anil.

Paul knew that if Anil needed guidance then, unlike many students, this was indeed true. He had learnt a lot about Anil's background from Claire.

Anil began tentatively, 'We believe X/2009/D2, alias Yakawa, is a long period comet. Although we don't know exactly how long it takes to go round the solar system. We could make an educated guess.' He paused to collect his thoughts, 'Calculations from the space agency predict that it takes around two hundred years to complete one orbit of the Sun. If your idea is right and the comet has slowed down, then something must have caused this to happen. Whatever energy the comet had before it entered the zone around the pole star must have gone somewhere. I can't understand where it could have gone.'

'You are right the kinetic energy lost in slowing would become stored energy in a gravitational field or taken away after a collision. This would affect the Comet's route around the Sun. I think we should build a computer model to find out what happened. Why don't you take Zihang's data for a solid angle about twenty degrees around the zone? You could build a computer simulation of the gravity interactions that Yakawa would have experienced over the last few thousand years. By the way I wouldn't use the pole star as the reference it is not exactly in the North. Use the Northern Celestial Pole instead.'

'Ok, ' said Anil.

'I've got a good book on gravitation. It could help you with the computer programming. You can borrow it if you like,' said Paul, feeling guilty.

He had not finished rereading it yet.

'That would be great,' replied Anil, making Paul feel guiltier still.

'So much for my biceps,' he mumbled.

'What did you say?'

'Oh nothing,' replied Paul.

# Five

# Flies

'Do you realize what it takes to reserve a bespoke Hubble search? When you said big telescope, I didn't think you meant Hubble! I've got a nine-inch Newtonian reflector in my back garden. Can't you use that?' asked Dieter.

Paul was impressed. He didn't know Dieter was an amateur astronomer. However he was beginning to get the idea that Dieter wasn't keen on using the international telescope in orbit around the Earth. He needed to get his arguments tight.

'It has to be a telescope above the Earth's atmosphere or we have no chance. We are looking for evidence of very massive dark objects, not previously discovered. The telescope must have cameras that respond to a wide spectrum of light and other radiation. There are so many reasons why Hubble is our best chance of seeing anything,' said Paul.

Dieter responded quickly, 'The 'chances' don't seem too good either way. You told me that there is only a 0.01% probability that the object is there at all. I've heard of null experiments but this is ridiculous! The trouble with you physicists is that you have big ideas that need big budgets to match. Couldn't you settle on the first big thing and skip the second?'

Ouch! Thought Paul, he could see this idea slipping away.

'What if I cut the field of search in half? I'll be quicker and it'll cost less. Would you be keener?'

'I'll think about it,' said Dieter.

Paul thought that was almost a 'yes' so he left while he was winning.

He wandered over to where Anil and Claire were looking at a computer screen.

'Hi, you two,' he asked, 'anything new?'

'Well,' opened Claire. 'It's not human contamination. The analysis says that humans and this gene share a common ancestor over eight hundred million years ago, give or take two hundred million. The closest gene codes for an enzyme that produces proteins for cellular walls.'

'I love it when you talk dirty', said Paul, ignoring Anil's embarrassment.

He went on, 'What does that mean?'

'It means,' started Claire, 'that this gene is as closely related to you and me as the fruit fly is to the elephant. And talking of fruit flies; it is has a similar gene, with a common ancestor around 300 million years ago.'

'So the genetic relationship is closer to an insect than a mammal,' Anil chipped in.

'Well, that effectively eliminates human contamination then. It also opens a lot more questions!' said Paul.

'You can say that again,' said Claire. 'For example have we found evidence of intelligent insect life elsewhere in the universe?'

'Intelligent?' queried Paul.

'Insects have brains you know!' replied Claire. 'Although I accept I've never met one with GCSEs.'

Ignoring the digression about insect IQs, Anil said, 'Depending on Paul's black holes and things, this insect life may not be very far away?'

'And how did it survive the conditions in a comet's tail anyway?' mumbled Paul almost more to himself than the others.

'Any progress on the search area Anil?' asked Claire, changing the conversation towards a more fruitful direction.

'Yep,' Anil replied. 'The model has worked out a probable track of the Yakawa Comet over the last 100 years. This is based on the position of known objects in the star map. If I try to go any further back I'll need all of the university's computer power. The potential error in the predicted result would be awful; too many gaps in the Zihang's data.'

Paul thought about the cost of using the Hubble telescope. Could he be wasting the research group's money?

'So you're telling us that we can only realistically go back 100 years. In astronomy terms, you know that's a flee bite don't you?' Paul said.

Anil looked downcast. Claire looked concerned. Paul felt guilty.

'Ok it'll do for now,' Paul said. 'The DNA thinks it's less than a year old any way. '

Then he thought to himself; there has to be another way of tackling this.

'Any progress on Hubble?' asked Claire, with a concerned frown on her face. Clearly she was expecting the worst.

'Dieter gave me a definite maybe,' said Paul. 'Your model will help though, Anil. Failing that we'll try to get time on the largest optical scope we can find and with luck, land-based radio scopes to boot. I wonder what they're doing at Jodrell Bank.'

Secretly he didn't fancy his chances,

'Either of you fancy a pint?'

'You do know how to treat a girl,' said Claire, smiling and what a smile.

'I'll have a cola,' said Anil cheering up.

They left for the pub.

\*\*\*\*

Late that evening Paul returned. He thought he'd have a look at Anil's results. He logged into his computer and brought up Hubble's library pictures of the night sky. He tapped in the four co-ordinates that outlined the patch in the sky that Anil had proposed. He changed the settings to look at pictures using different coloured light, then X-rays, then radio frequencies. He saw something; in fact two somethings. He zoomed in.

'Now that's interesting,' he mused.

# Six

## Old Friends

It was something Claire had said in the pub that gave him the idea. She had said that biochemists like her, knew there were still many unanswered questions and were not afraid to admit it. Physicists on the other hand seemed to think they'd solved everything and if they applied their established laws to every problem that came along then the answer would drop out. This was nothing more than a 'blind belief system'. In the spirit of lively, combative debate Paul defended physicists manfully, even though he knew this debate also went on inside his discipline. Claire had a point. He enjoyed discussing things with her. She was a worthy adversary, but he wished she'd picked on Anil not him…. Or perhaps not… Anyway it was closing time and after Anil headed home Paul asked Claire if she wanted to go up north to discuss their question with his astrophysics mates. Now, sitting opposite her on the train Paul realised Claire's reaction to his suggestion about the trip was strange. He wondered whether she was expecting a different question.

'So how do you know these guys?' Claire asked, waking him from his reverie.

'Sorry,' said Paul. 'I was miles away.'

He paused 'Prama and I did our first degrees together. Her family settled here when she was a child. Her father was a Gurkha and served in the Army. She did well at school and we met at University. She studied Physics. I studied Astrophysics'.

He seemed to be reflecting on something, then 'There weren't many girls in the class, so all the guys wanted to be her friend. She used to say 'The odds were good but the goods were odd.' So I must have been one of the least odd!'

'An ex-girlfriend then?' Claire enquired.

'Yes, but it didn't last long. Perhaps she wanted to find someone even less odd. So we moved on. We're still friends though.'

Paul was finding he could talk to Claire. He knew she looked nice but he liked her as well.

He continued, 'Jacques was one of my supervisors when I did my PhD. Over the years we've had a few beers together and many debates like last night'.

Claire was getting interested in probing Paul's relationship with Prama, but she had a problem to solve, so she asked about their academic backgrounds.

Paul had a go at their résumés, 'Jacques was educated in Paris and came over here as a postdoctoral researcher in astrophysics. He is an expert in plasma physics. I guess you know that as a comet passes the sun its tail becomes plasma. Plasmas are very common in space; hence there is a link to astrophysics. He does some consultancy work for the semi-conductor industry because they use plasmas a lot. This helps the university and the university helps his team do pure research. Synergy, I think they call it.'

'And Prama?'

'Prama's a theoretical physicist. Really that means she's almost completely a mathematician. She'd kill me for saying so. Her field is black holes and gravity. I have to admit it's a subject I still find very hard. It's full of weird algebra. Apparently Einstein was very good at it. I tend to prefer the more practical side. Prama said once in one heated discussion, that I only saw what was in front of me. She dubbed me 'her Engineer'. Originally she meant it as an insult, but I quite liked it.'

Claire was deep in thought.

Paul broke the silence

'We're drawing in. Better get our stuff down.'

They disembarked. Paul hailed a taxi just outside the station.

He gave his instruction to the driver, 'Dirac Laboratories please'

The taxi moved off into the traffic.

****

As they entered the building, Paul reflected that in the 15 years since he had first walked underneath the lintel bearing the name of the labs, it had hardly changed; except for the security that is. Paul pulled out his mobile and phoned Jacques.

Jacques, thought Claire, not Prama. That's promising.

'He'll be down in a few moments to pick us up,' said Paul.

After a couple of minutes Claire heard a voice.

'Bonjour mon ami. Bienvenue.'

The owner of the voice was a man in his early forties. He was just less than six foot tall, slim, dressed in Armani jeans, a tee shirt, a smart jacket and rather stylish shoes. He looked to Claire like a modern entrepreneur rather than a poor academic.

'Bonjour Jacques, tu est ca-va?' asked Paul, in an awful French accent.

'Ca va bien. Merci. And who is this, Paul?' said Jacques switching to English and smiling towards Claire.

'Let me introduce Claire. It's her puzzle we are trying to solve,' said Paul.

'Enchante,' said Jacques taking her hand. 'I am grateful for the opportunity to help.'

This man oozed charm.

'It's nice to meet you Jacques,' she said 'I've heard a lot about you from Paul.'

Jacques gave Paul a sidelong glance.

'Let me get you through the barrier,' said Jacques.

They followed Jacques through the barrier and up a flight of stairs. He showed them to his office.

Jacques's office was a complete contradiction to the way he dressed. The room was long and narrow. On one side there was a row of three desks pushed up against the wall. On the opposite wall there were a couple of four drawer filing cabinets next to which, at the far end, yet another desk. On top of the far desk was a printer surrounded by two boxes of unused printer paper and underneath this desk was a computer processor. There were other computer processors under the other desks. Claire counted four at various angles, with a mass of cables going in all directions. Above the desks there were shelves lined with books. On most other horizontal surfaces, there were piles of paper. Peeping out from some of the paper Claire could see the edge of a keyboard and then a monitor. She was sure she could find other keyboards if she looked hard enough. In the corner sat another computer, some circuit boards and a machined component, the size of a hen's egg, fashioned in a luminous blue stone - maybe part of some experiment he had been working on.

'I see you've been having ideas again, Jacques,' said Paul.

'You know how it is. There is much to absorb, no time to clear up. Why don't you two sit down?' said Jacques pointing to the one and only chair.

Paul carefully cleared a space on one of Jacques's desks for him and Claire. He placed the documents he had shifted systematically at right angles to the documents beneath. Paul and Claire perched on the edge. Jacques watched all this attentively, as if recording each movement in his head.

'Oh forgive me,' said Jacques as if a penny had dropped. 'No chairs, I'll get some. And I'll see if Prama is free at the same time.' He left the room.

'Is it always this chaotic?' asked Claire when they were alone.

Claire knew she was specifically talking about Jacques, but she could see Paul and Jacques were good friends and she didn't want to offend either of them.

'Oh you mean Jacques?' Paul laughed. 'No, he's actually very organised, but occasionally he get's a bee in his bonnet about a problem he's working on. He tends to throw himself into things. He's very tenacious and becomes so single minded that he shields everything else out; including tidying up.'

He continued, 'Each of these documents will be connected to a line of research he's interested in. He knows where each paper is and what it contains. I don't know whether you noticed that I was very careful when I moved that stack of literature so that nothing dropped out of place. Did you see how he followed my every movement?'

'No I didn't. I was too busy trying to find a chair under the paper!' she laughed.

Paul joined in with a chuckle.

'But what you're saying is that he's in the middle of a piece of work that is very important to him,' Claire went on. 'I can see he's a really nice guy, but now is probably not a good time to disturb him.'

Paul reflecting on her point, 'Yes, now you come to mention it, he does look very busy. I don't know why he didn't tell me that last night when I phoned him. We know each other well enough to postpone our meeting. But he seemed very keen'.

Paul paused. Then as an after-thought, 'Perhaps something has cropped up this morning.'

At that moment there was a commotion outside, as two chairs with lives of their own, appeared to be trying to break the door down. They were followed by Jacques who was trying to control the wayward furniture. Behind the chaos was a stunning woman, about Claire's height in her early thirties, dark complexion with deep brown eyes and long black hair. She was pushing another chair in a way that seemed somewhat more elegant than Jacques. Well, enter Prama, thought Claire.

'Hi Paul it's been a long time... too long,' said Prama leaning over her chairs to give him a kiss on both cheeks.

'Hello, you look well.' Paul said a little stiffly. 'This is Claire. Claire meet Prama.'

Verbal introductions over, Paul pressed himself against one of the desks so that they could see past him. It's getting crowded in here he thought.

'Hi Claire,' said Prama with a friendly smile. 'It's very nice to meet you. I reckon your puzzle is really interesting. I hope we can help.'

Prama glanced at Jacques who nodded in agreement.

Oh damn, thought Claire, I really hoped I'd dislike her.

'Hello,' she said, holding out her hand and smiling. 'It's good to meet you too.'

Paul watched the encounter noticing that the pitch of both their voices had gone up.

'Okay formalities over,' said Jacques, impatiently. 'Let's get down to it.'

They each took a chair and after a few seconds managed to get them into something resembling a circle. Given the size of the room, this would have been hard enough anyway, but with the piles of paper, not to be disturbed, it became a choreographic masterpiece worthy of a Covent Garden ballet.

After a few moments they had settled into a semi circle subtended by the desk Paul had cleared.

Paul said, 'Jacques, I can see you are in the middle of something big, so if this is a bad time we can ask our question and let you think about it later.'

Claire nodded in agreement, pleased to see that Paul had a sensitive side to his character.

Jacques winked at Prama. Prama returned a knowing look.

Jacques said he had all the time in the world, depending on its velocity that is.

Clearly an 'in joke' thought Claire.

Paul went on, 'The DNA from the tail of the Yukawa Comet has survived, in what I believe, was a hostile plasma environment. Having managed this, it shows no sign of damage or aging. We don't understand why. We have some ideas but they seem too far out.'

Jacques, collecting his thoughts, responded, 'Paul, Claire, what you see about you is the work of a poor, demented scientist trying to get to the bottom of an intriguing problem. To be sure, I am busy. However do not worry about using my, our, valuable time. We are all yours. It is your puzzle that has absorbed me. It is among the most interesting experimental conundrums I have met for a long time. I spoke to Prama this morning and she agrees.'

Prama nodded and Jacques continued, 'but first I would like you to bring us up to date with what you have found so far.'

Claire started to go though the background. To Paul, her voice appeared to have returned to normal pitch. It took just over an hour for Claire to explain the experimental methods, the data and their analysis. Jacques then gave them a brief overview of the environment in the tail of a Comet.

'I understand the DNA sample was taken as the shuttle's probe passed though the tail. This is not the ideal environment for complex molecules. As a comet approaches the Sun, it is bombarded with solar radiation. This causes part of the nucleus, sometimes called the head of the comet, to evaporate. In turn this creates a coma or cloud, around the nucleus. Some of the gas and dust particles from the coma then move from the nucleus to create the tail.'

Jacques paused and looked at Paul.

He asked Paul, 'Did you say the probe collected the sample when the comet passed through Ursa Minor?'

'Yes,' Paul replied.

Jacques thought for a second or two.

He mumbled to himself, 'That is still quite close,' reflecting on Paul's reply.

Jacques went on, 'Whilst it is in the Solar System all objects, planets, comets etc. are subject to the Solar Wind.'

'The Solar Wind?' asked Claire.

'The Solar Wind is a stream of charged particles flowing out of the Sun at speeds up to nine hundred kilometres per second.

They are the product of nuclear fusion going on in the Sun,' Jacques replied.

He continued, 'Any object in the path of the solar wind will be bombarded by this stream of particles, or to put it another way, bombarded by radioactive radiation.'

'Is that dangerous?' asked Claire.

'It could be,' responded Jacques, 'On Earth we are protected by the Earth's magnetic field and the atmosphere. It's a very sensitive balance. The further you are from the Sun, the weaker the wind. The sample was taken when Yakawa was about 100 million miles above Earth's North Pole. The Solar Wind would have been significant there.'

He continued, 'The radiation from the Sun causes the gases in the comet's tail to form an electrically charged cloud called a plasma. I have found a paper by a scientist called Finkelmann. His team has analysed the radiation signature of Yakawa comet's tail. This will help us to understand what chemical elements will be found there. It was based on data from the Lowell radio telescope last year.'

Jacques paused looking around his room. Jacques leant over to one of the piles of paper that Paul had moved earlier. He extracted a stapled document from one of his piles.

'Here is the article. The elements and molecules in the plasma include most of the components that make up DNA, and many others. It is a highly reactive and turbulent environment. DNA, being an acid, would attract particles to neutralise it. The plasma, being an electrically charged particle cloud, would contain a lot of candidate particles ready to oblige. In this environment, I would be surprised if a complex organic molecule like DNA, could last for more than a few hours.'

Jacques stopped speaking and waited for reaction.

'So what we've seen is impossible,' remarked Paul.

'Not quite,' said Jacques.

'Stop teasing them,' interjected Prama.

'I guess you're saying the DNA could have travelled in the head and become dislodged when the coma was created,' said Claire refusing to be teased.

'Mon Dieu, she's good Paul,' said Jacques. 'Yes, the nucleus is a bit more of a mystery we believe it is made up mainly of ice and all the elements I mentioned earlier. It could be an environment that would protect DNA for a very long time.'

Claire interrupted, 'But if you raise DNA above a certain temperature, it will denature. In other words the two DNA strands will separate. Our samples were intact. In other words the probe captured double-stranded DNA, not single-stranded. Wouldn't the process of evaporation have caused the DNA to break up?' she asked.

Jacques responded, 'Not necessarily. Don't forget the comet is travelling through a vacuum. In these conditions the boiling point of water, an important constituent of the comet's nucleus, is very low. So it would not need much thermodynamic energy, heat, to cause the DNA to break up.'

'You said the DNA may have been protected for a very long time. How long, thousands of years?' asked Paul.

'Possibly,' said Jacques. 'I can't give you a definitive answer, as we don't know the exact constituents of the comet's nucleus. I can tell you that there is a possibility that the DNA was preserved. I can point you to some earlier research that would help you produce a probability distribution. The big question is how did it get there? I think this is linked to where it came from.'

'Yes we were on that track also,' said Paul, looking at Claire.

Jacques had more to say, 'There is another conclusion in the results of Finklemann's paper. The comet is of long period and there is a seventy five percent probability that the comet was formed outside of the solar system. In other words it has probably travelled a very long way and is an interloper from another system. If this is true then the DNA could have travelled for millions of years, before it was encased in the nucleus' head. This is, to be sure, another factor to consider.'

He paused, 'I am also interested in Paul's other observation.'

Paul looked puzzled.

'Let's break for tea,' suggested Prama.

They all agreed.

****

Anil had now read three quarters of Paul's book. He was concerned that the software he had written was wrong. He decided to go and see Dr Zihang Wu to get some advice about how to write the corrections to his program. Zihang had a reputation for being a mathematical genius, so he wanted to be well prepared for their meeting. He'd arranged to see Zihang in thirty minutes. This didn't give him much time to re-read the chapter about Black Holes. Earlier he had realised that if it were a Black hole that was affecting the comet, the chances were that it would not be in Zihang's computer file of star information. The reason for this is that they are comparatively small and being black, they are very, very difficult to find; obvious really. He thought Zihang may have a way of handling this problem in work he had done earlier.

Missing data on black holes was a problem but it was not the only reason he thought his software was wrong. It seemed black holes came in several flavours. When he wrote his computer programme had assumed that black holes, like very efficient waste disposal units, swallowed anything that came too close. He had now read this was no always the case. If he didn't correct his programme he would be giving Paul and Claire the wrong answers. This was going to tax even Anil's brain. Oh well, he thought, I had better go and see Zihang.

****

They returned to Jacques room with their drinks. This time Jacques had cleared space himself for them to rest their cups. He did not want any accidents with his precious journals. Over tea Paul asked Jacques what he meant by 'Paul's other observation'.

'You told me about the results your that post grad had produced. Perhaps you could share your thoughts with Prama and Claire,' Jacques said helping Paul's memory.

'Oh yes of course,' he said.

The puzzled look had transferred to Claire's face.

Paul turned to Claire and explained, 'Last night I scanned last year's Hubble images that looked at the area of the sky Anil had suggested. I found two groups of objects on either side of the projected comet's path. They appeared to be the same in all respects: radiation profile, the orientation of objects within the group. I thought it might be evidence of gravitational lensing, so I mentioned it to Jacques. I can't see how it would be connected to the DNA problem though.'

'I think we'd better explain what we're talking about before we continue. Do you need an explanation Claire?' asked Jacques with sensitivity.

'Yes please,' Claire said. 'This is not my field'.

Paul was a little ashamed he had not taken this approach himself in earlier discussions between him and Claire.

'Prama, your field I think,' said Jacques.

Prama took a deep breath and began, 'Einstein's Theory of General Relativity says that gravity bends space and drags time.'

I wish I'd never asked, thought Claire.

Prama continued, 'It is possible that the two groups of objects Paul has seen in the images from the Hubble telescope are in fact only one group. The light may have come via two different paths. These paths have been bent so that the light forming their magnified images must have converged on the Hubble's telescope mirror next door to each other. The cause could be a large gravitational field. The kind of thing produced by a big star or black hole bending the light's path as it travelled towards us.'

'Oh is that all,' said Claire

'There is a problem though,' said Prama.

'I thought there would be,' said Claire.

Prama continued, 'The large star would have to be very close to a line drawn between us and the object in the image.'

'This should make it easier to find shouldn't it, because you know where to look?' asked Claire confused.

'Yes and we have looked. We could find no evidence of a single large massive object near the path of the incoming light. Given the distance between the imaged groups and the distance from Hubble it has to be huge to cause such an effect,' said Prama.

'So what you are saying is that if this was gravitational lensing, then there is no way we'd miss the star that caused it,' Paul interjected.

'Well almost,' continued Prama. 'The effect could also be caused by two smaller independent masses closer to Earth but still outside the solar system.'

'How would that work?' asked Paul.

Prama replied, 'To give you an analogy; if you can imagine you were looking at a yacht at sea through binoculars. Ten minutes earlier your little brother… you haven't got any kids yet have you Paul?' Prama teased.

Paul shook his head thinking she was getting worse than Jacques. Claire was intrigued.

Prama continued, 'your little brother had just dropped the binoculars on the ground. The impact had damaged the binoculars so that two optical halves had been knocked out of line. The effect would be that you would see two images.'

'So in our case each mass is one half of the binocular that bends one of the two light beams?' said Claire.

'Yes and each binocular half could be a large mass like a Black Hole bending the world-line of the light,' said Prama.

'World-line?' asked Claire.

'..sorry, the path taken by the light in space and time,' replied Prama.

Claire again, wished she'd never asked.

'So if you imagine that the two optical halves of our binoculars are equivalent to two black holes some distance apart in space, then we could get the image that the Hubble telescope saw. Now back to you Jacques,' said Prama looking at Jacques expectantly.

'As you can see I've being doing some research.'

Jacques made a Gallic sweeping gesture around the room, 'I have found evidence of two eclipsing binary systems on the periphery of the solar system. Their positions are next to the two stars SAO 2010 and SAO 4005 that are about five degrees, either side of Polaris, the pole star.'

He stopped looking around his room again. He got up and moved towards the window. There was a pile of books stacked on top of the central heating outlet. He removed one of them and placed it on the space on the desk that Paul had cleared earlier.

Leaning over the document, Jacques restarted, 'This is a space chart showing the area around the Celestial North Pole. Polaris is very close to this Celestial North Pole.'

Pointing to the star closest to the middle, Jacques went on, 'When you look up into space at night in the northern hemisphere, all the other stars appear to revolve about Polaris.'

'That's because it is above the Earth's North Pole and almost in line with the axis of the Earth's rotation,' Claire added to signify she understood.

'Yes that's right,' replied Jacques. 'It is the Earth that is moving, not the stars. They are moving, but they do it very slowly'.

Jacques continued, 'We have found two binary objects, possible black holes rotating around dense stars, here and here'.

He pointed to two points on the chart in a straight line either side of Polaris.

'You will notice the symmetry here. They are not only in a straight line with Polaris; they are also equidistant on either side. In fact, more accurately, they are symmetrical around the

Celestial North Pole,' Jacques paused enigmatically for it to sink in.

After a second or so Paul asked, 'But the Celestial North Pole is a point invented by mankind to map the universe from Earth. It is a feature of Earth's rotation which is only important if you come from this planet. Surely it has no real significance to the real geometry of space?'

'Good point,' replied Jacques 'For me also, it is an amazing coincidence. So I am thinking we need to find out more. My next step is to analyse the red shift of the binary objects. This may shine more light on our conundrum.'

'What will the red-shift tell you?' asked Claire.

Paul explained that if Jacques looked at the makeup of the light from the stars, he could estimate the distance that the stars are from Earth by finding out how much their light signature had shifted towards the colour red. Claire thought she'd understood but wasn't sure. She asked Jacques to continue. He did.

'So these two stars that are approximately equidistant on either side of Polaris could be responsible for the images Paul found in the Hubble data.'

Jacques stood up again and flicked though another of his document stacks.

'Ah here it is,' Jacques exclaimed, clearly pleased to have found whatever he was looking for. 'I have also analysed the stars' radio spectrum. I have here some data from Jodrell Bank.' He said, placing another document on the desk in front of them. 'It was collected at the same time as the Hubble photos were taken. I have found evidence that if you move the distance from Hubble's orbit to the surface of the Earth, the images, the images become one.'

'So it is probable that the radiation from the two binary stars converged on the radio telescope network on Earth's surface,' said Paul amazed.

'Yes, but I cannot be specific about exactly where the focal point was, simply it was on the Earth's surface, probably in Northern Europe.'

Claire thought his phrasing was interesting full of caveats, 'probabilities' and 'evidence', not very firm. Sometimes she wanted more certainty, but that was not the business they were in.

Paul thought a little and addressed Jacques again. Jacques saw it coming.

Paul started, 'You also said that these were part of a binary system. Presumably the two components of the system are continually rotating around each other. So their gravitational signature is continually changing. Given the Earth is rotating, orbiting the sun and wobbling on its axis..,'

Busy little things, thought Claire,

'…the focal point would never stay on at the same point on the planet's surface. This means the phenomenon will hardly ever repeat and certainly not in our life times,' said Paul.

'This is true,' said Jacques. 'You have probably seen a transient event that will only happen when all the celestial objects are in the right place. Quite a find! It is at least worth a submission to a scientific journal. You should write one and submit it to Physics Review Letters.'

'It won't be exactly ground-breaking, but it is a real discovery I suppose,' Paul, pausing for thought. 'Would you co-author it Jacques?' he asked.

'Of course', replied Jacques.

Claire was transfixed by their cosy academic chat but decided to bring them back to reality.

'So you've observed a big coincidence, but what this has got to do with my DNA analysis?'

Jacques replied 'Absolutely nothing, but interesting eh?'

Claire looked at Prama and asked 'Is he always so annoying?'

Prama looked thoughtful, smiled and said, 'Yes, he is'

They all laughed. These were scientists having fun.

****

Paul and Claire had been having so much fun with their hosts, that they had almost missed the train. Prama rushed them to the station in her little Fiat. They ran across the concourse to board the train just in time.

'That was close!' said Claire, catching her breath.

'Sure was,' replied Paul.

They started to make their way along the carriage looking for seats. The train was extremely busy and there were only few singleton empty seats dotted about the train. It was an unspoken agreement that they wanted to sit together. As they made their way along they saw an empty seat next to a businessman, opposite him was a young man dozing. The bag of the latter was on the seat next to him. Paul made his way towards the young man and tapped him on the shoulder. The young man looked up at Paul with a querying expression.

'Excuse me,' said Paul. 'Is this seat taken?'

'It's all yours mate,' came the reply.

'Do you mind if I put your bag on the rack then?' asked Paul.

'Be my guest mate,' said the young man, turning his head away to continue his doze.

The businessman looked up from his reading and nodded with approval, then returned to his book.

Paul lifted the young man's bag on to the rack and then searched for space to put Claire's and his own. Claire sat down in the seat next to the businessman. Paul, when he had finished his baggage handling duties, sat down opposite her.

'I'm knackered,' he said to Claire.

'It's good to get a seat. I wasn't looking forward to standing all the way,' said Claire with a sigh of relief.

Both of them knew that they could easily have got seats if they had split up. For some reason the idea of travelling separately had become unthinkable.

Claire looked around her. The young man next to Paul had fallen asleep with his head resting against the edge of the window frame. The businessman next to her, in his shirtsleeves was still concentrating on his book. His jacket was in a neat bundle next to his brief case. Both were on the rack above him. Claire had seen Paul carefully move the jacket to make room for their bags. The businessman had offered to take his jacket down during Paul's bag manoeuvres.

'Thank you but I think there's enough space,' Paul replied courteously.

The businessman smiled, nodded and returned to his book. Claire liked to see two strangers observing a protocol of old fashioned politeness. It made her feel safe.

She glanced at Paul, sensing he was going to say something.

'I'm going to get my book down,' he said. 'Do you want anything?'

'No I'm fine thanks,' she said. 'I've already got mine here.'

Claire placed her book on the table in front of her. She would read it later. Her thoughts had returned to their meeting with Prama and Jacques. She was still intrigued by the relationship between Paul and Prama. She was framing a question in her head.

'I like your friends,' she said, getting Paul's attention.

'Yes, they're fun aren't they?' he replied, looking up at her.

She was trying to find a subtle way of finding out more about Prama.

'Prama's very clever isn't she?' Claire said as an opening gambit. 'Has she been in Jacques department for long?'

'For ages,' said Paul. 'I think she will need to move on soon though. She needs to experience another university.'

'Do you think she will do that?' asked Claire, pleased that this thread of conversation was developing, not wanting the discussion about Prama to end.

'I think she would like to go back to the Far East,' said Paul.

'The Far East?' queried Claire, fazed by the sudden change in direction.

'Yes, she was brought up there. Her father was based in Hong Kong. He married a local girl and Prama was born.'

'So Prama's half Chinese?' asked Claire.

'Yep, she speaks English, Cantonese, and some Nepali. She learnt Japanese at school. So as well as being a theoretical physicist, she is a linguist. Clever girl, like you say!' said Paul.

Claire was quiet for a moment trying to take it all in.

Paul went on, 'She was sent to university in England and whilst she was away Hong Kong was returned to Chinese rule. Prama gained British Citizenship, but her father did not. Shortly afterwards her mother died, so her dad was a bit lost.'

'But I thought you said her father was in the Ghurkas. So he must have been in Hong Kong with the British Army! How could they split a family like that?' asked Claire, incredulously.

'Amazing isn't it?' Paul said. 'He fought in real battles and got real medals in the Falklands! In my opinion, this was not the UK government's finest hour. Anyway, after lots of pressure Prama's dad and his comrades got their citizenship. It's a pity our so called leaders didn't do the right thing the first time round.'

Claire was taken aback by the strength of Paul's feeling. She could see he was very passionate about the situation Prama's family had been in. Claire wanted to know more about Paul and Prama, so lightening the conversation she asked him about a comment he made on their outward journey.

'Why did Prama call you "her engineer"?' Claire asked.

'What?' said Paul, bringing his thoughts back.

'Oh yes,' he said smiling.

He had realised that the conversation had become rather too heavy. They were on a public train after all. He glanced up at the businessman opposite who was still engrossed in his book.

'It goes back to the difference between the engineer and the physicist,' said Paul.

'Is there any difference?' asked Claire, leading him on.

'Let me show you,' Paul said, closing his book and placing it on the table in front of him. 'If an engineer wanted to stop this book sliding as the train went round corners, he could do a little experiment.'

At that moment the train, travelling at speed, lurched to one side. The book slid along the table. The businessman briefly glanced down and then returned to his own book.

'That was impressive,' smiled Claire, amused by the coincidence.

'Good wasn't it?' Paul responded, with a smile. 'Anyway, I can stop it sliding by placing your book on top.' He took Claire's book and put it on top. 'This adds pressure on the surface between the table and my book. The result is that it is more difficult for the book to move.'

'But if we go round a really tight bend then the book may slide again,' said Claire, enjoying the game.

'Yes,' said Paul. 'So we do lots of journeys, add more books until it never moves. Then just to make sure, we double the size of our stack of books.'

Glancing to her left, Claire noticed that the businessman smiled. He was still engrossed in his book but was now maintaining a proprietarily strong grip on his text. Perhaps he thought his book was to become part of Paul's experiment.

'Alright I understand,' said Claire. 'The engineer works out the solution practically, and just in case he's got it wrong puts a big safety margin in. That makes sense to me, so how does the physicist do it.'

Lifting his book and pointing to the table surface Paul explained. 'The physicist finds himself an electron microscope.'

'I didn't notice one in the train,' interrupted Claire.

The businessman had found something amusing in his book.

Paul ignored her comment and keeping a straight face, he continued, 'The physicist takes samples from the surface of the table and the surface of the book. He examines both of these samples through his electron microscope. From what he learns, he works out "Mu".'

'What's "Mu"?'

'"Mu" is the co-efficient of friction. It's the Greek letter mu. We use lots of Greek letters,' he said. 'Anyway, returning to the subject of "Mu". This tells him how much weight he is needed to get enough friction to stop the book sliding. He then weighs each book and calculates the amount of friction per book. A year later, after lots of academic papers he has worked out how large the stack should be,' Paul stopped.

Claire had a feeling that Paul was leading to something but she did not know what.

She said, 'In the meantime the engineer has solved the problem and his book has been secured to the table for weeks!'

'Ah,' said Paul. 'But the engineer has only solved one problem; the physicist has solved hundreds.'

'Like what?' said Claire, knowing she was falling into a trap. The businessman had not turned a page for some time. He must have reached a difficult section in his book.

'Let me give you an example of the same problem,' said Paul.

Claire waited. The businessman turned a page.

'Imagine two cats are sat on top of a children's playground slide.'

'Ok,' said Claire fixing the image in her mind.

'Which one gets to the bottom first?' asked Paul.

Claire thought for a moment, 'I don't know.'

'The one with the smallest Mu, of course!' he said.

Looking into Paul's eyes, Claire thought for a second. She saw a twinkle. She laughed.

Paul laughed.

Paul liked women who laughed at his jokes.

The businessman suppressed a chuckle. His book was obviously hilarious.

The train came into a station. It was the businessman's stop. Claire got up to let him out. He alighted.

'He must have been reading a funny book,' said Claire, 'He was laughing all the way through it.'

'It had an unusual title,' said Paul, smiling. 'It was called 'Finance for Senior Managers'.'

They looked at each other and started to giggle. They were still giggling when they got to the other end. Their other fellow traveller was still asleep.

# Seven

## New Friends

Claire was already at work when Paul walked through the door at seven thirty.

'You look dead beat' she said as Paul walked over to his desk.

He felt very tired. After they'd got back from the meeting with Prama and Jacques, Paul had gone back to his research. He had probably had only two hour's sleep and he had to admit to himself that his body needed to rest. His mind however had too many questions to resolve.

'You know what it's like'

'Yes,' said Claire. She did. 'Come on, let's get a coffee.'

He threw his jacket over the back of his chair and they walked together to the tearoom where there was a kettle. It was on old disused laboratory that now doubled as a tutorial room and tearoom. There was no highly sophisticated drinks machine here; it was all manual labour. Paul filled the kettle and Claire selected two of the least encrusted mugs and used one of the laboratory-type sinks to wash them.

Paul sat down on one of the chairs that were dumped at higgledy-piggledy angles around the table in the centre of the room. He watched Claire as she worked at the sink.

'What do you want; tea or coffee?' she asked.

'Coffee please, I'll pay' he reached over and dropped a few coins in the cardboard box next to the small fridge. She put down the cups and walked over to him, opened the fridge and peered in. He liked her proximity. She wondered how a laboratory so concerned about absolute cleanliness in their labs, could grow such things in their fridge. Maybe these were special cultures for somebody's biology experiment. She eyed the bottle of milk suspiciously but took it back to the mugs anyway.

'Milk?' she said.

'No thanks just strong and black please,' he said.

'You need bed not caffeine,' she said, pouring the water into the mugs. She then dunked the tea bag a little, put it in the bin, added the milk, collected both mugs and sat down next to him.

Claire continued, 'Thanks for introducing me to your friends yesterday. It was a fascinating meeting. I've started some more PCR off with different primers to see if I can isolate any more genes. After listening to Jacques, I'm starting to think we have an even bigger biological question here'.

Amazed at the effect of the coffee, Paul was almost awake but not enough to understand any of the words that Claire had just said.

'You look puzzled,' she said.

'You read my mind,' he replied, starting to think that this girl was far too perceptive. 'I think I need a bit of a lesson on some of the techniques you are using. What is PCR?'

'Ok,' said Claire. 'We have been given tiny amounts of DNA collected from an expensive international space mission. The samples are so small that if we used the original samples for analysis, we would soon have none left. We'd then have to send our trusty shuttle off again and get some more.'

'And pigs may fly,' he interjected.

'Precisely, so we use a process called PCR or Polymerase Chain Reaction. This uses a mix of chemicals, natural enzymes and the DNA you want to copy. You then add a 'primer' which is two short DNA strands to kick-start the process.'

'I assume the primers are called that because they are the first few links in the new copy?' he asked, hoping the bits were starting to fall into place.

'You've got it. The problem with the primer is that you have to pick ones that the sample would recognise, so there is a bit of intelligent guesswork to do in advance. If you get the wrong one, then nothing will happen or you only copy a small bit of the DNA. Fortunately another team in Italy had already designed some primers, so we have had a head start and we've been able to get PCR going.'

'Okay, what about,' he paused, trying to get the words right. 'Poly-mer-ase Chain Reaction.'

She continued, 'Polymerase is a special enzyme that copies DNA. It's an enzyme; that's the 'ase' bit. It's like a machine that makes things from component parts. I guess, being a physicist you'd call it a biological catalyst. It produces the polymer called DNA. We also add chemical components into the pot, along with the DNA to be copied.'

'I thought it sounded like cooking!' he said.

'Well cooking is chemistry,' she said not insulted in the least.

'If we raise the mix to the right temperature the DNA double helix separates into component threads.'

'Ah that's what denatured means?' he asked.

Claire could hear the penny dropping.

'Yes, the heat breaks the links between the two threads of the double helix. In other words, it melts. As it cools, the primers and the enzyme get to work copying each thread. Finally hey-presto the DNA strands glue themselves together back into the famous double helix, but now you have twice as many. In one cycle we will have doubled the original sample. By repeatedly raising and lowering the temperature you can double the sample each time. In about a few hours you can have over a million identical copies of the original DNA section.'

'Amplification,' he said.

'Yes. Of course, if your original sample was contaminated and the primers match it, then you'll amplify the contamination also. So the whole process needs to be very clean and carefully controlled,' Claire continued. 'And then we analyse the products from the PCR process to give us the famous A G C T coded sequences of DNA bases, but that's another story.'

'So the gene we talked about yesterday may be one of many in the sample,' said Paul

'Yes,' Claire replied. 'There are the three Italian primers, there may be more.'

Paul realised he was looking too deeply into her eyes and when Claire had finished there was an imperceptible pause where she held his gaze. His mind had gone blank. Get a grip Paul, he thought, coming to his senses. She's more than just another conquest.

'Hi,' a voice at the door.

The moment had passed.

'Hi Anil,' said Paul, disappointed at the interruption.

'Hi,' said Claire her cheeks a little flushed.

'I've got some more stuff for you,' said Anil, still standing by the door.

'Come in; have a coffee,' said Claire.

'A drink of water will do fine thanks,' said Anil.

He wandered over to the water purifier that stood in the corner, the highest-tech thing in the room and drew himself a cup of water. He sat down.

\*\*\*\*

Just as Paul arrived at his desk, his mobile rang. It was Jacques. He had some news and he needed to talk. He asked Paul to bring that delightful Claire along with him. They arranged a meeting and Jacques rang off.

# Eight

## It's All Relative

They had decided to use Dieter's office as he was out raising money or something. Paul had suggested to Claire that they use the internet video phone system in the shared office, but she thought it would be quite disruptive to anybody trying to do real work. So Paul had brought his laptop into Dieter's office and plugged it into the network.

After a few seconds a message came up 'Incoming Call – Jacques'

Paul clicked 'Answer' and Jacques', face started to form in the window below Paul's camera. In spite of the size and graininess of the picture Claire could see that Jacques was excited.

'It's great to see you mes amis. You are a real picture, the two of you there.'

He couldn't resist the chance to tease them.

Paul said, 'Ok, Jacques, enough of the flannel. I can see you're excited. What's happened?'

'Oh don't be so British Paul, Let us Latins have our fun.' He took a breath, 'Do you remember your not-so ground-breaking discovery?'

'Yes,' said Paul.

'Alors, it's breaking more ground than you think.'

'What?' said Paul, staring at the little picture in the corner of the screen.

'I have Prama here and she agrees.'

He moved a little to let Prama come into view.

Claire in a normal voice said, 'Hello Prama.'

Prama in a normal voice said, 'Hello'

Paul just wished Jacques would get on with it.

'Hi Prama,' he said.

'She agrees with what?' said Paul, bringing them back to the point.

'Our latest extraordinary find,' replied Jacques.

'What find?' said Paul, none the wiser.

'Your focussed images have re-appeared.'

'What?' said Paul, 'but that's impossible.'

'Exact, so we're in new territory here and I have no idea what's going on. Wonderful isn't it?' replied Jacques.

Paul seemed to have been struck dumb, so Claire asked Jacques to explain what they'd found.

'After you left, Prama and I decided we needed more data to help you with your journal article.'

'Thanks,' said Paul.

'What are friends for?' Jacques replied with an extravagant shrug. 'We decided to ask Jodrell Bank if they could look for your star group again when our two binary systems were back in the same orientation in the night sky as they were when the Hubble image was taken.'

'And you saw the image again?' said Paul excitedly.

'No,' said Jacques.

Paul and Claire looked at each other exasperatedly.

Enjoying the moment, Jacques continued, 'But we did half a second later! Mon Dieu. This is bizarre!'

Paul really wished Jacques would hurry up.

'Based on the rotation of the Earth, our orbit round the Sun and the 'wobble' as you call it, our two binary systems were almost in the same part of the sky last week. Prama has now extracted data from several telescopes around the northern hemisphere, to see if any of them happen to have been looking at that bit of space at the right time. She has been looking for similar images that have been captured, in focus or otherwise. Why don't you tell them what you've found?' Jacques said, keeping up the suspense for as long as possible.

Jacques made space for Prama and she moved herself in front of the camera.

'We have found no less than four other occasions which have the same spectroscopic profile as your image,' said Prama. 'There is even an academic paper that suggests that the observer has discovered a new Mira type pulsating star where in fact we now believe this is an optical illusion caused by the scanning of our two binary systems.'

She waited a moment for any comments. Paul looked aghast but he said nothing.

Prama continued, 'As Paul pointed out at our last meeting, Earth's movement in space is quite complex. For a pair of stellar objects to remain synchronised to a repeating scan pattern of Earth's northern hemisphere implies some kind of resonance and communication between the Earth, and the binary systems. This would be difficult enough to understand if they were ninety three million miles away like our Sun. But these systems are separated by many light years and in turn many light years from us. If the Earth were to wobble, just a tiny bit because of a passing comet then the whole system would stop working. This does not seem to be happening.'

Paul had regained his composure, 'So you're telling us that two binary systems separated by hundreds of light years have synchronised the rotation of component stars so that they can focus energy on an insignificant little planet in an average solar system in an adjacent galaxy. And to do this they must communicate faster than the speed of light.'

'What does all this mean?' asked Claire.

'It means,' said Paul looking at Jacques, 'by some bazaar accident, we have found that the Earth is the focal point of a huge gravitational telescope that is tracking us and breaking one of the most important laws of physics – the speed of light.'

'Does this happen very often?' she asked.

'No,' said Paul 'because it's impossible.'

'Oh,' she said. 'Does it have any bearing on my DNA problem?'

'Well it might do,' said Prama 'Your DNA was piggybacked on a comet that went through this area of space. I can't quite believe it but if the sample didn't get there on the back of the comet then, perhaps it's no coincidence that the space concerned could be having all kinds of troubles with time. This is the kind of thing science fiction writers call a rift. Contrary to popular belief, no one has ever seen this before or if they have, they haven't told me. There's a small probability that Paul's 'far out' fourth option is right. Maybe your comet has been in a different time dimension. It's still too far fetched for me though.'

'And me,' said Paul, with a worried frown.

They said their goodbyes and hung up. They all needed to reflect.

'What next?' asked Claire.

'I wish I knew,' said Paul.

\*\*\*\*

'Ah I'm glad you two are back.'

Claire was wondering why everybody was referring to them as 'you two'.

Anil continued, 'Do you want to see the results from my gene search?'

'Yes,' said Paul and Claire together.

'I've managed to input the two of the sequences that Mike gave me into the computer. I've run the program and found some interesting matches. So far the closet match is in two genes of Drosophilia Melanogastor; the fruit fly to you and me, Paul.'

'I knew that,' said Paul joking.

Claire smiled amused, 'So you've found the second gene is close to the fruit fly also.'

'Yes,' said Anil, 'with a common ancestor at about two hundred and eighty million years ago.'

'It can't be from a fruit fly though.' said Claire, 'Drosophilia Melanogastor is far too complex to be in space; unless it came from Earth.'

Paul had wondered why the fruit fly was thought to be 'complex', but he realised that if you compare it to a single cell organism, the most basic form of life, there must be hundreds of millions of years of evolution in between. Compared to bacteria, the fruit fly was very complex.

Anil went on, 'The genes appear to be from a eukayote.'

'What the hell does that mean?' asked Paul near desperation.

'It means,' said Claire a little concerned, 'that they are not from the most primitive single cell organism that you would expect to find in a sample from space. It's a bit worrying because it has started me thinking about contamination again.'

'However,' interrupted Anil, breaking their train of thought. 'They are sufficiently different from the fruit fly as to be a completely different species. So you don't have to worry about an extra terrestrial invasion of huge insects.'

'Yet that is,' said Paul with his tongue firmly planted in his cheek, but not sure whether he was still joking.

'That's an image to conjure with!' said Claire thinking aloud. 'A giant fruit fly flying to Earth on the back of a comet, you think he'd find a better form of transport wouldn't you!'

'Any one for tea?' said Paul, feeling all today's conversations were far too weird.

'Yes please' said Anil, 'No milk thanks'.

'I think I will,' said Claire. 'I'll come and help.'

She was quiet as they walked back to the tea room. He had a feeling that she was mulling something over. Not surprising he thought after all the stuff they'd learnt today.

'Paul,' she said as she was filling the kettle with her back to him.

'Yes,' he said, expectantly.

'I don't want you to take this the wrong way but,'

Oh dear, he thought. He could not see her face so he had no idea what was coming.

'I've got my sister and her boyfriend coming over tonight for dinner. And I don't want to be a gooseberry. Would you like to come too?'

Yet again Paul was aghast. 'Are you asking me on a date?'

He had read about this kind of stuff, but it'd never happened to him before.

'Maybe,' she said enigmatically.

'I'd be delighted,' he replied, beaming.

She returned one of her smiles, her eyes sparkling.

****

'Come on Prama think!' She mumbled to herself. Prama just couldn't get her mind round this. Paul used to say if she got stuck she would just make something up and 'hey presto' she was off again. Just like a theoretical physicist, never bounded by the real world. They had laughed about that then. Once she had said that at least she was not afraid of committing to some of the realities. The comment had more bite than she had intended. Then they were sad. She wished she'd never said it, but it was true; it was true then, anyway. Perhaps he'd changed. Ah well, water under the bridge. Let's think something up! Jacques was always good with ideas. She would chat with him.

'Hi Jacques, can I hijack you?'

The old ones are always the best thought Prama.

'Mais oui. What would you like my dear?' Jacques replied smiling at the joke.

From anyone else the 'my dear' would have triggered fury in Prama, but not with Jacques; it just seemed natural.

'I can't get my head around this binary star problem. It makes no sense. I simply can't believe we have a relativity violation,' Prama said with a wrinkled forehead.

'Would it stop those wrinkles on that pretty head of yours, if I said I had the same problem?' he queried.

Again, if it were another person, she would have thought he was flirting with her, but she knew he was devoted to his wife and scores of children.

'I can only think of entanglement,' she said in a manner that resembled a question rather than a statement.

'Go on,' he said, interested.

'It goes back to the EPR idea from the 1930s'

'1935,' chipped in Jacques, 'it was an idea of Albert Einstein, Podolsky and Rosen to demonstrate why quantum mechanics was wrong if Relativity was right'.

'I know that entanglement is a very trendy research area at the moment, but I think we are seeing similar mechanisms in Paul and Claire's problem,' she paused.

'Yes, it's trendy because of quantum computing. What will they think of next? Go on,' he said encouraging her to speak.

'If you remember Einstein had a problem with quantum mechanics because he felt it violated the velocity of light limit. So with his colleagues Einstein wrote an article about a thought experiment. They described a situation, predicted by quantum mechanics, where two particles that were originally close to each other could influence the other instantly after they had moved apart. He called this "spooky action at a distance".'

'Yes they wrote the paper to show how silly this was because the communication would have to travel faster than the speed of light, or travel backwards in time. Go on.'

'As you know experiments were done and these proved that their experiment did indeed work. So quantum mechanics was right; QED. This has now become known as entanglement.'

'Yes and as I said earlier, they now use the phenomenon in quantum computing. Please go on.'

'From what I understand about quantum mechanics it is only important at microscopic, sub atomic scales,' said Prama.

'Even smaller, I would say and gravity is usually only important on the astronomical scale, but go on,' said Jacques, starting to get involved.

'As you know over the last forty years there has been a huge amount of work bringing the various theories of physics together culminating in the standard model. But this, again only applies in the microscopic scale. There have been many attempts to reconcile the standard theory with the 'big stuff', gravity, but they have failed to gain acceptance.'

'True, but ideas like string theory have never been tested by practical experiments and because of this they must remain unproven,' he interjected.

'I have just read some material about entanglement and it appears to work at distances of several metres, so that is certainly not microscopic!' she said.

Jacques nodded.

Prama continued, 'Although the current theory of particle physics predicts most things very well, there are known problems with the Standard Model. I've mentioned one: it doesn't include gravity. Also it assumes all particles have no width, depth or height. This causes some bizarre theoretical effects that have never been seen, like infinite forces and density. If they existed we should have seen them.'

'Modern physics is full of bizarre things like that!' interjected Jacques.

Ignoring the interruption, Prama continued, 'Everything I've read about string theory tells me that they have invented an idea that particles can be represented as waves that are vibrating on strings in dimensions that we can't see. This seems to work mathematically but nobody has yet been able to see them or prove they exist. This is often cited as an example where theoretical physicists have gone off the rails. Are they working on assumptions that have never been tested experimentally? So how can anyone prove or disprove them? Well I was thinking; what if entanglement and string theory are linked in a way that explains what we are seeing. What if Paul and Claire have found the experiment to prove it?'

Jacques looked at her, 'You know, sometimes I think you are mad, at other times I think you are brilliant. Right now I'm not sure. So I'll opt for the last one. Let's put some meat on the bones shall we'.

Then they started to work it all out.

# Nine

## Sad Little Sister

Just as Claire had suggested, Paul arrived at a quarter to seven, fifteen minutes before Claire's sister and boyfriend were due. He had arrived at the door with some flowers and a bottle of wine, wondering whether she was ready. Perhaps she had thought he would be fashionably late but unlike Jacques whose roots were on the Mediterranean coast, Paul had a thing about being on time. My God I'm boring, he thought. Well this is it. He raised his finger and pressed the doorbell.

He heard the latch on the door click. It opened and there before him stood an apparition in white.

'Oh wonderful, you've arrived,' Claire said.

And it could speak too, Paul thought, but he seemed to have lost his voice.

His vision was drawn instantly to her eyes. They somehow looked bigger and sparkled more than ever. If she was wearing eye make-up, it was very subtle. He could see she was wearing lipstick but it was so close to her natural colouring, it too was barely discernable. Her hair was down and flowing over her shoulders. She wore tiny gold earrings where the studs had been and a simple chain around her neck, she needed no more.

'You look beautiful,' he said, relieved he could speak again.

'Well thank you kind sir,' she said with a smile, blushing slightly. Looking at the flowers, 'Are those for me?'

For a moment he wondered what she was talking about.

Then waking from his daydream, he said, 'Yes sorry.' Not sure why he was apologising and why he felt awkward and clumsy.

Pulling himself together he passed her the flowers and gave her a polite kiss on the cheek. Smiling, she returned the gesture.

'Come in. They haven't arrived yet. Everything is just about ready.'

She led him into the flat. The door opened into a small hallway there were three doors, presumably it was a one bedroom flat.

'Why don't you hang your coat just there,' Claire said, pointing to a small alcove in the corner.

There were four coat hooks screwed to the wall. Paul recognised a coat she often wore to work. He hung his coat next to hers. He followed her through the door into the living area. It was a good-sized room. A gold coloured sofa was placed at a jaunty angle in the middle. In front of it was a low wooden coffee table. On Paul's right he could see a small dining table laid out for four people. Behind this there was a kitchen area that seemed far too orderly given a meal was being prepared. On the other side of the room, opposite the dining area, there was a large window that overlooked the garden below. There was a television and DVD to the left of the window. The TV was about half the size of the one he had in his flat; he supposed big TVs were a man-thing. Against the wall next to the television, stood her desk, on top which a laptop was symmetrically placed. There was a framed photograph at the corner of the desk and a couple of books with bookmarks at the other corner. Above the desk there were shelves full of science books. There were other books of many different genres in a small bookcase that fitted into the gap between the desk and a radiator. He glanced across the titles. He notices a James Joyce and a number of other literary classics. The next shelf held thrillers and detective stories. No science fiction, perhaps she prefers science fact, he thought.

'I like your flat,' Paul said. 'It looks really comfortable.'

'Thanks,' Claire said, her voice a bit more distant than he had expected.

'You certainly have a broad reading list' he said, looking towards the bookcase.

'Yes,' she replied with a smile, 'I suppose it's obvious; my tastes are quite catholic.'

'You can say that again,' said Paul. 'There are some titles here I can't even pronounce, let alone read!'

Claire laughed. She is beautiful when she laughs, thought Paul.

She had made her way over to the kitchen area that was separated from the main room by a work surface containing a sink and draining board. He followed her over to where she was putting some water in a vase.

'This is for you,' Paul said, offering her the wine.

'Oh thanks, that's kind. Can you pull the cork for me? There's a corkscrew in the drawer there.'

He pulled the cork and put the open bottle on the table.

'Hasn't it been a lovely day?' he said feeling embarrassed that the only thing he could talk about was the weather.

Normally he only ever talked to her about science. Paul realised that Claire had many other interests. He was beginning to become intimidated by her bookcase. Sad but true, he thought. He needed to read a book on small talk.

'Yes,' Claire said. 'I love this time of year. The trees are full of fruit, and the evenings are still light and the weather is mild. Somehow the colours look different as well. Just look at that sky.'

She came to join him at the window and together they looked out at the shades of red around the sun as it disappeared behind some trees.

'You know, it's that kind of sight that got me into science and astronomy,' he said, saying what he was thinking, rather than worrying about talking work stuff.

'The colours are truly amazing…' she said softly.

The doorbell rang. The others were early. Yet again, the moment was gone. She went to answer the door whilst he waited by the window.

'Oh dear, you poor thing.'

He could hear fragments of conversation coming from the hall. He knew something was wrong.

Claire appeared in the room with her sister. Sarah had clearly been crying. Her eyes were red. There was no sign of her boyfriend. Paul had expected her to be the elder sister; in fact she looked a couple of years younger than Claire. There was a clear family resemblance, except Sarah was blond.

'Paul, this is Sarah. Sarah meet Paul,' said Claire.

Paul was instantly embarrassed; feeling like a 'spare part'.

'Hi Paul,' she said putting on a brave face.

'Hello Sarah,' replied Paul. Then addressing Claire, 'I can see something is wrong, I think I should leave you two alone', feeling more awkward than before.

'Oh no, Paul please don't go. Claire has gone to so much trouble and I've heard so much about you,' said Sarah emphatically, holding back the tears.

'Could you just give us a few moments Paul?' said Claire, her eyes pleading with him to stay. 'Why don't you pour yourself a glass of wine and make yourself comfortable.'

'Ok' he said, feeling that he was cornered.

He was not good at "people stuff" like this. He just wanted to be somewhere else. But he did as he was told, sat down on the sofa and sipped a glass of wine. Oh bugger, he thought and gazed through the window into the evening sky.

It was only a few moments later when Claire returned.

'I really should go, you know,' Paul said.

'No please don't. She's just dumped her boyfriend. He was a rat and she needs company. I don't want to spend the next few hours talking about, no offence, how all men are rotten,' said Claire smiling.

'None taken, but I'll be in the way.'

'No please stay, if you can put up with being outnumbered,' said a voice at the door. Sarah had recovered her composure. 'Come on Claire are you going to feed us?'

Unbelievably the dinner went well. Sarah and Claire got over their empathetic men-hating very quickly and Paul listened while Claire and Sarah told him about their adventures as children. After she had left school, Sarah had studied to be a meteorologist. He joked that she didn't mind talking about the weather then. They laughed. Paul's earlier embarrassment about small talk had evaporated but at the end of the meal, he knew he'd better make his apologies and go home. He felt good that Sarah looked happier, but the two sisters needed time alone to talk. Claire saw him to the door and Sarah discreetly moved to the kitchen out of earshot.

'Thanks for staying,' said Claire looking into his eyes.

'Thanks for having me,' he said.

There was a short silence. He could feel her breath on his face. He bent down and kissed her gently on the lips. They were cool and soft. She felt the warmth of his body next to her. She slipped her arms around him and pulled him gently towards her he could feel the soft pressure of her breasts through her dress. He cradled her head in his hands to hold the kiss for longer. She knew if they continued she would not let him go and by some mutual understanding, they separated.

'I must go,' he said gently. 'Sarah needs to talk to you alone'.

'Yes you must,' she said softly.

He turned and walked down the stairs. She watched him as he disappeared from sight.

****

When he hit the street he was elated. It was a beautiful moonless evening. In spite of the orange glow of sodium streetlights, he could make out some stars twinkling. He paused under one of them and looked at his watch. It was 11 o'clock. He would walk home. He moved away from the light and looked up.

Through the glow, he could just make out some stars forming a large square.

'Pegasus,' he said to himself.

He turned round and headed in the other direction. He lived north of here.

It was a quiet, tree lined, suburban street and as he followed the pavement around a corner, he noticed that next to a small park, a couple of street lights weren't working. Because of the open space of the park and the shade from some trees, the light from other lamps couldn't penetrate that part of his route. As he moved closer the sky seemed much darker. There was still an orange glow but far less dominant. His eyes were becoming accustomed to the new darkness. He stopped and looked up. He saw a magnificent river of stars over his head, appearing in the south west then disappearing behind distant street lights in the north east; The Milky Way. He looked away from the streetlight to get his night vision back. The more he stared up, the more stars seemed to appear. Whenever he looked up at a clear night sky he was awestruck. He knew each star was probably the centre of its own solar system and may have its own planets. One of those could be another earth. He was looking into billions of stars forming our galaxy. How could there not be other life? He tracked along the Milky Way until he came to the 'W' shape of Cassiopeia. He then looked to his left to find The Plough. He could see why it had so many names, the Plough, the Big Dipper, the Great Bear; you couldn't miss it. He identified the star in the body of the constellation just below the handle. Phecda – eighty four million light years away. He identified Dubhe – one hundred and twenty four light years away, and tracing a line between the two about the same distance again he thought he could see a faint dot. I wonder if that's it? He thought, but he knew it was unlikely.

He was looking for the M82 galaxy. Through a large telescope, it looks like a fly with its wings opened out. There are flies in space, he thought. This was another galaxy like our own Milky Way, one of billions of galaxies each one holding as many worlds as each other. If there isn't life out there, then that's really very very odd, he thought, we are safe though; that one is twelve million light years away.

He looked back to his old friend Dubhe and the other bright star at the back of the constellation, Merak. He followed the line back in the direction of Cassiopeia and found Polaris. the Pole Star. Against all this background, it looked alone and almost insignificant. It was not very bright, or distinctive. It was not very close either, being four hundred and thirty light years away. He looked at the space around the star. There were a few faint dots, but it was not the densest area in the sky. What secrets are you hiding? He mused and walked home deep in thought.

# Ten

# Oh Bugger!

Having slept really well, Paul was back at his desk bright and early. He was gazing into his computer screen at the latest set of results from Anil's programme. He was being bombarded with too much information and he needed to consolidate his thoughts. Let's list the facts, he thought. He took a sheet of paper from his desk and started to write. The old ways are the best, he thought.

He'd filled a page, so he stopped and scanned his notes. This wasn't helping. He needed to stand back from the problem for a bit. He found that he had the best brain waves when he was thinking about something completely different. He looked up and Claire was just hanging her coat up.

'Hello all,' Claire said to the whole team.

She was met with mumbled hellos from the other three people in the room.

He thought, for some reason, she didn't want everyone else to know about last night. He decided to follow her lead.

'Hi Claire,' asked Paul, trying to keep a straight face, 'Did you have a good evening?'

Her eyes sparkled, 'It was very nice thank-you. I had friends over. They were really good company.'

'That sounds great,' he said, grinning. 'Fancy a coffee?'

'Thanks I'll join you,' she replied, grinning back.

They headed for the tearoom.

'Who do they think they're kidding?' mumbled Anil, smiling to himself.

****

'How is she?' asked Paul in a quiet voice. The walls were very thin in the tearoom.

'Oh she's fine. She's going to stay with me for a few days. Do you think that would cramp our style?' hoping it did not seem too forward or disloyal.

Paul was relieved that she was still interested in him. 'Probably, but we've lots of time, no need to rush.'

She smiled at him, not the same sparkly smile as usual, but something more tender. He smiled back and brushed an imaginary hair away from her cheek. Her head moved almost imperceptibly towards his hand. Tiny gestures, but very poignant.

'Well we're at work now and I've been trying to get my brain operating properly. I'm afraid 'ze little grey cells' are slow today. I've done a list,' he said, lightening the mood with a parody of an Agatha Christie character.

'Good for you,' she teased.

'Shall we go through it together?'

'I'd like nothing better,' she said, 'but I must see how Mike and Anil are getting on'

'Ok,' Paul said, 'let's meet back here in an hour.'

'It's a deal.'

She topped up her coffee mug and went back to the rest of the research team.

'Ah there you are,' said Dieter, sticking his head round the door. 'I've been looking for you'.

'Why, what have I done?' Paul said jovially.

'I'm not sure. Is there something I should know?' asked Dieter sharing the joke.

Paul shook his head.

Dieter went on, 'I have some time on Hubble for you.'

'Blimey,' he said. 'How did you swing that?'

He wasn't expecting Dieter to come through.

'I'm not sure; maybe they like my Germanic charm. Either way, you've got a slot. You will need to e-mail the guy in NASA to work out which cameras are available, the field of resolution you require and other details. I'll forward his address to you.'

'Great I don't know what to say.'

'"Thanks" will do fine,' said Dieter

Paul said thanks and went back to his sheet of paper. He added extra points to his notes.

'Well that's it,' said Claire walking back into the tearoom. 'It's contamination! Damn!'

'How do you know?' asked Paul, seeing that she was downcast.

'Anil's found a match for five of the genes we've sequenced.'

'Yes?' prompted Paul.

'It's Apis Mellifera.'

'Which means?' prompted Paul again.

'Our DNA came from a honeybee.'

'Oh bugger,' said Paul.

****

They spent the rest of that day going over every step the DNA had taken between the space probe and their laboratories. As it went though the comet's tail, the probe had found several small samples of DNA. These samples were kept apart in separate sterilised containers then further separated, in ultra clean conditions in the International Space Station. This is in orbit around the Earth. It was difficult to see how the original samples could have been contaminated in space. When returned to Earth, meticulous precautions had been taken at every step for all the universities taking part in the analysis. Paul and Claire could not see where it had been contaminated. It must have been in their laboratory. This would be extremely embarrassing and Claire was really worried that she had failed to follow some fundamental laboratory protocol. The problem was that she couldn't see what she had done wrong. If it were true, it would damage their reputation badly. All because of a bumblebee, she thought. I'm starting to hate honey! It had to be done; she would have to update Dieter with the bad news.

'Do you want me to come with you?' asked Paul.

She said no. It was her mess and she should face the music. Claire knocked on Dieter's door and walked in. He could see by her face that there had been some kind of disaster. He braced himself for the bad news, when the phone rang.

'Yes, I'm speaking,' said Dieter into the phone.

'I understand but why the urgency?'

'Yes I understand, but these things take as long as they take. I'll try my best,' Dieter said tightly. He paused, 'Goodbye.'

Claire was not really listening. She was deep in her own thoughts. She felt she had must have made one of the most serious errors in her career, and one of the most basic! How could she have allowed the samples to get contaminated? What a mess! She was devastated. After this, the whole department's competence would be in question. Dieter had put the phone down and was looking at her expectantly. He didn't seem to be in a good mood.

'You would not believe this Claire,' he said angrily. 'They want our results now; they're telling me we're too slow. That's rubbish!' Looking at her expression, he paused. 'Alright what's up?'

She looked at him and took a deep breath, bracing herself took the plunge 'Dieter, I've cocked up.'

'By that you mean what, exactly?' asked Dieter.

'I've made a colossal mistake,' she said, exasperated.

'I can see that by your expression,' He said without compassion.

'I have the results from the genes sequencing. I believe I am responsible for their contamination,' she was at least pleased to get it off her chest.

Now she must brace herself for the onslaught. Dieter was known to be a perfectionist and intolerant of poor science, as he called it. This is why he was in charge of this department. His reputation for running a tight ship had gone before him. He had always argued that science was difficult enough without adding to the complexity by making stupid mistakes. Because of this, all protocols in his laboratories were thoroughly proven and crosschecked. He encouraged all his team to stick to the script and keep excellent records. Some would say that this left no opportunity for innovation but he argued that in experimental work, even innovation has to be disciplined. At least when you came to the analysis you knew that the experimental method was sound. If anything weird turned up, it was weird, not a mistake. Whilst Dieter was in charge, this was the way they did things around here.

'I need you to explain why you think that,' he said, his voice softening.

He knew that Claire was a meticulous scientist. He found it difficult to believe that she should make such a basic error with any samples, let alone some as valuable as these. At this point he preferred to believe that her only error was in interpreting her results and not in her laboratory work.

'The gene sequences come from a bumblebee,' she said.

'A what?' he exclaimed, hardly believing his ears.

'Apis Mellifera, the common bumblebee,' she repeated. 'We have found a match with the modern Apis Mellifera. I cannot see anyway that it could have been in the original sample.'

'Oh my God,' said Dieter

'You're the second person to use a phrase like that,' she said, wondering why men had such small vocabularies.

Claire explained how she had retraced all the steps during the handling of the samples. Having eliminated everything else, the only thing left was an error in performing one of her protocols. She had gone though those as well and found nothing wrong.

Dieter looked thoughtful, 'I have been through your protocols myself. They are well documented, some of the best I have seen. You have clean rooms, reserved areas for producing mixes, PCR and sequencing. You have secured the routes between these areas, and you label and record your samples meticulously... I could go on.'

He paused. She was surprised he knew so much about the details of her work.

'Thank you for your support Dieter, but the fact remains something has gone wrong. I have let the team down,' she said, trying to keep professional.

'I hadn't finished,' he said. 'I have reviewed your protocols and believe they are sound. So that makes me as culpable as you.'

This did not make her feel any better.

Dieter continued, 'Is it possible that one of your team did not understand the protocols and they have not followed them properly?'

'As you know, that is the most likely reason but there are many checks and balances supervised by me. Yet again, I am responsible,' said Claire firmly.

'What about sabotage or vandalism?' Dieter asked.

'The same applies. I should have detected it.'

Claire had now convinced herself that, as she had made the error, she did not want to hide behind any of her team. Dieter thought this was admirable but it may have clouded her judgement.

'Ok Claire, this is what I am going to do. I am not going to inform the space agency yet. I want to get to the bottom of what has gone wrong. I know you feel that the problem is in these labs. If so, I want to know exactly what has happened. So I'm going to ask an old colleague from the Biology department to cross check everything. In the meantime I'm afraid you'll have to stop work in the labs. Let's keep it low-key for the time being. I will need to tell the team that they can't use the labs. I'm sorry can I have your keys please.'

Claire handed him the keys to the laboratory and made her way back to the tearoom. She hoped it was empty. It was. She was horrified that she could have made such a mistake. It was even more horrifying that she could not reconcile the facts she had in front of her. She knew Dieter had to bring someone else in to investigate and she was fearful that whomever Dieter brought in would find she had missed something really basic. She knew Dieter was doing what he had to do. He was giving her all the support that he could offer.

'How did it go?' Paul had stuck his head around the door.

'Just as you would expect, really,' she replied.

She looked dejected.

'You alright?' he asked.

'Yes thanks Paul,' she was not. 'I need some time alone to think.'

'I'll be in the team room if you want to talk.'

'Thanks,' she said coolly. 'Everything is fine.'

Although they both knew it wasn't.

****

Later that evening Dieter told her how his ex-colleague was going to go about his investigation. He thought it would be best if she worked from home for a few days, whist they got on with the investigation. Feeling even worse than she did before, she agreed. Dieter gave her some sympathetic words; she smiled only partially hiding the emotion in her eyes. She packed up her working papers and left for home. She wondered what Sarah's day had been like.

# Eleven

# Contamination

Anil was now deep into Paul's gravitation book. Being a mathematician he was fascinated by the beauty of Einstein's equations, but he had to admit he wondered what the great scientist had been smoking when he had thought of them. It would take Anil some time to get his head around the complex matrix maths underneath the equations, so he'd have to read the book a couple more times. He wanted to understand fully the implications; he was confident he would, eventually.

'Good morning,' said Paul, as he threw his jacket over the back of his chair; performing a ritual that was becoming familiar. However the morning coffee ritual was missing.

'Hi Paul, this book is fascinating,' Anil said, holding up GRAVITY. 'I'm nearly halfway through.'

'Careful you'll break your arm,' he joked, as Anil lowered the book. 'It's the basis of much of what we know about stars and things in astronomy. There are still a few mysteries left though.'

Paul knew it was a good idea to lend Anil the book. Anil seemed to have an affinity with numbers and equations. He was able to grasp the underlying message that is often hidden behind complex algebra. Paul had an intuition about things he could visualise. He could work with equations, indeed he had to, but he found it easier to relate to numbers that meant something physically. Anil seemed to have this ability, but he had the talent to handle abstract concepts with ease.

'Have you spoken to Claire,' and not waiting for the reply, 'how is she?'

Paul replied a little distantly, 'I called a couple of times last night, but her phone is off. I guess she's a bit down.'

Paul was unsure what else to say. He had told a white lie. In fact he had called round to see her but he wanted to keep their brief conversation private. Claire had built a shield around her. She believed something had gone wrong and she would take full responsibility for letting the team down. She was not prepared to transfer blame. Paul did not see it like that. He explained that in different times, the whole team would share the glory, so they should share responsibility. Whatever he said it seemed to make the situation worse. Paul had had a few minutes alone with Claire's sister where she told him about her concerns. Sarah said she had not seen Claire like this before and she felt Claire needed support from both of them. At that moment Paul should give Claire space. Sarah would talk her round. Paul was feeling quite down. He missed Claire; they all did but he missed her more. The whole team respected Claire. They desperately wanted to support her but her fate lay in the hands of others.

'Come on,' said Anil sensing the mood, 'let's get some coffee'.

'I thought you didn't drink coffee?'

'I don't.'

\*\*\*\*

Anil, sipping water from a plastic cup, was gazing at some program code on his computer screen. He put his cup down and picked up the book they were discussing earlier. He flicked backwards and forwards over a few pages. He was looking for something.

'Paul,' he said, still looking at the book.

'Uh hh,' mumbled Paul, engrossed in a message on his screen. 'Have you a minute?'

'Right I'm all ears,' he said tuning towards Anil. 'Shoot.'

'I've been trying to write a simulation for a comet passing close to a black hole. If the incoming angle is oblique, the comet would experience changes to time and space, but it can still fly close to the black hole and survive. If it survives it can continue with time and space running as normal. On the other hand, if it hit the black hole head on it will be captured and never escape.'

'So far so good' said Paul, encouraging him.

'There is a boundary around a static black hole that determines what happens to our comet if it approaches from any angle in between the two extremes I just mentioned. If our comet crosses what is called the gravitational radius, alias "horizon", it will be sucked into the centre by massive gravitational forces. Having crossed the boundary, it cannot return. It is lost for ever.' Anil waited for confirmation.

'Yes, it is like a one-way membrane if anything crosses it cannot get back. There is a theory that if you could escape, you may turn up in another part of the universe. Unfortunately, it is likely that matter on the other side of the membrane would be crushed into the centre first. So anyone who tried to use it as a gateway would not be able to escape from the middle of the black hole. That is, in the unlikely event that they had survived being crushed to a pulp in the process. So if there is an opening to another universe it's a one-way street to the centre or in other words there is no exit!'

'That sounds pretty conclusive,' said Anil.

'Well it's the best theory around. Mind you, I don't know anyone who's tried so you can't be sure.' said Paul, trying not to be too dogmatic.

'I can't find what happens if the velocity and angle of approach are such that it is exactly parallel to the horizon?'

'Time stops,' answered Paul. 'That's another way of explaining why the hole is 'black'. Light is a vibration, vibration measures time, time stops, light stops, everything goes black. You can get stuck there also'.

A light dawned. Anil understood. He went back to his book.

Paul went back to his e-mail. It was from Prama. She had some ideas about 'time dilation'. She wanted to set up another meeting with him and Claire. His mind went back to Claire. He was convinced she'd made no mistake. Some very odd things were happening. Maybe there was a connection after all!

****

Dieter didn't believe Claire had missed anything either, but he had to be sure. He had briefed his old colleague thoroughly and given him the run of the labs. All he could do now was to wait until the investigation was complete. The problem was that the wider scientific community were becoming impatient for results. He could stall them, but not forever. He hadn't spoken to the Italian team for some time. They too must be getting closer with their results. He picked up the phone. He dialled a number and after a couple of Italian rings he heard a familiar voice.

'Bonjourno Massimo. It is Dieter. How are you?'

'I hear your Italian is as good as ever my old friend,' Massimo joked ironically. 'I am well. How goes it with you?'

'I am well also. How are Margaretta and the kids?'

He wanted to get straight to the point, but this was not Massimo's way. They did small talk for a few moments. Then he sprung the question, as subtly as he could.

Dieter asked, 'How are you getting on with the Yakawa samples?' trying not to be too specific.

'We seem to have had some problems sequencing the DNA samples,' Massimo replied cryptically. 'I am sure we'll resolve it. And you?' he enquired.

'We have the same experience here, I am quite worried about contamination,' said Dieter, feeling guilty about not coming completely clean. 'We're re-checking some of our results. It's probably nothing though'.

They chatted a little more about the project and then they rang off.

'Interesting,' mumbled Dieter to himself.

And then, in another place, interesting, thought Massimo.

\*\*\*\*

Jacques and Prama were getting bogged down. They'd gone back to their respective offices and pulled out everything they could that would give them a quick crash course on string theory. Jacques' office was more chaotic than normal, and Prama's was almost as bad. They had been together in Prama's room and had been talking for over two hours.

'Everything hangs together but nothing seems to explain how we get these two systems to communicate with each other without violating one of the universal constants,' said Jacques.

For a moment they were both deep in thought.

'In areas of massive gravitational fields, like next to our binary systems or black holes, space and time are quite different to our experiences here. What if these other dimensions become important to such an extent that our normal three dimensions plus time becomes secondary?' she said.

'Yes,' he said, 'that is not a new idea.'

'Let's try this one,' she said, warming to her theme. 'You said that we kept violating one of the universal constants, Plank's, Newton's Gravitational constant and c, the velocity of light. In my maths I have always set these equal to 1. They are constant after all and this simplifies the maths.'

'This is common practice,' confirmed Jacques.

'It may be a mad idea, but what if the constants are only constant in three dimensions? What if in the other dimensions the speed of light is twice as fast? Nobody has ever seen these other dimensions so how would we know?'

'But it would surely predict weird things in the dimensions we can see.'

'But perhaps that's exactly what we're seeing. What if, in these dimensions, the constants are not constant at all? The ratios between constants may be fixed but a change in one compensates for changes in the others? No one would ever know this unless you could tap into a world where three dimensions were unimportant. Perhaps this is what we are seeing. Perhaps this is the mechanism for entanglement. If this were the case then, dependant on which space you were in, time would behave differently. If you were able to move between spaces, say at an oblique angle to these different dimensions, you could pop in and out of places where the clocks run at different speeds,' Prama stopped waiting for Jacques reaction.

Jacques was thinking perhaps she was mad after all.

# Twelve

# Bumblebee Conundrum

It was getting late. Dieter had just been given a verbal update on the findings of the investigation into Claire's laboratory work. He now had no choice. He would have to call the space agency about the situation. He was on the phone for over an hour. He stood up and went into the team office.

'Does anyone have Claire's address?' Dieter asked. 'Her phone doesn't seem to be working.'

He took the details down from Paul and left. Paul was really worried for her. He'd call her tonight.

\*\*\*\*

Dieter arrived at Claire's flat about twenty minutes later. Sarah answered the door and showed him in. Sarah made her apologies and went for a walk. They talked for some time.

\*\*\*\*

He wasn't sure how he was going to open the conversation. Paul picked up the phone and dialled. It was ringing. He felt awkward and clumsy again. This was going to be difficult. He took the plunge.

Paul's call came in shortly after Sarah had arrived back. Dieter had left.

'Hi, it's Paul.'

'Hello you,' she said.

He couldn't make out whether she was being brave or she really was cheerful.

'Anil's doing really well with his software,' he said. 'He's had some good ideas. I'd like to encourage him to work on them.'

He'd decided to broach the subject of the investigation only if she did.

'Good idea,' said Claire, cheerfully.

'You know what?' she said.

'What?' asked Paul.

'The Italians found bumblebees as well.'

'Thank God,' Paul said relieved. 'I knew it was ok.'

Claire then told him all about the conversation with Dieter.

\*\*\*\*

Earlier, Dieter had received a systematic, almost pedantic explanation of what had happened in Claire's analysis of the DNA strands. He could not work out from the explanation what she had done wrong. So he had to ask.

The reply was 'Absolutely nothing is wrong, it's a very well run laboratory. In fact if she wants another job she can come over to my laboratories.'

'That's a relief. Thanks.'

His friend left.

Having heard that Claire's lab work was exemplary, he was proud, relieved and puzzled in equal measure. But Dieter still had a problem. From his point of view the results accurately reflected the samples they had been sent. He may still end up in a pissing contest with the Agency, who always felt they could do no wrong.

That afternoon Dieter had no choice but to contact the space agency and tell them about Claire's findings. This is when the shit would hit the fan, he thought. Let the battle begin.

Dieter made the call and explained they had found Apis Mellifera genes in the sample. He used the Latin name because somehow it sounded less like a cock-up.

'Yes,' came the reply. 'So did the Italians.'

Dieter guessed as much. This was helpful.

'But they had a separate sample,' said Dieter incredulously.

'This is true. So either the sample was contaminated by the probe or we have just found a bumble bee in a comet's tail.'

'What? That's impossible!' again, incredulously.

\*\*\*\*

The next morning Dieter asked Claire to join them in his office. He told Claire how impressed the investigator was with her work. She blushed. He didn't tell her that he had offered her a job.

'We need to decide where we go next,' he said. 'Can you get Paul in here?'

They squashed in together in Dieter's small room. It reminded Paul of his and Claire's meeting with Jacques.

Paul and Claire updated Dieter with what they knew, including their discussions with Jacques and Prama. Paul missed out some of the wild speculation and just stuck to facts and inevitable questions. Claire explained that the genes they had matched were from a modern terrestrial species of bumblebee and unless there was an exactly parallel evolution going on somewhere else in the universe, the DNA most probably came from Earth. Given the Italian samples had found the same genes. It looked like the samples had been contaminated in space. If not then a terrestrial bumblebee had somehow flown into space, hitched a ride with a comet and bits of it had come home care of the probe. Paul explained that as the comet was passing through the constellation of Ursa Minor, it was about 100 million miles away from Earth. This was when the sample was collected. The bumblebee must have had a lot of stamina to survive the journey.

'The whole thing is beginning to look like a massive hoax,' said Dieter.

Paul wasn't so sure but he kept his thoughts to himself.

Paul and Claire returned to the team room.

'Prama's sent me a text,' he said. 'They've had some more ideas. Do you fancy another day trip up north?'

After a tense few days, she felt quite relaxed again. So she replied 'Yes, I'd like that. We could talk about your list on the train'.

'Do you fancy a drink to celebrate your award for excellence?' Paul asked.

'I'd love to, but I can't. I must get back to Sarah,' Claire replied.

He was downcast but determined not to show it.

'Never mind,' he said. 'We can talk tomorrow.'

'Sarah's going out at eight thirty, why don't you come round then. We could look at your list over a bottle of wine and a takeaway. I don't feel like cooking,' she said smiling.

Suddenly Paul was downcast no more. It was great to see the old smile back.

'That would be great. See you at eight thirty.'

# Thirteen

# The List

They got to the train just in time. The train was not busy so they had plenty choice about where to sit. They selected a section of two double seats on either side of a table. Paul put his bag on the rack and helped Claire with hers. They automatically sat side by side. Last time they had sat opposite each other.

'What have you got in here?' he asked, grinning broadly. 'I can hardly lift it!'

'Only my trusty old computer and some results to show Prama and Jacques,' she replied smiling. Then as an after thought, 'Now we're sitting comfortably, don't you think we should go over your list.'

'We were 'sitting comfortably' last night and it slipped our minds,' he said with a glint in his eye.

'Well, that was then and this is now,' she said in a mock schoolmarm voice. 'Come on let's at least give it a try.'

'Okay,' said Paul in mock abashment.

He reached into his bag to find his note pad. He placed the paper on the table between them.

*The DNA is contaminated — it came from Earth*

*DNA is from space and appears to be undamaged – Options:*

*It is young - Options*

*It has been in a different relativistic time frame and It has travelled through time*

*It was produced nearby, just before the probe went by*

*It was teleported ... Silly!!!!*

*It is not young Options:*

*It spent most of its time in the head of the comet...*

*What is the longest time it could stay in tact in the head of a comet?*

*how did it get there?*

*It has been floating in space for millions of years and captured as the probe went by*

*The analysis is wrong*

*Somebody's taking the piss!*

*There appears to be a ~~Galactic~~ Interstellar binocular telescope tracking Earth's northern hemisphere - Options*

*This happens naturally all over the universe — we're just the first to see it*

*Some kind of natural phenomenon linking us, the lens and the image*

*A freak co-incidence of geometry and star distribution*

*historically connected — back in time (time travel bollocks!)*

*action at a distance — communication faster than light assumption is wrong*

*Communication does not have to be infinite, just faster!*

*Other dimensions — stringy things- yuck!*

*There must be other examples,*

*we just need to look - What do we look for?*

*What about the southern hemisphere? —*

*Some intelligence has built this*

*Why? — we're insignificant!*

*The 'God' option — spirits and stuff. I prefer beer!*

*it happens naturally, but Some intelligence is manipulating it. — more than I can cope with!*

*Who?*

*Why?*

*The data is wrong or we've misinterpreted it.*

*Someone is taking the piss!*

*What data should we look at?*

*Hubble — point it where and when*

*Old fashioned land based astronomy?*

*Radio astronomy*

*DNA data bases*

*Physical locations. — focal points*

*How does a bee get inside a comet?*

Claire scanned the list for a few moments.

'If you take out the words of limited vocabulary, this is quite good. Maybe you've got a brain after all,' she said with an amused smile.

'And I thought you were only after my body,' he replied grinning stupidly.

'Behave yourself. Let's see what I can add to your list,' Claire paused for thought. 'I am now pretty sure that the DNA came from a terrestrial bee and it was no more than a few days old. From Jacques' description of the comet's tail, I cannot believe that our DNA sample could have survived more than a few hours. You have eliminated contamination, which is very touching but it still remains the most likely reason. We must include contamination by the space agency, because the Italian samples were contaminated also. Mind you, knowing the precautions they take, I've no idea how that is possible.'

'Ok,' said Paul obediently adding a 'stet' mark on his list.

'Also you need to add the point that the sample most likely came from Earth, Where would you put that?' Claire asked.

Paul thought a moment.

'I think it should read 'the DNA is young AND it came from Earth',' he paused again, his mind churning.

'Now that's an interesting thought,' he said aloud.

'What is?'

'We've been concentrating on the movements of the comet. And, because it's really difficult to work out, that's where I've put most of my effort. Maybe I've been looking at the wrong thing.'

Paul stopped deep in thought.

'How do you mean?' Claire asked.

'We've been asking how the bee got into the nucleus of a comet. Well, it probably didn't. We know where the bee came from, you've told us. It was from Earth and not millions of years ago. So that rules out a journey in the comet's head. We also know where it arrived and when. It could not have survived there for long, so it must have arrived within a few hours of the probe. We need to concentrate on the bee, not the comet,' said Paul.

Claire thought that was what she was doing but she was pleased Paul had caught up.

****

This time Jacques had booked a spare seminar room. He explained that they could have used his office, but all the chairs were now buried in paper, so there was still nowhere to sit. They all enjoyed the joke, even though it was true.

Claire explained about the bumblebee genes and the fact that her lab did not seem to be responsible for any contamination. She missed out the details of the investigation and the stress they had experienced before they knew about the Italian laboratory results. Jacques said he guessed both labs would have been under incredible scrutiny. He seemed to understand the pressure Claire had been under.

Claire was just summarising the position when she said, 'The question of the DNA samples now seems to come down to two alternatives. One: was the DNA contaminated by the equipment used in space? And if not: How did a bumble bee materialise in space whilst the probe and the comet were passing by?'

Jacques looked quite surprised, 'Why do you think it would be a whole bee and not just its DNA?'

Claire replied, 'Don't forget, when we first started the DNA analysis we were expecting to find very basic forms of life. When I found soft, cellular material with the sample, I had assumed it was part of a simple animal. So I was not worried about what happened to the rest of it. Then I found out it was a more complex animal. So I thought I'd test for the proteins it contained. This might have given me some idea of what cells the DNA came from. It turned out to be keratin, a protein found in hair and bone.'

'What does that tell you?' asked Prama, her curiosity aroused.

Claire continued, 'From what Jacques has told me, no animal could last very long in the plasma environment.

I know from talking to Paul that an animal with an exoskeleton, like a bee would last longer than us mere humans in the vacuum of space, but within a few minutes, the body would still break up because of the differences in gas pressure.'

'That's right,' said Paul.

'My theory is that the bee's body had exploded because of the difference between its internal pressure and the vacuum outside. The probe then picked the sample up just after this event, but before the keratin and DNA had time to separate,' said Claire.

'So the time window to collect the sample would have been quite small,' said Prama.

'That's right,' replied Claire. 'So if the original sample was not contaminated, then the next option is that the probe and the bee arrived within a few minutes of each other. We know where the probe came from but the bee?'

Claire looked into each face for reaction and true to form Jacques obliged.

'The odds of that must be miniscule!' said Jacques.

'My thoughts exactly,' said Claire 'Paul had said to me we should concentrate on the bee, a bee from Earth. Well I am now convinced the probe and the bee arrived together. Now you can see why I am reluctant to dismiss the contamination option!'

'The odds of the alternative are tiny unless there is something connecting the three parts together,' said Prama.

'Are you suggesting there is something odd about that point in space?' asked Paul.

'Not really, my question is: Is there some prior connection between the probe, the comet and the bee that have caused them to be in the same place at the same time?' replied Prama.

'I assume you don't mean like a dentist's appointment?' asked Claire wishing they would accept the obvious conclusion.

'Not quite,' said Prama laughing with the rest of them.

Prama then explained her ideas on quantum entanglement and gravity to them.

\*\*\*\*

In the taxi back to the station they had argued. Claire could not understand why Paul and Prama could so easily dismiss the obvious solution of contamination.

'The three of you, seem to be preoccupied with some fanciful science fiction stuff,' she said.

'But science can only advance if people challenge the traditional answers,' he replied, a little more sharply than he had intended.

Claire was irritated by the implication that she was blocking scientific discovery. They were quiet for a moment.

'Science is not about making things up, you know. It is about having ideas and then testing them by experiment,' she replied, somewhat heatedly.

It was strange thought Paul; Claire had used the kind of argument that he used to use on Prama. She did not know that he had a good reason to act out of character. Paul was confused and he was unsure how to explain what was really going on. He was annoyed by Claire's comment about "making things up".

'If you want to prove our theories wrong then you are free to do it,' said Paul, coolly.

'I will,' she said, icily

They sat in silence for the rest of the journey to the station. Then their interactions became professional and cold, quite unlike their taxi ride earlier that morning.

Yet again the train was not full and there were plenty of seats. Like before, Paul offered to help Claire put her bag in the rack. She said no thanks and placed it in the seat next to her. Paul sat on the seat opposite her bag. The train trundled along whist they sat in silence; Claire reading a journal, Paul looking at the scenery.

I cannot win, he thought to himself. Paul was trying his best, but if he explained his motivation, she would only rebel. Claire was too independent for her own good. He didn't know what to do.

'Alright,' he said. 'How are you going to prove we are wrong?'

'I haven't thought about it yet,' she snapped, 'but I will'.

'Why don't you do an isotope analysis of the material around the DNA,' Paul suggested. 'If it is contamination, then the chemical profile will not match the comet in any way. The paper Jacques gave us contains all the data you need.'

Why is he helping me with this? She thought. Paul must know that there is very little chance of Prama and Paul being right. This experiment will either prove nothing or prove that the samples were contaminated. They were ganging up on her and helping her at the same time. She too was becoming confused.

'You mean the Finklemann article,' asked Claire in a flat voice.

'Yes,' said Paul, 'If you speak to Jacques I'm sure he's got similar papers buried under those stacks of his.'

Claire smiled reflectively picturing Jacques office and then she checked herself, remembering she was supposed to be annoyed.

She replied curtly, 'Yes I'll give him a call.'

Claire went back to her journal. Claire knew Paul thought she was being stubborn; perhaps she was. Claire was not sure why she was jealous of Prama and Paul. They always seem to be on the opposite side of the argument to Claire. Why was that? Was it because Claire wanted to be in opposition? Was it because Paul and Prama were a team or still an item? They go back a long way after all. Claire found it hard to dislike Prama. Claire wondered what Paul really thought about Prama; Paul had really got under Claire's skin.

The train stopped at an intermediate station. People were getting on and off the train.

'Excuse me,' said a lady to Paul 'Is that seat taken?'

'No, it's free. Can I help you with your bag?' asked Paul, standing up.

Paul lifted her case in the rack over their heads. It was heavy.

'Thank you young man, I'm going to visit my daughter. I don't know why I pack so much. She says I always bring the kitchen sink,' said the lady, with a chuckle.

Paul smiled politely.

The lady looked at Claire, glanced at the title of Claire's journal and asked, 'Are you two travelling together?'

'Yes, we work together,' replied Claire.

Paul was a little disappointed by Claire's reply. The lady glanced at him noticing his reaction.

Addressing Claire, 'Are you studying at university?' asked the lady.

'Yes. We work there. The studying never seems to end,' said Claire smiling. 'How did you guess?'

'Well your book is a bit of a give-away,' replied the lady. 'I always think learning keeps you young. Anyway I'm disturbing you. I think I'll read as well.'

The lady pulled out a novel and buried herself into its pages, only occasionally glancing around her and exchanging knowing smiles with Claire and Paul.

The train drew into the next stop and the lady stood up. Paul helped her get her bag down.

'Thank you, you are very kind,' said the lady and then in a whisper to Paul. 'She's both pretty and clever that one, I wouldn't let her go if I were you!' The lady winked at him and got off the train. Claire did not hear the lady's words.

'You've made a conquest there,' said Claire, with a thoughtful smile.

Paul was embarrassed but Claire did not notice. Her mind had shifted away from their travelling companion, to an earlier conquest of Paul.

They left the train at the next stop.

They parted at the station. Their goodbyes were professional and cool; Paul did not know why. They went home, each to their respective flats.

# Fourteen

# Rivalry

Paul had been on the phone to Prama for a couple minutes or so. After he hung up he went over to Claire's desk and addressing Claire and Anil together he asked them a question.

'Prama has followed up on some of my ideas. She's on the train right now. I asked her to come down for a meeting this morning and she'll be here in about fifteen minutes. I'd like you two to take part. Are you busy?'

'No problem,' said Anil.

'Claire?' prompted Paul.

'I'm afraid I can't,' she said, coolly. 'I have to do some work in the lab. I'm getting a bit behind.'

'Ok just Anil and me then,' said Paul in a "suit yourself" kind of way.

He knew he was being petulant, but her attitude was annoying him. He could feel her drifting away and he did not know why. Claire put on her white coat and left for the laboratory. Anil watched her go in silence.

Paul spoke to Anil, 'Let's take my laptop into the tearoom. We can show Prama the output of your software in there.'

When they arrived at the room Paul busied himself connecting his computer to a projector.

'Is there something wrong between you and Claire?' asked Anil.

He felt he had got to know them both well enough to ask this kind of question and besides, the tension was affecting the rest of the team.

'Don't worry, it's nothing,' said Paul.

Paul's mobile rang.

'Hello,' said Prama. 'I'm downstairs.'

'Ok,' he said. 'I'll be right down.'

Paul told Anil that Prama had arrived. He left the room to fetch her.

'Who else is with you?' she asked.

'Just me and Anil,' Paul replied.

'Oh, no Claire?' asked Prama.

'I'm afraid not,' said Paul, without elaborating.

They arrived at the room where Anil was waiting.

'Hi Anil, I've heard a lot about you. How is your programming going?' she asked to break the ice.

'Fine thanks,' he replied, pleased that she knew who he was.

Anil certainly knew who she was. He had read several of Prama's papers and he was hugely impressed. Now that Anil had seen her for real, he was even more impressed. Prama looked around the room. Something had amused her.

'You've had too much of Jacques' company,' said Prama, laughing.

'Probably,' replied Paul with a chuckle and seeing Anil's confused face he whispered. 'Sorry, in joke!'

Anil nodded, still a little overwrought by being in Prama's presence.

'Paul, it's your meeting,' said Prama, inviting him to start.

Paul opened, 'I've had a number of ideas that I'd like to check with you, Prama. As some of the ideas are a little far out Anil and I would like to bounce them off you before he commits them to his computer.'

Anil was pleased to be involved, but not so sure about re-writing his software. Anyway, for now he would listen.

'I think I may have come up with a way in which DNA from an insect from Earth could end up in space. But before I begin I must ask,' Paul looked at Anil. 'Anil, do you know how lasers work?'

'No,' said Anil, 'is it important?'

'It could be,' said Paul.

'Do you want me to explain?' Prama chipped in, wanting to be part of the conversation.

Anil nodded, quite curious about this woman he had heard so much about.

Paul cautioned, 'The simple explanation please Prama,' knowing that Prama could talk for hours on the subject.

Prama started, 'LASER stands for light amplification by stimulated emission of radiation. It works by doing exactly what it says on the can,' borrowing a phrase from a famous advert.

She continued to give a detailed explanation for the next fifteen minutes. Then she stopped. Anil was enraptured. He liked people who tested his intellect.

'I couldn't have put it better myself,' said Paul, not without irony.

Prama smiled flattered, knowing his comment was a compliment. Anil could see these two knew each other very well. With the concept of the laser firmly planted in their minds, Paul started to explain his own theory.

'My idea is that we are seeing a laser effect not with light waves but with gravity waves,' Paul went on, 'and I suspect the phenomenon is very common in space because it happens naturally. The problem is that you need to look the right way and even then it is hard to detect.'

'So you think we've discovered a gaser?' asked Anil.

'Yes, swap 'light' with 'gravity',' replied Paul, 'and I think with the correct geometry, concentration of mass and triggering radiation you could be produce a sharp gravity wave pulse, with its power concentrated in one direction.'

Paul continued, 'Gravity waves are disturbances in space time.'

'Like radio waves except with gravity?' said Anil.

'Yes and gravity waves are normally very difficult to detect. But if they were concentrated, or beamed like a radio transmitter aerial concentrates radio signals,'

Prama interrupted, 'and they were amplified like a laser amplifies light,' enthusiastically adding to his sentence.

'Then,' said Paul regaining control, 'anything in its path would experience significant bending of space and time.'

'In short, a high power, beamed gravity wave travelling through space would wreak havoc to clocks and geometry for anything in its path,' said Paul

'But how could this work?' asked Anil.

'Do you remember Anil, when you asked about static black holes?' asked Paul.

Anil nodded.

'I think we need to use the mathematics of rotating black holes, not static ones,' said Paul.

'Why?' asked Anil.

Prama chipped in, 'I believe most black holes in space are not static. They are more likely to be rotating and this changes their properties.'

'Yes' said Paul, 'In a rotating black hole there is an outer membrane and an inner membrane.'

'The inner membrane is a point of no return, if you cross it and you get sucked into the singularity by massive gravitational forces.' said Prama.

'Like a static black hole?' asked Anil.

'Yes,' she continued, 'but the outer membrane is different. If you cross the outer membrane you can escape. But whilst you are in the gap in between you experience changes to space and time.'

Paul took back the lead, 'There is a gap in between these two membranes where space and time behave strangely.'

'It is called the ergosphere,' said Prama, 'which means the sphere from which that you can extract energy. This is different from a stationary black hole from which it is impossible to extract any energy.'

Paul went on, 'I'll call it 'the gap'. My idea is that each of the binary systems we have found near Polaris, are made up of a very dense star and a black hole rotating together around their common centre of gravity.'

'A reasonable assumption,' added Prama, helping him along.

'As stuff falls off the normal star, it gets sucked towards the black hole. It goes through the outer membrane and spins inside the gap. I'm assuming it does not go through the inner membrane. This makes the system very unstable building up more and more energy,' Paul paused.

'Like pumping energy into a laser?' said Anil.

'Yes,' said Paul, 'then an external gravity wave appears from somewhere triggering all the stuff in the gap to cross the inner membrane and go into the black hole.'

'The stimulation bit,' said Anil. 'It would be like pulling the trigger of a loaded gun.'

'If you like,' said Paul. 'The energy involved in operating the 'trigger' as you call it, does not have to be big; just enough to kick-start the process. This produces a massive pulse of gravity wave radiation that bursts out from the binary system.'

'Like firing our gun,' said Anil.

'Yes, but more like a giant light house equipped with a powerful laser beam.'

'But this does not explain how the bee has moved from Earth to space,' said Anil waiting for Paul's explanation.

'Good point,' said Paul.

****

Claire returned back from the laboratory window that overlooked the street. She had been daydreaming; that was not like her. She needed to concentrate on the job in hand. Claire had always enjoyed working with the nuclear magnetic resonance system and the mass spectrometer. They were amazing devices.

She felt they allowed her to look into the innermost secrets of the molecules with which she worked. She supposed that was what Paul felt like when he looked into the stars.

'Oh that man again!' she mumbled to herself.

What gave him the right to pop into her mind when he felt like it? She thought. She did not have an answer. She just needed to concentrate to make sure she had set the machine up properly. So Paul could clear out of her head for a few moments. She might let him back later.

Claire had prepared a sample for the spectrometer a few hours ago and varied some of the set-up parameters to allow her to crosscheck the results. This would enable her to calculate the statistical probability that her results, whatever they would turn out to be, were right. She had now taken 100 sets of results and she had started to download them into her computer system. She was now waiting for the program to finish its analysis.

While she waited she reflected on her experiment. As Paul had suggested, Claire had called Jacques earlier that morning. He asked about how she was and chatted about the kind of work they did. He was very helpful with the published articles she wanted. He told her which ones he thought were rubbish and which were good. He had a lot of information that would help. He had agreed to e-mail everything he could find. She had now printed the most important bits and the key details were sitting in front of her now. There was something he had said just before he rang off that made her think…

She woke from her reverie as the computer screen lit up scrolling pages of numbers, followed by a graph. The graph had many peaks. Each one represented an element or molecule in her sample. She zoomed into a section that corresponded to one of the articles Jacques had sent her.

'Well I'll be damned!' she said to herself, subconsciously imitating Paul's tendency towards profanity.

She hit the button to print the results. She had decided she needed to see Dieter and she needed to see him now!

****

Anil had been listening patiently to Paul's idea, hoping he would have a solution to their puzzle about the bee. Prama had remained quiet, deep in thought.

'I'm afraid I haven't worked that out yet,' said Paul, reflectively. 'I haven't got an answer.'

Paul and Anil looked at each other with puzzled expressions.

'I think I do,' said Prama.

Paul looked into the screen surprised, 'You do?'

'I do,' she said, in an amused voice. 'You have forgotten the other binary system.'

'I couldn't think how the two systems could be connected. They are too far apart to operate together,' countered Paul.

'You said it yourself Paul,' said Prama enjoying her moment, 'The gravity pulse is stimulated by an external gravity wave. What if the source of this was halfway between our two binary systems and it sent out a gravity wave to each of our black holes simultaneously?'

'Whatever simultaneous means!' said Paul, now very confused about time and space.

Prama continued, glossing over Paul's comment, 'The two gravity waves would be entangled. Your two "lighthouses" as you called them, would be sending out rotating beams of gravity radiation. These would be highly co-ordinated pulses but crossing in space in different places as the stars rotate. Given their position in space they would occasionally cross near Earth.'

'But this doesn't explain how our bee got teleported,' said Anil, getting to the nub of the problem.

'Oh yes it does,' said Prama. 'Have either of you heard of optical tweezers?'

They both shook their heads.

'Well you should look them up, they allow experimenters to move tiny objects by using coherent laser beams,' said Prama. 'Of course they only do that in three dimensions. But you are talking about gravity waves. They impact on time and space. I think you may have discovered two things, not one: GASER and Gravitational Pliers.'

'What are Gravitational Pliers?' asked Paul, reverting to his stupid mode.

'I think I've just made them up. They are like LASER tweezers, but they are bigger and work with gravity. In the right situation, they could pick things up and move them in time and space.'

'Like our bee,' said Anil.

'Just like our bee,' confirmed Prama.

Paul was dumb-founded. Anil was impressed.

'Paul, I think this is worth testing,' Prama said. 'Anil, why don't you put all this into your computer program?'

Paul could think of nothing else to do but wind the meeting up. They agree that Paul would help Anil with the design of his software and they would call Prama if they needed help.

Before Prama left Paul said that he would like to introduce her to his boss. The three of them chatted for a few moments and Paul walked Prama to the taxi rank across the street. They stood together until a free taxi rolled up.

Claire was gazing out of the window of the laboratory, not looking at anything in particular. Her eyes suddenly focused on Prama giving Paul a peck on the cheek as she got into her taxi. Claire now knew why she was being so unreasonable with Paul.

****

Claire knocked on Dieter's door and went in.

'Hi Dieter, am I disturbing you?' Claire asked, knowing she was.

'Of course not,' he said, looking up from some undergraduate marking he was doing.

He pushed the papers aside and said, 'I'm all ears.'

'Dieter, as you know, I have been convinced that our sample was contaminated, if not here then somewhere else. In my opinion the sample had never been anywhere near the comet's tail. It was too improbable. So I thought I'd prove it.'

She put a sheet of paper in front of him. These were the graphs she had just picked up from the printer.

She explained, 'These are the results from my mass spectrometry analysis of the Yakawa sample. You can see the peaks denoting the chemical structure. I've labelled the molecules and the elements that are present in the sample.'

Dieter looked over the graphs.

'These are the results from earlier work that analysed the composition of Yakawa comet's tail,' Claire laid down a second sheet extracted from one of Jacques' reports.

'At the high molecular end,' she said, pointing to the right of her graph, 'there are peaks reflecting the organic molecules. You would not expect to see a match here with the earlier work.'

'So we should only look at the lower molecular weights?' asked Dieter.

'Yes, so compare the left hand side of both graphs,' she said.

Dieter moved them so that one was above the other.

'They are exactly the same,' he said, 'What does that mean?'

'It means,' said Claire, 'that the sample did indeed come from the comet's tail and it is not contamination. If this is a hoax, then it's a very good one!'

'Good grief,' said Dieter, 'then the bee was in the comet's tail after all.'

Claire wasn't listening. She knew it was good news, but she still felt sad and alone.

'Oh God he'll be smug now!' she mumbled.

He had done it again; floated into her mind!

'Sorry, I didn't quite catch that.'

'I was just thinking how smug Paul will be when he finds out that I have found the problem is not contamination,' Claire explained.

'I don't see why,' said Dieter. 'He told me that the odds of his theory being right were miniscule.'

'So why has he been pursuing them?'

'Because I asked him to,' he replied. 'You've got more friends here than you think!'

'Oh,' she said as Dieter's comment was sinking in.

\*\*\*\*

When Claire had revealed that Apis Mellifera genes had been found in the samples, Paul knew that contamination was the most obvious cause. Up until that time he was convinced by Jacques' explanation that any ancient genetic material must have come from the comet's nucleus. Paul even thought it possible that the organism had evolved in the comet's nucleus; stranger things had happened. Maybe it had been there dormant, for thousands of years. Who knows? Either way the DNA was most likely to have come from a very primitive organism. The find of terrestrial bee DNA therefore killed most of the more plausible extra terrestrial theories for its origin, leaving only contamination.

Paul had absolute trust in Claire. The whole team could see how professionally she ran her laboratory. So he believed that whatever Claire found in the samples she analysed, was in the sample before it had crossed the threshold. The problem now was that she had shown that the source of the DNA was a modern animal. Not only that, but a comparatively complex animal. Paul had confidence that if Claire had found it, then it was indeed there. He was worried that others would assume Claire had made a mistake. He knew how the world political outside could cruel and unforgiving. Also unlike her attitude to science, that was open and honest, the wider community may take a different approach. As soon as the news broke, there were other people in the chain of events who could be implicated by poor science. Many of them would be scrambling to protect their backsides and shift the blame. Paul knew he could not explain his thoughts to Claire; she would think him cynical. Perhaps he was, but she could be naïve. Paul would not change her for the world. A few days earlier immediately after Claire had broken the "bee DNA" news, Paul felt that he needed to talk to someone about his concerns. He had arranged to meet with Dieter to ask how he could help. They were sitting together in Dieter's office, pondering the situation.

'Claire must know that the source of contamination will take forever to be proven, not guilty or otherwise, mud would stick. My god she is stubborn!' said Dieter a little irritably.

Paul responded, 'I'm not sure she looks at things like that, Dieter. She trusts the integrity of the processes upstream of her, just like we trust her.'

'Alright,' said Dieter 'What about your time travel theories, are they all as improbable as they sound?'

'If you think about it, my last two theories are the same. If the bee's DNA was there when the probe and comet arrived, then the next question is how did it get there? The alternatives seem to be: it came with the probe. That is my favourite. And secondly, the crazy one: relativistic travel from Earth. Well to the best of my knowledge, we don't yet have that technology on Earth.'

'So it leaves contamination of the probe's scavenging apparatus before it left Earth,' mused Dieter aloud.

'Yes and we can both see that an error like that would take a long, long time to get into the public domain.'

'And in the meantime we are in the middle of a pissing match,' continued Dieter.

They both sat in thought for a few moments. Then Dieter broke the silence.

Dieter asked Paul, 'What do your friends up north think about your crazy ideas, as you call them?'

'Jacques is being very tolerant, going along with it and Prama is enjoying the intellectual challenge of a new problem. There is a real puzzle here after all!'

'Is there any scientific value in the research you are asking them to do? I don't want you to be wasting other peoples' time,' said Dieter.

Paul could see Dieter's point. He did not want to send anybody on a 'wild goose chase' especially two friends that he respected and admired.

Paul thought a little, 'I have been concerned about this. I have been honest with both of them, but they are theoretical physicists who are as happy to think about 'toy' models as real ones. They understand the probabilities involved as well as us, if not better.'

'I've never met Jacques and Prama, but I've looked up some of their work. They are well-respected scientists. What will they get out of it if the work turns out to be a hoax?' asked Dieter.

'They know that's a strong possibility, but both of them, particularly Prama, have told me that whilst working on the problem, they have gained new insights. Prama has been pushing at some of the most basic laws of physics for some time; in fact I think she's thrown the book away!' said Paul smiling reflectively to himself. 'She can be quite cavalier with the laws of physics.'

'They're enjoying themselves then,' said Dieter amused. 'They sound like fun. I'd like to meet them someday. In the meantime I'd like you to keep this thread of research going. You never know you may come up with something ground breaking.'

'I'll make that my objective,' said Paul still smiling.

'In the meantime I'll tell the wider community about your area of research. I'm sure they'll think you're mad, but it may stimulate other ideas and it will definitely pull contamination out of the limelight for a bit. Thanks for your help Paul.'

'Don't mention it,' Paul said leaving for the tearoom. Paul felt a little guilty, as he was not doing this for Dieter. He was doing it for Claire, though he would never tell her that.

****

Paul and Anil were in the tearoom pouring over star maps and pages of data from Anil's computer program. They had taken over the tearoom because the large table in the middle made a good surface to lay their documents out. They were starting to adopt the Jacques' school of research methods.

Paul was saying, 'This seems to be fitting together very well. How much data have you got on our two binary systems?'

Anil was about to answer, when a head appeared around the door and said, 'Is this a private party, or can anyone join in?'

Claire was smiling her old warm smile.

Paul and Anil both smiled back, but Paul's eyes seemed to have some hesitancy as if he did not know whether Claire's smile was for him or both of them.

'What are you up to?' she said, moving into the room and bending her head, slightly sideways, to look down at the table.

Paul was mesmerised for a moment as he watched the graceful movement around the smooth outline her neck where it joined her shoulder. A memory from a few nights ago entered his head. Anil was answering her question.

'After our meeting with Prama this morning..,' started Anil.

'Oh yes. How did it go?' she asked, glancing at Paul then looking at Anil for an answer.

'Paul and Prama came up with some really cool ideas about gravity waves and they've asked me to modify my computer program to accommodate them,' said Anil enthusiastically.

'I'm not sure they're cool, yet. For the moment, I think we should keep them into the category of 'far fetched',' he said trying to temper Anil's enthusiasm with a little realism.

'How far have you got?' asked Claire.

'Paul's been helping me with the analysis. I haven't written any code yet. That may take some time,' replied Anil, with no sign of his enthusiasm waning. He was clearly excited. 'Would either of you like a coffee?' realising that the air had changed somehow.

'A tea would be nice,' she said.

'Coffee for me thanks Anil,' replied Paul.

Anil moved to the sink and started to fill the kettle.

'I've got some news,' said Claire, with a warm smile and looking directly into Paul's eyes, 'I've done the isotope analysis, as you suggested.'

'Oh' Paul said stupidly.

That was all he could say. At that moment, he was finding it difficult to operate the speech paths in his brain.

'I've just briefed Dieter,' Claire said, keeping the suspense as long as she could. 'I've collected evidence that our DNA sample was in space next to the comet, because there are fragments of the comet's tail in the sample.'

'My God!' said Paul, sitting down.

There's that small vocabulary again, but not smug at all she mused.

'That's brilliant!' exclaimed Anil from the corner of the room, next to the tea bags. 'Maybe Paul's theory is right after all!'

'Good grief!' said Paul, still looking at Claire.

Anil cleared his throat and put their tea and coffee on the table.

'I'm just going to check through my code.' He said, picking up his glass of water and leaving them to their thoughts.

They were quiet for a few moments.

Then Claire lent forward and kissed him.

'What's that for?' he asked, unsure of himself.

'For believing in me.'

# Fifteen

## Rational Conclusions

Prama was talking to Jacques in his room. She had gone through the details of Prama's meeting with Anil and Paul.

'Your meeting seems to have ended with some wild conclusions,' said Jacques.

'You think so?' queried Prama.

'Yes, but not as wild as violating every constant in the known universe,' he teased, referring back to an earlier conversation. 'By the way, I have acquired some red-shift information about our two binary stars.'

'You have?' she queried. 'So do you know how far they are from Earth?'

'Yes,' said Jacques, 'but the distance is not what I find interesting.'

'What is interesting then?' asked Prama always susceptible to Jacques way of keeping one in suspense.

'It turns out that the two binary stars are, as well as we can measure them,' said Jacques, being a real pain, 'exactly the same distance from Earth'.

'I can't have heard you correctly. You are saying they form an isosceles triangle with the Earth at the apex?' she enquired for clarification.

'Yes,' he clarified.

'And you say I have wild conclusions!' she exclaimed.

'Exactement!' he said accepting the irony.

****

Paul was in high spirits again. He reflected that he did not want much from life. A smile from Claire seemed to be enough. He wanted to spend more time with Claire, but she was busy and he had work to do also. It was nearly time to leave for the evening but Paul had just received the incredible finding that the two binary stars were the same distance from Earth. Paul was very keen to see what difference this new data would make to the predictions from Anil's software. He had given the information to Anil for him to put into his database. Anil had asked why the finding was so 'incredible'.

Paul began, 'Think of all the coincidences. We have found two binary systems that are virtually mirror copies of each other.'

'That does not seem to be so strange. There are perfectly rational explanations for remote objects sharing similar attributes, critical sizes and things,' interjected Anil.

'On its own that is not so strange. But then consider these stars are exactly symmetrical about the Celestial North Pole. Despite its impressive name it is not a constant in the universe. It is an arbitrary point in the sky decided by humans.'

'Ok, but that's only a coincidence if there are only two binary stars. I understand there are billions of them. I reckon that improves the odds significantly,' Anil retorted.

'And you could apply the same argument to the finding that the two stars are the base of an isosceles triangle with Earth at the apex. But if you multiply those probabilities together and bet on it at a bookie's, I feel very strongly you'd lose your money,' Paul concluded.

'I don't bet,' said Anil.

It's just as well thought Paul.

Paul and Anil worked on very late into the evening. Paul looked at his watch. It was ten thirty. Oh shit, he thought. He had wanted to see Claire. He called her mobile.

'I missed you,' he said.

'Hello you,' she said softly, 'you looked busy, so I didn't disturb you.'

'You can disturb me any time,' Paul said, feeling it was a corny thing to say.

'Can I?'

'Yes you can. Where are you now?' Paul asked.

'I'm playing Scrabble with Sarah,' Claire said, 'I could have done with your extra vocabulary. She's winning.'

They laughed lightly, a private joke.

'Can we spend some time together tomorrow?' Paul said, speaking quietly so that Anil would not overhear.

'I'd like that,' she said and as an emphasis, 'very much.'

'Good night,' Paul said.

'Good night,' she said. 'Don't stay there all night will you?'

'No,' he replied softly.

They rang off.

Paul and Anil worked until three o'clock in the morning. They loaded their data and started the programming running. It would take the rest of the night to finish. They left it to complete its meditations.

****

Despite their lack of sleep, Paul and Anil were in the team room bright and early. Well, Anil was bright. Paul was tired out. He had too much on his mind to sleep well. He needed his shot of caffeine. Anil's program had still not finished running, so he asked Anil if he wanted a drink and headed off to the tearoom. As he got to the door he met Claire on her way in.

'You look worn out,' she said concerned. 'You haven't been here all night have you?'

'No but it was pretty late, nothing a spot of caffeine won't cure,' he said. Then with a twinkle returning to his eyes he added, 'It would be nice to find somewhere soft to rest my weary head though.'

'The rest would do you good,' she said deliberately missing any double entendre.

'How's Sarah?' Paul asked really wanting to know about Claire, but not finding the right words.

'Oh, she's fine,' said Claire. 'She'll be going back to her own flat tomorrow.'

'It'll be good to have your freedom back,' he said, a little ineptly.

'Yes, I suppose so,' she said reflectively.

Claire had taken over the coffee making process and handed him his mug and sat down next to him.

'What are you doing this evening?' Paul asked tentatively.

'Nothing, why are you asking me out on a date?' she teased.

'Maybe,' teasing her in return, 'there's a restaurant in the park across the road from your flat. I wondered if you fancied dinner. They cook better than me. It's a really nice place. If it's warm enough we could eat alfresco. Given the hours we've put in we deserve a holiday.'

He was starting to think he was overselling his idea, so he shut up.

'It sounds lovely, I'll need to change,' she said concerned about her informal clothes.

He stood her up and took her hand and turned her round in a pirouette.

'You're perfect,' he said, 'very perfect.'

'Maybe, but I'll change anyway,' Claire said.

****

Two hours later Anil's program had finished. Paul and Claire were standing behind him looking over his shoulder at his computer monitor.

Anil explained, 'I've just down loaded all of the output from my software on to a PC. This machine,' he said, tapping the box beneath his desk, 'is simply not powerful enough to run the simulation. So I used one of the university's largest computers to process our data; even then it took over eight hours. So I hope I've written the code correctly. My next step is to produce a graphical display of the Earth and our two rotating star systems containing one black hole each.'

'The binary stars,' said Claire.

'Correct,' said Anil concisely

'Right,' said Paul, 'let's see the animation.'

Anil typed a few parameters into his keyboard and hit the "Enter" key.

A tiny blue dot marked "Earth" was linked by two curved lines to two other objects marked Star A and Star B. There was a white dot close to Earth marked "Yakawa".

Anil explained, 'I have plotted the distances on a logarithmic scale. That's so I can fit all the objects on the screen. It makes the lines joining the objects look curved.'

'That makes sense,' said Paul.

Anil continued, 'When I start the simulation it will step though Earth time showing where the objects are in space and where the laser, sorry gaser, beams are shining. It gives you a view as if it were taking a picture from space every 10 minutes. I'll start the run 1 hour before the probe rendezvoused with the comet.'

Anil keyed some more parameters into the keyboard, and clicked the mouse.

They watched as the comet tracked its way across the solar system. But nothing else happened.

'Ah I forgot,' said Anil. 'I need to add the trigger!'

'You mean the radiation source that causes the Gaser stimulation?' asked Paul.

'Yes,' said Anil. He clicked at a point midway between the two binary stars and ran his program again.

This time the binary stars sent out two curved coloured beams that traced the screen like radar beams. Occasionally the beams from the two stars would cross.

'Stop there, Anil,' said Paul excitedly. 'Can you step it back?'

Anil clicked the mouse a few times and the display started to reverse. He continued until Paul said stop.

'Look,' said Paul. 'This is the situation one hour before the comet and the probe's rendezvous. The beams are crossing on the surface of the Earth. Can you step forward again please Anil; in five minute steps?'

Anil keyed some more information into the keyboard and clicked the mouse. The intersection between the two beams gradually moved toward the rendezvous until the probe, the comet and the crossing point of the two beams were all in the same place.

'Amazing!' said Claire.

Everybody else was speechless. Another sign of small vocabulary thought Claire.

\*\*\*\*

They were all very excited by the result. It seemed to show how a humble bumblebee could be picked up from Earth and transported through space by a pair of intergalactic tweezers! To all of them this was amazing. To Paul it was bizarre evidence of a random event without any intelligence behind it. Otherwise why pick a bee? Paul knew that before they could come to any real conclusions, they needed to check the data very carefully. This would probably mean another late night. There was no way he was going to miss his date with Claire. Paul decided to phone

Prama and Jacques to tell them about the results. He would start the detailed analysis tomorrow after they'd all had time to let the implications sink in. Anil agreed to call Prama also and demonstrate his program over the Internet. He was rightly proud of his work. For some reason, he wanted to talk it over with Prama.

****

Paul arrived at Claire's flat at about eight pm. Sarah had answered the door. She said Claire was just getting ready. She looked just as beautiful as she did the last time he was at her flat. He should be getting used to her, but he still felt awkward with his words.

'You scrub up well,' said Claire with one of her warm smiles.

'So do you,' said Paul.

Sarah coughed interrupting them. 'You'd better go hadn't you?'

They turned towards the door and left for the restaurant. It was a warm evening and with the protection of her shawl, Claire and Paul were able to sit outside. To anybody listening to their conversation it would not have appeared very romantic, as there was a lot of talk about bumble bees and stars. Anybody out of earshot would have seen two people teasing, laughing and joking, comfortable in each others company, but still learning about each other.

As they walked back to Claire's flat they paused to look at the space where their comet had been. It now held even more mystery for them then it did before.

'Do you want to come in,' she asked as they reached her front door.

'I'd love to,' said Paul, 'but Sarah may not want to play gooseberry, as you call it'

'Yes I suppose you're right,' said Claire.

She pulled a sad face.

He giggled and kissed her. She hugged him.

'Thanks for a lovely evening,' she said.

She turned, unlocked her door and with one last tender look disappeared behind it.

He returned to his stars.

\*\*\*\*

'The odd thing is why was the bee deposited next to the comet? In the computer simulation, the crossing points of the beams continue all the way back into space; they go far beyond the rendezvous point of the comet and probe,' Jacques was saying.

They had all decided to meet together in Jacques' office. There were five people rather than four; Anil had come along as well. Somehow it seemed less crowded than before. Claire was puzzling about this when she realised Jacques had taken two of the filing cabinets out of his room and put them in the corridor outside. His shelves were still loaded with books and the old stone used as a bookend.

'Maybe there was something in or near the comet that caused the beams to drop their load,' said Prama.

'The other odd thing is; why did the beams pick up only a bee?' said Paul. 'The beams must have passed many solid items as it moved along the Earth's surface.'

'Alors! Prama, Anil, idees encors? What could have caused this?' Jacques asked them. 'You are the ones having the best ideas today.'

'Perhaps the same kind of material was near the bee causing it to get picked up in the first place,' said Anil. 'Some compound that responds to gravity waves differently to other materials.'

'Ok,' said Claire dragging herself back to the conversation. 'I did an isotope analysis of the comet's tail and found nothing unusual, except for the DNA that is. So I suggest that the "something" was in the comet's nucleus.'

'And that something was able to absorb and re-emit gravity waves,' said Paul latching on to Claire's idea. 'If we were able to isolate that material, it would be amazingly useful for gravity wave detection!'

Jacques was amused with the interplay between Claire and Paul. They seem to be well suited.

'Let us all let our imaginations get the better of us,' said Jacques, smiling indulgently at Paul and Claire. 'If your ideas are right, then there must be a similar material on Earth adjacent to where the bee was captured. Perhaps it settled on the material as the beams came past.'

Anil could not work out whether Jacques was pulling their respective legs, or was he being serious? He was soon to find out.

'Bonnes idees,' said Jacques, 'but too fanciful. For me, there is not the evidence. We still have three mysteries.'

'Three?' asked Anil.

Jacques replied, 'One: what caused the bee to be picked up? Two: what caused it to be deposited? And three,' he paused, in his inimitable style, 'and three: What triggered the gaser beams in the first place!'

'I'm not sure I can cope with this, we solve one puzzle and get three more,' said Claire. 'I thought we were winning!'

'One door closes and three doors open,' said Paul. 'Weird eh?'

Claire glanced at Paul with her smile. Paul returned it; a silent, private dialogue. Paul and Claire looked at each other again like two naughty children sharing a secret. They would have giggled if it was not too immature.

'Very philosophical,' said Jacques, noticing every nuance, 'but not very useful!'

He realised that he would not get any more sense out of them today.

\*\*\*\*

It was late in the evening when Claire, Paul and Anil got off the train at the railway station. Anil said good night and headed off home. Paul offered to see Claire to her door. She accepted gracefully. When she asked him if he wanted to come in this time, he said yes. He watched attentively as she slipped the key into the lock. It turned quietly and she opened the door. He followed her up the stairs watching her every move. He followed her into her flat.

'Isn't Sarah here?' he asked quietly in case she was.

'No, she's gone back to her own flat. She's ok now,' Claire replied.

'Oh, that's good,' Then realising his comment was ambiguous 'I didn't mean…'

She put a finger to his lips. It had stopped him babbling anyway. He did not want to talk. He dropped his bag. The computer made a bang as it hit the floor. He did not care. She lifted her face and put her hands around his head. She pulled him closer. He wrapped his arms around her and felt the pressure of her body against his. They kissed a long lingering kiss. She gently pulled away and looked into his eyes. Her eyes sparkled more than ever. Her smile was warm and tenderer than he could remember. He smiled in return, a loving smile. She led him gently into the next room.

****

It was quite late when they woke up the following morning. Paul had gone into the kitchen to make her a coffee. He noticed his computer bag on the floor so he picked it up and put it on Claire's desk. A sheet of paper fell out of his bag. What's this? He thought and picking it up, he found it was a photograph. He did not notice Claire come up behind him. She slid her arms around him from behind. He smiled an inner smile.

'What's that?' Claire asked.

'It looks like it's a one of the photographs from the Hubble telescope,' Paul replied.

'It's beautiful,' said Claire. 'Look at the colours.' Then looking more closely over his shoulder, she asked, 'Where is the trigger for the gaser beams?'

"It should be here in the centre,' he said pointing to a blank space on the photograph.

'Where is it then?' asked Claire, more interested than she expected.

'That's what I was wondering,' Paul said. 'It's not there! So where the hell is it?'

'Didn't you say it should be equidistant between the two binary stars?' Claire asked.

'Yes that's this point here,' he said pointing to the same spot on the photograph.

'Didn't you also say that the binary stars were the base of an isosceles triangle and the Earth was at the apex?' she asked, rhetorically.

'Good grief, Earth is equidistant between the two binary stars' he said, excitedly. 'That's why we can't see the trigger; we're sitting on it! The gasers were triggered from Earth, but when was the trigger fired?' he asked, mostly to himself.

'As they are about two hundred light years away,' she responded, 'probably around two hundred years ago.'

'You're brilliant!' he exclaimed impressed.

'I'm glad you think so,' said Claire, 'Now put your photo down and come back to bed.'

'Anything you say, my lady'

He did as he was told.

# Part Two

# Crystals at Dawn

# Shi-liu

# Earth and Sky

Xu Kuang-hsien had been up all night watching the falling stars. At first he thought he had discovered more comets, but he soon realised it was a meteor shower. He was looking at the heavens using a telescope. The images he saw delighted him. He wished his colleagues would accept the French telescope for what it was; a powerful instrument. But because the Emperor had said that China had no use for Barbarian products, it was conventional not to acknowledge the value of the device. His viewing position was ideal. At nearly fifty feet above the ground, on top of the Ziwei Palace in the Beijing Observatory, he had a glorious view above him. Xu had all the equipment he needed to chart the sky accurately. Most of the tools around him dated back to the Ming Dynasty. They were much older than the foreign telescope but with this new instrument and the ancient measuring equipment, he was able to look much deeper into the sky than any of his ancestors. For a moment or two, his mind thought back to the wonderful things he had seen recently. It was autumn 1825. Earlier in the year, he had seen four comets. Only one of them was visible to the naked eye but with this telescope, he had seen and charted them all. He put his eye back to the eyepiece.

It was a few hours before dawn when he saw it. A falling star much brighter than all the others had broken though the upper atmosphere and was continuing its onward journey to Earth. It disappeared over the horizon to the south, beyond the Grand Canal. There was a slight flash when it hit the Earth. He made his entry in the observatory's diary.

He wrote, 'Hour of the Tiger: Bright falling star impacted in southern provinces. Beijing Observatory must order local authorities to find fragments for examination.'

The next morning he sent a message to the Governors of Henam, Hubei, Hunan and Guangdong provinces, ordering them to return any fragments of the meteor to Beijing.

The intense heat due to friction with Earth's atmosphere had broken the meteor into many pieces. However some large fragments survived the fall. The largest piece fell into a lightly populated area on the boundary between the provinces of Hunan and Guangdong. The impact created a small crater, so it was easy to find. The authorities of Hunan province had found some fragments of luminous blue stone. The governor had arranged for them to be sent overland to the Observatory of Beijing. The Guangdong fragment was much larger. The governor of Guangdong province was not sure that the overland journey from his province would be secure so he arranged for the sample to be placed in a sturdy cabinet made of ebony. It was then sent by ship, as this was the quickest way to transport it to Beijing.

# Shi-qi

## Sweet Revenge

As the crew of *the Perseverance* rowed back from the stricken Chinese junk, they were still savouring the sweet taste of victory. Jefferson, in particular, felt an elation that came from taking revenge on a swindler who had duped him. When aroused, he was a man of certainty and he had no doubt that his actions were justified. It would be sometime later, when the excitement of their exploits had died down, that some part of his brain might question his decision to engage the Cheng He. In the meantime his body was still pumping adrenalin. This masked any subconscious qualms. Jefferson was not aware that he had killed the sons of a Chinese mandarin and a revered sea captain. The fact that he was missing this nugget of information would have serious implications for him and his crew. At that moment the thoughts of Jefferson were focussed on his increased wealth and how he would spend it. Some of the more observant members of the crew had seen something in the manner of the Chinese Captain that unnerved them. Often superstitious, these sailors would later reflect on the curses on their heads. Jefferson was not concerned about Chinese curses. He felt that the day had gone much better than he could have expected. Having seen the damage he had inflicted, he expected the junk would sink. He was not a murderer but they had brought it upon themselves. Besides they had plenty row boats aboard, he thought.

About a day after quitting their position off Hong Kong Island, the crew of the *Perseverance* headed through the Formosa Strait towards Taipei. This was a Chinese designated overseas trading port and Jefferson wanted to fill the remaining empty space in his hold with tea. Even though the wind was in the east, he decided that it was time to go home and he had already plotted his course to San Francisco. Jefferson had become uncharacteristically prudent. He was starting to have doubts about whether the Captain of the junk was the same man who had swindled him. There was something about his manner; if he had made an error, then so be it. He thought he may give Chinese ports a wide berth for a while. On Jefferson's next voyage, he would ply his trade in Japan. As the *Perseverance* approached the tip of Formosa, Jefferson decided that he would take the tea on board then wait in Taipei until the wind direction was more favourable.

# Shi-ba

# Vengeance

*HMS Vengeance*, a member of the Royal Navy Pacific Squadron was on a westerly heading, patrolling just north of the Tropic of Cancer. Captain Henry Thomas was sitting at the desk in his cabin trying to collect his thoughts before committing them to the Captain's log. He had written the date, 13th June 1826, followed by the ship's position and course. Thomas had written nothing else. Even though he felt that the last few days had been dull and uneventful, something must have happened to be worthy of note. He racked his brains but no inspiration came. A concern started to form at the back of his mind. If I find it dull, perhaps the crew do also, he thought. I must speak to the officers about keeping them busy. He knew that a crew that is bored is a crew with low morale. Thomas returned to his log. He flicked back over earlier pages. These were in the hand of his predecessor Captain Wightman RN. Thomas settled on the entry October 4th 1825. It related to their sighting of a comet in the constellation of Ceti. It was the day after his ship, *the Vengeance*, had quitted the squadron at Conception bound for Mazatlan. Thomas remembered it well. There had been much excitement when they first saw the comet. Sailors have a special relationship with the night sky and to find a new object was to excite wonder like the most famous comet that was named after Captain

Edmond Halley. They watched the comet for several nights afterwards, but it had disappeared from view soon after they crossed the equator. There was a knock on the cabin door.

'What is it?' shouted Thomas, frustrated that he had written nothing.

'Your meal sir,' said a voice on the other side of the door.

'Then bring it in, Smith,' said Thomas.

'Where would you like me to put it Sir?' asked Smith, looking at the papers on the Captain's desk.

'On the table in the corner,' ordered Thomas.

'Aye aye sir.'

Smith placed the tray down carefully on the table.

'Thank you James,' said Captain Thomas. He knew all the first names of his crew and would use them when informality seemed appropriate.

James Smith retired. Captain Thomas went back to his thoughts.

It was at Mazatlan where Captain Wightman had contracted a fever. He died a month later. Lieutenant Thomas, being the senior officer, took command of the *Vengeance*. At twenty-five he was very young to be the captain of a man of war. Thomas, like all the crew, mourned the loss of a true leader. Wightman had become his role model. Thomas had learnt much under Wightman's command and had grown to like and respect the man. He wanted to emulate Wightman but Thomas was not sure he was made of the same stuff. As a sixteen-year-old Midshipman, Thomas had first served on a forty-six-gun frigate. It was a big ship with a crew of over three hundred men. As was normal on a large man of war, the discipline was harsh. He had learned to live with it, but in spite of weight of numbers, the Navy had seen some talent in Thomas and he earned his commission. He was sad that his first command came through the loss of his mentor. Wightman had had a distinguished career in the Royal Navy. His apprenticeship must have been quite different to Thomas'. England had been at war with the French for years. This contrasted with Thomas' time in the navy, most of which had been in peacetime. He had seen some conflict in the Indian Ocean where he had served with distinction. He did not like the brutality of war but he liked action. He was a fighting man and the master of a Royal Navy man of war. There just did not seem to be any wars. He lent forward and wrote some words in the log.

*Trades light to moderate. Continuing on patrol as ordered. No land or vessels sighted for fifteen days.*

*Vengeance* was a one hundred foot, brig-sloop. She had a complement of only seventy; fifty officers and men, ten boys and ten marines. In keeping with Navel regulations, she was continuing Captain Wightman's orders until the ship could rejoin the squadron in Singapore. The orders were to protect His Majesty's' shipping. Trade with China was becoming increasingly important to the British Empire and the *Vengeance* was to be a small but important component in the Empire's commercial machine. *Vengeance* had been patrolling at a latitude of thirty degrees North, which was a popular parallel for British and American shipping. It had been very quiet for the last few days and they had not seen another sail since quitting the Marshall Islands. He would shortly be changing course south towards the Loo Choo archipelago.

There was a knock on his cabin door. He looked down at his log. He had wanted to write something more inspiring. Damn, he thought.

'Yes,' he called out, 'come in.'

It was Lieutenant Crispin Greville his second in command.

'Yes Mister Greville,' he asked, 'what is it?'

'We've sighted a sail. You asked to be informed of such an eventuality,' said Greville.

Captain Thomas was relieved. Some activity at last, he thought. 'Oh yes, thank you Crispin. I'll come up top momentarily,' he said.

After a little more thought, Thomas put down his pen and followed Greville up to the forecastle. He took out his telescope and looked in the direction where the sail had been seen. He could make out that the ship was a forty two gun frigate. She was flying the white ensign of the Royal Navy.

'Mr Greville, it's the *Helena*,' said Thomas.

'Signal her and ask if we can come along side, she may have orders.'

'Aye aye Captain,' replied Greville.

The sea was calm and the breeze was light so it took an hour or so before *Vengeance* and *HMS Helena* could rendezvous. Greville ordered one of the longboats to be lowered. Thomas was rowed across to the *Helena*. The crew of *Vengeance* watched as he was given permission to go aboard. They wondered whether he would still be the captain of *Vengeance* when the longboat returned. It was likely that the navy would decide to replace Thomas with a more senior officer from *HMS Helena*. If that happened the crew would have been disappointed. They were growing to respect their interim captain, Lieutenant Thomas.

An hour later the longboat returned with some provisions and a familiar silhouette. It appeared that the commanding officer of the fleet had decided to continue with Lieutenant Thomas as *Vengeance's* captain. The officers and crew were relieved. A few minutes later he was aboard his ship. Captain Thomas instructed his officers to meet him in has cabin in ten minutes. They had new orders.

\*\*\*\*

After a few days moored off Taipei, the wind improved. The renegade merchant ship *Perseverance* weighed anchor and headed on a north easterly tack into the East China Sea. The ship's master, Walt Jefferson, had put the incident with the Chinese junk behind him. His mind had moved on to another challenge. He was about to navigate his ship across the vastness of the Pacific Ocean to their home port of San Francisco. It will be good to be home, he thought.

In variable winds, *Perseverance* picked her way towards the southern tip of Japan. She continued on this heading until she was fifty leagues south west of Kyushu Island. There, *Perseverance* tacked, making a new course on a south easterly bearing. There's gold and silver to be gained from there, he thought looking over his left shoulder at the southern most island of Japan. Although Japan was also a closed country, he believed there was opportunity to trade. He was already forming the plan for *Perseverance*'s next voyage. On their new heading they would pass the Loo Choo archipelago. Jefferson had done business there before and he knew the islands well. His charts were already marked correcting errors or omissions that he had found on previous voyages. One day this knowledge would become useful, he thought.

They had been sailing for many days without putting into port. *Perseverance* needed to take on water and supplies before she headed out over the expanse of the Pacific. Jefferson decided to put into one of the few inhabited islands in the group.

For a moment his mind went back to *Perseverance's* confrontation with the junk. He was sure that the Chinese authorities at Loo Choo would have had no news about it. Even if they had, his battle was with a thieving, opium-running merchant. I was within my rights. The crook tried to swindle me, he thought bitterly.

'No one will care,' he mumbled optimistically to himself.

He knew that in any case the Loo Choo authorities would persist with their tiresome rule of allowing no westerner to set foot on their shore. It meant that he and his crew would be kept at arms length. He realised that for once, this would be helpful.

In spite of the regulations, once they had dropped anchor, the local people brought them water and enough supplies for their onward journey. If Jefferson had been another person, he may have been touched by their kindness, but he was not. Whilst anchored in the bay, the winds dropped and veered. On the third day at anchor, Jefferson was bored and tired of waiting for the weather to freshen. He went below to count the gold in the boxes that he had liberated from the Chinaman. He ordered two of his crew to bring the boxes to his cabin. Each box was a cube of about fifteen inches on each side. Jefferson opened the first one with a crowbar. He found it was packed with gold ingots. The other, an ebony box, was much lighter and he levered the lock with a feeling foreboding. The lock gave way without damaging the ebony box. Jefferson peered inside and looked at the contents with a mixture of indignation and dismay.

'Damn his eyes,' screamed Jefferson in a rage. 'He's swindled me again!'

'Are you alright Captain?' asked a voice through on the other side of the door.

'No I am not!' shouted Jefferson in exasperation.

Calvert, the first mate, came into the cabin to find out what was amiss.

'This second box is naught but stone!' he said. 'It's a damned rock! Take it up top and throw it over board!'

Calvert looked into the box. It contained a grey crystalline stone with large flecks of blue crystal.

'Perhaps it's a precious stone,' said Calvert without any conviction.

Calvert knew that his captain was quick to anger and he was alarmed that if Jefferson thought he had been swindled again, the captain might decide to go back and finish the job he had started near Hong Kong. Calvert was not convinced that their earlier action was not piracy. He did not want to spend the last seconds of his life dangling from a rope. The idea of repeating their earlier adventure with the Chinese junk did not fill him with enthusiasm.

The whole escapade was becoming too dangerous especially with European ships of the line nearby.

'Alright, put the goddam thing in the hold and we'll break the stone up later,' said Jefferson, calming down, 'There may be something valuable inside.' He paused, 'At least we have one full case of gold.'

Much relieved, Calvert closed the box down and took it away to be secreted in a safe place. Calvert did not believe it had any value, but he wanted to go home.

After a few days the wind freshened and they were able to get under way again. The whole crew had had enough of this voyage and they wanted to get back to California. Jefferson gave the order to set *Perseverance* on an easterly heading into the Pacific; a heading that would lead them directly into the path of HMS *Vengeance*.

\*\*\*\*

*Vengeance's* orders were clear. She would have to seek out and apprehend the Perseverance. Her Captain, James Jefferson had killed the son of an important Chinese mandarin. If necessary Captain Thomas was ordered to sink the buccaneer's ship. If Jefferson was not caught, trade with China would be seriously damaged. Helena had the same orders and was tracking back along a sea route that Perseverance was likely to take. *Vengeance's* role was to head for the Loo Choo islands that were northeast of the last sighted position of the renegade privateer.

\*\*\*\*

It was two days after they had quitted the Loo Choo Islands, when Jefferson's look out spotted the masts of a Royal Navy brig. Jefferson did not expect to be pursued, so he continued on his course. He remained alert to any change of course by the English ship. However *Vengeance*'s course changed to intercept them. His old enemy was clearly on his tail. Jefferson decided to head back towards the archipelago, where he could lose them, or trap them between the islands. The navy vessel had added more sail to close the gap between them, and she seemed to have a better share of the wind. Before nightfall, *Perseverance* had made it to Amami Island, one of the islands of the archipelago. She was in a good position to start the cat and mouse game. At that moment *Perseverance* was the mouse. Jefferson hoped that she would soon become the cat.

*Vengeance* was some four leagues behind their quarry when she disappeared behind an island. The pursuers had lost sight of her and *Vengeance* hove to. In the failing light, there was little chance of interception. Captain Thomas was reluctant to simply follow Jefferson into these waters. It was probably a trap. Indeed, most of the area was uncharted and *Vengeance* could easily run aground on an uncharted sandbank in the dark. Thomas gathered his senior officers together in his cabin. They stood together around the chart table examining the incomplete charts of the area.

'The island to the north west is not even on the chart!' said Greville, in exasperation.

'That's our problem,' said Thomas. 'Jefferson has been sailing these waters for years. He will know every nook and cranny. I'm going to play this game by my rules, not his'

Thomas was wondering what he would do if he were in Jefferson's position.

'Do you think he'll make a run for it sir or fight his way out?' asked Lieutenant Smythe.

Smythe was newly commissioned just before he boarded the ship. Although he spoke with a plum in the mouth, he was more grounded than Thomas would have expected. At twenty one, he was the youngest of Thomas' senior officers. He came from a navy family. His father had been a Captain at Trafalgar and the son had some of the same grit.

'If I were him,' said Thomas, 'I'd try to sneak out under the cover of darkness.' He was thinking about *Perseverance's* most likely course out of the archipelago. He glanced down at a pair of islands on the chart. Captain Thomas continued, 'I'm sure he'll try to fight his way past us if he has to.' He paused and looked more closely at the channel between the islands. 'I think we should spring a trap here,' he said pointing at a channel on the chart. 'What do you think Mister Greville?'

Greville looked at the spot where the captain was pointing. He mused for a few seconds.

'If we waited in the middle of the channel, the buccaneer would have to pass us at one end or the other. I suggest we put some marines and crew ashore here Sir,' said Greville pointing at a beach on one of the two small islands, 'They could signal us of Perseverance's approach from the top of the peak.'

'An excellent plan, Mr Greville,' Thomas said, enthusiastically. 'Mister Smythe, I'd like you to organise a landing party to scale the peak. I doubt that the island is inhabited, but if it is, I don't want a damned blood bath. The marines' role is to protect the look-outs with minimum force.'

'Yes sir,' said Smythe, crisply. He turned and left.

'Mister Greville, now let's set our trap.'

'Aye, aye, Sir.'

*Vengeance* made its way between the islands. The landing party had rowed their way across to the island. They were making their way to the top of a small peak. After half an hour the look-outs were in position.

Greville was looking at the landing party through his telescope.

'Are they in position yet?' asked Thomas.

'Yes, they are Sir,' replied Greville.

'Then the trap is set,' he said, continuing quietly, 'now all we have to do, Crispin, is wait.'

*Vengence* waited in the wide channel between the islands. The sea depth was poorly marked on the charts and therefore Greville was not sure how much water there was beneath the keel. He took some soundings, but could not find the bottom. Clearly it was deep enough. *Vengeance* was positioned ready to make way at a moments notice. She was well hidden and her lookouts could see any ship passing at either end of the channel.

The next morning the lookout spotted *Perseverance* crossing the western end of the channel. *Vengeance* was ready to make way quickly. She fired a warning shot across *Perseverance*'s bows. *Perseverance* was quick to return fire from her starboard guns. Jefferson had assessed his enemy. He thought *Perseverance* was more than a match for this small brig-sloop. He altered course so that *Perseverance* headed straight for *Vengeance*. Jefferson would never to accede to King George's authority. *Perseverance*'s cannon fire was not well aimed and had done little to damage *Vengeance*. *Vengeance* was making more headway than Jefferson had anticipated. He thought he had caught her sleeping. Thomas ordered his eight port gun crews to return fire. A broadside hit the oncoming vessel. *Perseverance* was hit in several places. Even though she had lost her mainsail, *Perseverance* was still underway. Typical of Jefferson's innate aggression, he ordered his crew to return fire from guns positioned in the bow. A cannon ball tore a hole in *Vengeance*'s mainsail and killed one of her crew in the rigging. *Vengeance* tacked so that the two ships were heading straight for each other.

'What is the goddam idiot doing?' shouted Jefferson incredulously. 'He's going to ram us!'

Thomas knew exactly what he was doing and just as the ships were about to collide *Vengeance* altered course to port, on the windward side of *Perseverance*.

'That will take the wind out of her sails!' said Captain Thomas, calmly. 'Mister Greville, order the crew to fire as our guns bear.'

Greville gave the order.

The ships' starboard guns would be in line as the two ships passed. However Jefferson was too slow to reposition his gun crews. *Vengeance* fired her guns in sequence as they passed alongside. Explosion after explosion resounded as the cannons fired; the sound echoing off the islands on either side of the channel. There was a massive explosion as one of the missiles had entered *Perseverance's* powder magazine; the deafening noise repeating off the sheer walls of rock around them. *Perseverance* was split in half. The decks were listing precariously. Those of her crew who were on the upper decks, dived overboard to swim away quickly before the sinking ship sucked them under. Those below decks were not so lucky. The damage was terminal and *Perseverance* sank within a few minutes.

*Vengeance's* crew launched the boats to pick up survivors, but Jefferson was not amongst them. The landing party returned to the ship. *Vengeance*, her mission completed, set course for Singapore.

\*\*\*\*

They had fought their naval battle above a trench between two islands. The water was very deep there. As *Perseverance* sank, her descent slowed due to the buoyancy of her cargo and trapped air. However descend, she did.

The box containing the blue-speckled rock, that had so annoyed Jefferson, was airtight. As *Perseverance* descended the water pressure increased. The box resisted for a time but even the strength of the ebony walls could not hold back the forces surrounding it. The box was crushed. If anyone had been watching from above they would have seen bubbles rising gently to the surface as air escaped. The blue speckled rock rolled into the hold that was now full of pressurised water. As the pressure increased, a blue aurora seemed to form around the rock. The rock started to shake, slowly at first, until a distinct vibration became apparent on the surface of the water one hundred fathoms above. The rock was glowing, like the light of a giant blue anglerfish in the deep. The rock started to emit electrical sparks. These formed bright blue tracks of lightening as they found their way to metal objects from the wreck. The rock was vibrating, making a low underwater thudding noise. The sound waves travelled to the surface. Although the *Vengeance* was now more than two leagues away, tiny water vibrations surrounded her. If any of the crew had looked overboard, they would have seen rhythmic ripples breaking the surface superimposed on the natural swell of the ocean.

As *Perseverance* sank deeper, the turbulence created by the thudding appeared to resonate with the structure of the ship. Planks of timber came away from the decking. Some of the hollow cannons cracked under the stresses caused by the severity of the vibration. Not only deck planks, but also the oak planks of the hull were breaking away from the ship. Cannon balls were shaking in a violent frenzy; they smashed into the timbers of the ship, splitting them like matchwood. When she hit the bottom, the destruction did not stop. The blue rock seemed to be affecting the seabed. The rock was producing a slow incessant thudding. The intensity was completely disproportionate to the rock's size. In the dark of the deep water a blue glow was eerily bright and getting stronger. The electrical discharges were almost continuous like cataclysmic lightning bolts of a hurricane. The thudding penetrated into the rocks below, travelling down through the layers of rock until at nearly six leagues beneath the sea bed, the vibration encountered the boundary between tectonic plates. With the thudding came molten lava that slid between the layers of rock, freeing them to slide over each other. The vibration was so pronounced that it began to eliminate the frictional forces between rocks. A vibrating line could be traced along the conjunction of tectonic plates. Sulphurous gasses were escaping from it. The outpouring of gas over the length of the fissure rapidly became more vigorous. A crack was forming in the Earth's crust many leagues long, extending in opposite directions from the wreck. The blue rock had released underground forces that had been in frustrated tension for nearly a century. The Earth's tectonic plates were moving. But then the fault reached an obstruction, a position where the plates were welded together. The movement became stuck. It had become locked. The pent up forces pushed harder and harder at the locked obstruction.

Then, as if the ground could not take the strain any more, the seabed exploded. One of the two islands above the wreck was no longer supported. It collapsed beneath the water, falling thirty feet in an instant. All around the island the sea level had collapsed. The seabed on the other side of the fault had risen upward and under the immense forces of two continents colliding; it was pushed upward some twenty feet into the air. The ocean was instantly at two different levels. It was like a huge waterfall supported by seawater. The water from above rushed into the void below, generating a wave forty feet high. The water currents shot the blue stone to the surface but it did not matter, it had done its damage. The wave was moving. As it came into shallower water, the wave increased in height. The malevolent wave front was thirty leagues wide, consuming everything in its path. Onward, onward it pressed.

*Vengeance* was now fifteen leagues away. The sea was calm. Her crew had heard nothing. Lieutenant Greville turned to look astern. Then he saw it. Some of the crew had seen it also.

'Oh my God!' he exclaimed.

Thomas turned to look. He could not speak. There was terror and inevitability.

A few moments later HMS *Vengeance* was engulfed by the tsunami of 1826.

# Shi-jiu

## Eastern Magic

Although the Guangdong stones never arrived at the Beijing Observatory, the Hunan samples did. The samples were delivered to Xu's lodgings and for a while he left them collecting dust amongst the array of astronomical instruments that littered his room. One afternoon his servant noticed that some of these instruments were behaving strangely. Xu wondered whether the meteorite samples were interfering with them, so he decided to investigate.

When Xu examined the stones he found that the meteorites were an amalgam of blue crystals embedded in pumice-like rock. With a small hammer and chisel Xu extracted two of these blue stones from their soft enclosure. Occasionally these crystals emitted a faint blue glow, but this property was erratic and he could find no explanation. He tried many times to reconstruct circumstances that caused the glow but he could find no pattern, or cause. In the end he gave up, putting the phenomenon down to a mystery of the heavens. He could not know how right he was.

Some time later an old friend came to visit him at the observatory. His friend offered to take the remaining samples to a monastery where a group of alchemists could examine them. He thought that the monks could be better qualified than Xu to find out what the meteorite was hiding. Xu agreed. They performed many tests on the Hunan stones, but Xu was told very little about their findings.

Xu kept the original crystals that he had chiselled out, for his own amusement. These were roughly formed rocks; one the size of a goose egg and the other a hen's. He had no idea what more he could do with them, so he asked an ivory carver to carve and polish each one into the shape of an egg. The hen's egg was a slightly lighter blue than its partner. On this stone was carved the symbol for Sky. The goose egg stone was darker and slightly denser. Xu had the symbol for the Earth carved on it. Considering where the stones had come from Xu thought that this was fitting. Xu had a bronze stand made for each one. He kept them at the observatory as ornaments. For the rest of his life, he enjoyed them as things of mystery. They were objects that had fallen from the heavens. For him they were full of wonder.

****

Nearly fifty years after Xu Kuang-hsien's death, the Old Beijing Observatory was still operational. That was soon to end. An alliance of European countries and the US, occupied Beijing. Along with many other items, two blue stone eggs disappeared. With the exception of the thieves, no one knew who had stolen them. Perhaps some of the Chinese scientists who examined the other stones understood their significance. The thieves however had no better idea of their properties than did Xu. Some years later some of the instruments were returned. However this act of reconciliation did not include the stone eggs, called Earth and Sky.

# Part Three

# Rocking the World

# Twenty

# The Parting

'Come on Claire, you'll be late,' said Paul, getting impatient.

They had been married for just over a year and this was the first time they would sleep apart since their wedding. Claire was due to take a plane in just over three hours time and she was not ready.

'I'm nearly packed,' she shouted from the bedroom. I'm just trying to find somewhere to put this pot of Marmite.'

'What,' said Paul exasperated, 'why Marmite?'

'Prama said it's the one thing she misses,' said Claire, struggling into the living room with her case.

'Well, don't get arrested for importing illegal substances. Besides, I'm sure there's more than Marmite she misses,' said Paul. 'What about Anil.'

'Ah therein lies a tale,' said Claire enigmatically. 'Right I'm ready. Is the taxi here?''

'Yes he's been outside for ten minutes, with his meter running all the time. Have you got everything; tickets, passport, money, something to read?' he asked.

She nodded.

'I don't want to leave you,' she said with a soulful expression.

He put his arms around her and cuddled her.

'I know, I don't want you to leave either, but you must. You won't get many chances to present at a conference like this; especially in Japan.'

Paul kissed her on the lips and released her.

'Right, you've got to go,' Paul said, taking her case.

He led Claire to the door and into the street where the taxi was waiting. He put her case in the boot.

'Are you sure you don't want me to come to the airport with you?' he asked, obviously not for the first time.

'No it's very sweet of you, but I'd feel even sadder waving goodbye at the gate,' Claire replied.

'Alright, remember to phone when you're in Tokyo.' Then as an afterthought he asked, 'Have you got the hotel details, they were on the table last time I looked?'

'Yes mummy they're here,' she said teasing him.

She kissed him again and got into the taxi.

'Terminal three please,' said Claire to the driver. She looked back at Paul.

She was both excited and sad. The taxi moved off into the traffic. Claire blew him a kiss as the taxi rounded a bend. He stood a while until she was completely out of sight.

Paul turned back to their front door. He went back into the flat. It was odd; before he had met Claire he had lived alone for years, but within a few seconds of her departure his world seemed empty.

'Pull yourself together!' he scolded himself, 'time for a brew.'

Being ten o'clock on a Saturday morning, he thought it was a bit early for a hard drink so he put the kettle on. When he had made himself a cup of tea, he went into the living room and sat down on the sofa. He put his cup down on the coffee table in front of him.

Paul and Claire had lived together in her flat for a year before they got married. They had decided to sell his flat as it was smaller and as Claire had said "in need of a steam clean". At the time he didn't know what she meant but thinking back, he now understood. He smiled to himself. He was thinking about those first few days before they had solved, well almost solved, the "bee" problem. Claire was behaving so oddly he did not know what was going through her head. He could not believe his luck when he found she was carrying a torch for him. He had known he loved Claire, but he had been convinced that she had thought differently. God, it's quiet, he thought. He looked around the room for something to occupy him. Claire had only been away for ten minutes; how was he going to survive for a week? He reached for his teacup and saw their wedding album on the table in front of him. They had been looking through it the night before. He opened the book at a group photograph of the research teams. They were all there; Dieter, Jacques, Prama, Anil, Darren and the rest. So much had happened over the last two years.

Claire, Anil and Dieter had published their paper on the DNA analysis of the Yakawa samples. Paul, Prama and Jacques had published their papers on gasers and gaser pliers. Anil published a groundbreaking paper on simulation of gravity wave radiation that contributed strongly to his PhD. It was not until these papers were all in the public domain that the scientific community realised something quite revolutionary was happening. The resulting furore had kept them all very busy. Both Jacques' and Dieter's teams were in demand to present papers at various prestigious conferences. More money started to come into the university. This gave Dieter and Jacques much more freedom and gave the rest of the team more opportunity. Paul and Claire were given full time lecturing jobs. In the meantime, Anil had become an expert in astronomical computer simulation. Paul was pleased that they had managed to get a grant to retain him as a research assistant.

Paul had not noticed it until Claire told him, but Prama and Anil were becoming very close. Claire was convinced they were going to become an item. Then, all of a sudden, without warning, Prama announced that she was going to take up a post in Osaka's University of Astronomy. All of them, including Jacques, were amazed. Anil looked like he had taken a bullet. Claire had become very good friends with Prama, and Paul was sure she had an insight into what was behind her decision. Claire was very evasive on the subject; she could be so annoying sometimes. Paul suspected Claire had been asked to keep a confidence, so he did not push it. That was six months ago. Anil seemed to have got over it. He was now a research assistant, working on Paul and Claire's projects.

Anil's software had come a long way since the early days of the "bee study". He had included a capability to include information from old astronomical records. He was using his model to look for links in history that could be correlated with the times when the gaser beams from the two binary stars may have intersected. Paul hoped this would help them pinpoint a search area for the trigger material they had proposed two years ago.

Paul's research focus was to look for materials that could absorb gravity waves. He hoped that Anil's software would lead him to a natural source of the material. As no one else had yet isolated the material, he thought he had the right to name it "Gravitum". As gravitum was a key component in his gaser theory, he was sure it must exist. Unfortunately there had been no other reports of teleportation that could be attributed to their gaser theory. This was surprising because Anil's model showed that the gravity wave beams would, in theory, intersect somewhere on Earth every few days or so. Paul reflected that he would continue searching until he dropped; all he needed were the right tools.

Paul had just been give responsibility for a gravity wave detector. His plan was to reposition it at a place where the gaser beams would intersect most often. Anil's software came to the rescue. It had provided Paul with a list of locations most likely to be exposed to gaser radiation. Paul and Anil scanned the co-ordinates of over a hundred sites and found the ideal location. It was a disused fire station, near an old industrial estate. The facility was no longer required by the fire service because it supported an area of the city that had been largely demolished. The old fire station was on council owned property about fifteen minutes away by train. For a peppercorn rent, the University had been given permission to set up a temporary laboratory there. Paul and Anil could not believe their luck.

It had taken a year to prepare the site for the experiment. Both Paul and Anil were excited that they would soon be starting the first trials of the equipment. The gravity wave detector would be commissioned in its temporary home tomorrow. The device, an interferometer, consisted of two, three-meter long arms supporting mirrors. Lasers were reflected off these mirrors and tiny differences in the time it took light to travel along the arms, would indicate the presence of gravity waves. Paul had inherited the device from an earlier gravity wave experiment. Unfortunately in spite of nearly twenty years of operation no gravity waves had been detected. More recently much larger, more sensitive interferometers were built in Europe, US and Japan. These devices were based on the same idea but the arms were several kilometres long. Paul accepted that their detector was obsolete. However, he and Anil had other uses for it. Their obsolete detector was the ideal device to test materials that might absorb gravity waves. He now had the tools to start his search for gravitum.

Paul took another pull at his tea. He was lonely and bored. He had decided what he was going to do. He picked up his keys, put on his old leather jacket and headed for the university. He was going to look at the plans for his new toy: the gravity wave detector.

****

Claire had arrived at the airport in good time for her flight. She was used to air travel so the queues and security checks were no surprise to her. She used to quite like flying; it was just the airports she disliked. They were so full of suspicion with nobody trusting anyone else. Claire wondered if travel had always been like this. She made her way to the head of the queue for the security check. At least she was able to take some hand luggage on board. A thirteen-hour flight would have been a nightmare without her books and computer. She placed her small bag on the conveyor belt and walked through the metal detector. A female security guard waved Claire forward to frisk her. Claire wondered if she looked like a criminal. The male security guard asked her to open her case. He looked closely at the charger for the computer then waved her though. Thank goodness, she thought, I'll be able to sit down soon. She knew that she would have plenty time to sit down on the flight but all this security made her feel tense and tired. The lounge was full of people milling around, struggling with their cases and buying duty free goods. She thought she would buy a bottle of perfume for Prama. She showed the assistant her boarding card and paid for the gift. Claire made her way towards the departures board. She saw an empty seat nearby and headed for it. Thank goodness she could sit down. Claire had an hour to wait. She opened her book and started to read. There was too much going on around her. Claire's mind started to wander to the last time Paul and she had seen Prama. It was at her leaving do.

During the eighteen months since Paul and Claire had lived together Claire, Prama and Anil had worked on a number of joint projects. After Claire had realised that the relationship between Paul and Prama had burnt out long ago, Claire no longer saw her as a rival. Claire had grown to understand that Prama was a scientist with a remarkable talent and as they got to know each other they had become good friends. The week before Prama had announced she was leaving for Osaka, she had phoned Claire. Claire thought back to the conversation.

'Hi Claire, it's Prama,'

'Hello, how are you?' replied Claire.

'I need to talk to someone and I'm afraid you've drawn the short straw,' said Prama. 'Can we have lunch tomorrow, I'll pay?'

'Why,' asked Claire,' are you in town?'

'Yes, I've got an interview.'

'With whom?' asked Claire.

'I'll tell you tomorrow,' Prama responded. 'I need some advice. Will you come?'

'Of course'

They made their arrangements and met the next day in a small Italian restaurant near the university.

Prama was already at their table when Claire arrived. Claire joined her and they ordered their lunch.

'So Prama,' said Claire. 'What is this new job?'

'It's a one year assignment with the Centre for Gravitational Research in Osaka, Japan,' replied Prama.

Claire was taken aback but she soon recovered her wits.

'I thought you were happy in Jacques' team. Have they run out of funding or something?' asked Claire, puzzled.

'No,' said Prama. 'That's not it. I need a change. Besides it's only for twelve months and I'll go back to my old job afterwards.'

She paused to collect her thoughts, 'Did I ever tell you why I went into physics?'

'No, you didn't. I have often wondered,' said Claire, now curious.

'Did you know I was brought up in Hong Kong?' asked Prama.

'Yes,' said Claire. 'Paul told me.'

'Well, we were an Army family. My father was away for much of the time fighting in various wars. Ghurkhas were involved in most of the big British campaigns, you know. So I spent most of my childhood with my mother.' Prama paused, as if she were trying to get a picture of her mother in her mind.

'Did Paul tell you that my mother was Chinese?'

'Yes,' said Claire.

'My mum was quite spiritual you know. She was searching for "enlightenment" through her beliefs. I did not share her views, I suppose that came from being brought up in the hectic life of Hong Kong, but I had her curiosity.'

'So you were both looking for answers?' asked Claire.

'I looked for my answers in science. I suppose you are right,' said Prama, reflectively.

'Anyway mum died whilst I was away at university. Hong Kong changed and my childhood culture has gone forever.' A look of sadness briefly crossed her face.

'I've wanted to go back to the Far East for some time. Just to feel the difference again. This Japanese job seems to be the best opportunity available,' Prama stopped deep in thought.

Claire understood Prama's words, but she felt the argument was weak. Claire could not believe that Osaka had any nostalgia for Prama, unless there was something she was not saying.

'You have another reason for going don't you?' said Claire.

'You are very perceptive,' Prama paused, as if she were deciding whether to say any more. 'I think I'm falling in love and I don't see how it can work out.'

'With Anil,' asked Claire.

'Yes,' Prama replied. 'I think I love him, but the traditions of his family and mine, aren't compatible.'

'Oh I see,' said Claire. 'Like Romeo and Juliet,' said Claire.

'Yes, and do you remember how that turned out!' said Prama, her eyes watering.

'But Prama, you are both over twenty-one. If you love him and he loves you, why can't you follow your heart?' asked Claire with concern on her face and her head tilted sympathetically.

'I can't do that. Anil loves his parents. It would destroy his relationship with them,' said Prama, a tear rolling down her cheek.

'I need time to think it through. He needs time to understand what he is doing'

'Have you talked to Anil about how you feel,' asked Claire.

'Not explicitly, he wants us to live together. Anil says his parents will have to accept it but I can see how much a breach with his family would hurt him. I've told him I can't move in with him. He says he doesn't understand. Deep-down we're both confused.'

Claire could see the irony this. Ever since she and Prama had become good friends, Claire had come to know a person who had such certainty in her life. Prama was organised about everything she did. It was unusual to see Prama so vulnerable.

'Oh, I am so sad for you,' said Claire, her eyes watering. 'Is the only answer to go away?'

'Yes, for now.'

'I don't seem to have helped you very much,' said Claire reflecting Prama's sadness.

'You have,' said Prama. 'You listened.'

That was the last time Prama had talked to her about Anil. Perhaps it would be different when she and Claire next met.

The airport's public address system broke into life. Claire's thoughts suddenly came back to the present.

Claire's flight was being announced.

'Flight JL402 for Tokyo Narita is now boarding. Please make your way to gate 12'

Claire picked up her hand luggage and headed for the gate. She was on her way to Tokyo. Prama and Claire were presenting their papers in a conference. In a few hours Claire would see Prama and find out whether she had managed to get her life under control again.

****

Paul walked over to his desk and ritualistically threw his battered leather jacket over the back of his chair. He sat down and pulled up the screen on his computer that described the equipment they had installed in the old fire station.

'Hi Paul,' said a voice.

'Hello, Anil, I didn't expect to find you here on a Saturday.'

'Nor, you,' said Anil. Then as if a light had dawned, 'Of course, Claire's left for Japan hasn't she.'

'You're too smart for your own good,' said Paul, with a straight face.

'That's right,' said Anil. 'Keep telling everybody that and I'll be happy.'

Paul laughed.

'What are you looking at?' asked Anil.

'Oh, just the diagrams of the detector' he replied

'I've been reading up on the latest gravity wave detectors. They're amazing devices,' said Anil.

'Yes, using lasers, they can make incredible measurements of distance.'

'It's basically the same technology as a modern builder uses on a building site,' Anil remarked.

'You mean laser tape measures?' queried Paul and then answering his own question, 'yes they use the same principle, but the gravity wave detectors are far more accurate.' He continued, 'Do you know what the accuracy is?'

'Ok, let me guess,' said Anil, peering under the corner of a sheet of paper in front of him. 'My guess would be they would be, er.., accurate to ten to the minus eighteen metres.'

'That was a lucky guess,' Paul said smiling. 'To put it another way, if you used one of these devices to measure the one hundred and fifty million kilometres gap between the Earth and the Sun, it would be accurate to less than a thousandth of a millimetre.'

'When you put it like that I see why our detector is obsolete!' said Anil, truly amazed.

'Don't knock it,' said Paul. 'That's why we got the device for free!'

Neither of them did much work that afternoon. They were both lonely and wanted to chat. A few hours later they went back to their empty flats.

As Paul opened the door into the flat it was still quiet and empty. He sat in front of the television for a while. Paul looked at his watch. Claire would be almost there, he thought. For the first time for ages he was in bed and asleep before ten thirty.

# Ni-jyu-ichi

## The Meeting

Prama was waiting on the Shin Osaka platform for the one o'clock Nozomi bullet to Tokyo. She was standing between two painted marks drawn on the platform, at ninety degrees to the track. She looked at her watch. She need not have bothered because the train was drawing in exactly on time. It drew to a halt and the doors opened directly in front of her between the two lines where they disappeared over the platform edge. She found her seat towards the middle of the carriage. A group of four people had got on the train together. They had swivelled one of the double seats behind her so that the four of them could sit face to face. Prama was always impressed they could do that on this train. They apply science and engineering well in Japan, thought Prama. A television screen, mounted in the wall at the end of the carriage, flashed a commercial message. She was no longer sure about her earlier thought.

Prama was going to the Seventh Bioastronomy and Planetary Research Conference, in Tokyo. She had been asked to present a paper titled "A theory of moving objects using coherent gravity wave beams." She felt the title lacked pizzazz but it seemed to fit the occasion. She was leaving Osaka a day earlier than necessary because she wanted to meet her closest friend, Claire at the airport. Prama had persuaded Claire to present a paper at the conference also. Claire had come up with the catchy little title "Analysis of Terrestrial Apis Mellifera DNA collected from the tail of the X/2009/D2 (Yakawa) comet". Prama thought that would draw the crowds. She looked out of the window, smiling to herself thinking that science could be funny.

Prama turned her head away and looked out of the window towards the west. The train was going at speed now. In her peripheral vision, she could sense the flash of objects as the train went past railway signals pylons and the like. Her eyes shifted focus to the distance. She could see the Mount Fuji in the background. Its pure white snowy top was resplendent, contrasted against the clear blue of a cloudless morning sky. Although a distant object, the mountain subjugated the landscape like an ominous reminder of the volcanic character of Japan; Fuji's presence both reassuring and menacing. Then the mountain disappeared behind shoebox shaped buildings that appeared to have been made to a standard design based on alternate layers of concrete and glass. Suddenly the concrete buildings disappeared to reveal Mount Fuji again, this time much bigger; more dominant. The train was now forty to forty five minutes from Tokyo. The green plain in the foreground was punctuated with small white buildings. They all seemed to have the same green or blue roofs made from shiny enamelled ceramic tiles; all glinting in the soft morning sunlight. Every house of them has a family unit in it, she thought. The number of people who lived along this route was amazing. Over the five hundred and fifty kilometre journey from Osaka, it was very unusual to have a panorama without some sign of dense population. Prama was astounded that most of the population of Japan seemed to be clustered together along the narrow coastline. She wondered whether there was a practical reason or did they just like each other's company. Two and a half hours after leaving Osaka, the Nozomi drew in to Tokyo station. Prama made her way to the Narita express station. Almost immediately, she stepped on to the train for the next leg of her journey. Prama arrived at the Narita Airport an hour and a quarter later.

Prama had been waiting at the terminal two of Narita airport for some time. In contrast to the Japanese railway system, Claire's plane was late. Prama was excited about meeting Claire again; excited to meet her friend from home and excited to get news of the other person who was very important to her. After a painful break, Anil had written to her. There was something about the written word on paper that made letters special. This one in particular was a lovely letter and she had replied in a similar vein. Prama was beginning to think it was time to go home. Perhaps she and Anil were ready. She looked up at the arrivals board and noticed that the Claire's flight had landed. Prama looked at her watch; it was nearly five thirty in the evening. It would be half an hour before Claire collected her luggage and passed through immigration. They were very efficient and thorough at Narita, but not fast. Prama made her way to the meeting point closest to where Claire would exit. Then Prama saw her. Claire looked tired and confused, not surprising after a long flight. Claire's face lightened up with relief when she saw Prama.

They made their way towards each other and hugged.

'It's good to see you. How long have you been waiting?' said Claire, garrulously. 'I had this dread of missing you in the crowds, but as usual your planning worked.'

'It certainly did,' said Prama, beaming, pleased to see her friend.

They had the usual conversation that people have when they arrive in airports. Both Prama's and Claire's cases had wheels. They made a loud rumbling noise as they wheeled them across some corrugated concrete flooring.

'It sound's like we're causing an earth tremor with these cases,' joked Claire, above the noise.

'I hope not,' said Prama, smiling. 'Not around here!'

They arrived at the terminal's bus terminal. The bus would take them directly to the conference hotel in the Shimbashi district. It was not until they had sat down on the bus that they could talk.

'So how are you?' asked Claire, opening the conversation.

'I'm fine thanks,' Prama replied, hesitantly.

'It's your auntie Claire, remember. You can tell me.'

'I will,' said Prama, 'but not now, you've had a long journey and I want to interrogate you before you fall asleep. How are all my old friends?'

'Well,' she said with a teasing pause. 'Paul is enjoying himself. He has been given a new toy to play with and they will be testing it tomorrow,' she paused and remembering the time zone, 'I mean today, I think. Jacques is the same as usual. He misses you terribly. He has no one like you to bounce his silly ideas off.'

'That will do him good,' said Prama. 'He'll have to think for himself.'

They both giggled.

'And Dieter is just the same: a man of fearsome reputation, but a pussycat really,' said Claire and then pretending to be thinking, 'and who have I missed? Don't tell me. I'm sure I can remember...'

'Stop teasing,' said Prama. 'Is he missing me or not?'

'He most definitely is. For the first few months he was useless,' said Claire. 'I don't know what you put in his tea, but it worked.'

'Poor lamb,' said Prama.

Then seriously, 'Have I hurt him very much?'

'Nothing he won't get over,' said Claire. 'But you don't want him to, do you?'

Prama did not answer. She changed the subject.

'Are you prepared for the conference? You know you're in the third slot tomorrow, don't you? Is your presentation ready?' asked Prama.

'No. I thought I'd do it tonight, before I go to bed,' said Claire, pausing. Then with a mischievous smile, 'Of course I'm ready, who do you think I am, Paul?'

They both laughed. Prama was really pleased that Claire had accepted the invitation to speak at this conference. The bus pulled up outside the hotel exactly on schedule. They both checked in.

Prama asked, 'Do you want to go up to your room and sleep, or do you want a meal and a gossip?'

'I managed to sleep on the plane, so I'm not too tired, just a bit confused,' said Claire. 'I'd like to go to my room, phone Paul, have a shower and get changed. I'd love to have your company for dinner if you're up for it.'

'Of course I'm up for it,' said Prama. 'It's great to have some girl talk in this misogynist place. Shall we meet back here in three quarters of an hour?'

'That will be lovely,' said Claire. 'I'll see you here in forty-five minutes. Then you can give me the whole lurid story over dinner!'

\*\*\*\*

The phone was ringing. It was morning. Paul pushed his coffee cup to one side and picked up the receiver.

'Hello darling,' said Claire.

'Hello gorgeous,' said Paul.

\*\*\*\*

Prama was waiting for her as Claire stepped out of the lift into the lobby.

'What do you want to eat,' asked Prama, 'European or Japanese?'

'I'm feeling adventurous. I'd like to try Japanese,' said Claire, continuing a little cautiously, 'but I'd rather not sit on the floor. I'd probably fall over.'

They both laughed. Obviously, Claire was not feeling too adventurous.

They made their way into the street.

'Have you ever eaten sushi?' asked Prama.

'Yes,' said Claire, uncertainly. 'There's a sushi bar around the corner from the university. Paul and I have been there a few times.'

'Would you like to try a traditional Japanese one?' asked Prama, with a mischievous glint in her eye.

'What are you up to Prama?' asked Claire, reading her face.

'You'll find it will be a different cultural experience,' said Prama, with a smile.

'Ok, it sounds like fun.'

As they walked along the street Claire noticed how polite people were to each other. They would step aside to make space for other pedestrians automatically. Somehow the flow of people seemed more orderly to that she was used to, almost a little too regimented. Everybody seemed to be happy enough though. Claire saw many people chatting and smiling as they walked. Some of those who were not chatting to their companions were talking into their mobiles. As she looked more closely she noticed most people had mobile phones. One or two were taking pictures, others tapping on the miniature screens. A group of young people were giggling and smiling as they looked at an image one of them had down loaded. They certainly like their technology, Claire thought. Like streets in many cities, there was a lot of noise and bustle, but Claire did not feel pressured or threatened. People seemed to be used to crowds. They were comfortable. A lady walked past her with a surgical mask on her face. Claire was curious.

'Prama, I've noticed people wearing white masks. Is there some disease going around or is it pollution?'

'It's probably because they have colds. It's ill mannered to blow your nose or sneeze in public. So they wear a mask over their nose and mouth,' replied Prama.

'We're here,' she said.

They had stopped outside of a door in the middle of a row of shops. The door appeared to open into another shop except there was a curtain with intricately decorated Japanese characters covering the window. There was a wooden lectern displaying a menu in Japanese. There were no European characters on it, even the prices seemed to be in Japanese script. Claire was glad to be with a friend who could speak and read Japanese.

'This is a Sushi-ya,' said Prama. 'There are some special cultural conventions to follow.'

'Oh,' said Claire. 'That sounds frightening!'

'We are not Japanese, so they will make allowances for us. Mind you being women won't help,' she said with a mischievous smile. 'If you follow my lead they may be impressed!'

Prama opened the door and they entered the lobby. There was a curtain in front of them that screened the entrance into another room. There were four pieces of material hanging down from the top of the screen. Prama parted a curtain at the gap in the middle and walked into the room behind. Claire followed. Prama said something in Japanese to a lady dressed in a silk kimono and made a "Vee" sign with her right hand. Claire realised in Japan the sign meant Claire and Prama were a party of two.

The lady smiled and said, 'Hai.'

'I like the kimono,' said Claire to Prama.

'Thank you. You are very kind,' said the lady, with a smile.

As in other sushi bars that Claire had visited, there was a counter surrounding a food preparation area. There were also high seats around the counter for the customers, most of whom were men. Claire had expected to see a conveyor belt distributing food to the customers around the counter but there was none. The only conveyer here was the fearsome looking man in the middle; this was definitely a low-tech sushi bar. Claire thought of the contrast with the high tech world they had left outside. Prama and Claire followed the kimono-clad lady to the counter. There was a space for two people between a female party of four and male diner.

Prama whispered, 'At least there are some businesswomen in here; we'll feel less out of place. Let me ask permission before we sit down.'

Prama said something to the woman on Prama's right.

The woman replied, 'Doe-so.'

Prama gestured Claire to sit down. The women next to her made a polite bow and smiled. Claire did the same in return. Prama went through the same process with the gentleman to her left. When the formalities were over Prama sat down next to Claire. Prama explained that courtesy is very important in a sushi-ya restaurant.

'I will never understand all the rules,' she said. 'I always find the best way is to be painfully polite, and bow a lot.'

Prama subtly pointed out the man on the other side of the counter.

'He is the Taisho, a special chef,' whispered Prama. 'The best way is to ask him to recommend some things, and then we won't get confused with the array of choices.'

Claire nodded, slightly bemused. Prama entered into a dialogue with the Taisho. He placed a small saucer and a teapot in front of each of them followed by a small wooden platform of fish on a bed of rice, and various other preparations. The Taisho put a rolled up towel and some chopsticks next to the platform. Prama said something in Japanese to him. He went to the back of the room and returned with two bottles of beer. He opened one for Claire and placed an empty glass next to the full beer bottle. He did the same for Prama. The Taisho went off to serve another customer.

'Now,' said Prama. 'Do what I do.'

'Ok,' said Claire, starting to enjoy the game. 'Anything you say.'

Prama poured some of the dark liquid out of her tea pot into the saucer.

'This is soy sauce,' she said.

'I thought it was tea,' said Claire. 'I'm glad I didn't drink it neat.'

Prama smiled, amused at the thought. Claire picked up the little tea pot and poured some of the soy sauce into her saucer.

'The wooden platform is a "geta",' said Prama. 'If you like, you can take it home with you afterwards and wear it as a shoe.'

'What would I do with one wooden shoe?' asked Claire, amused.

'If you want, you could have mine and make a pair. I suspect they would smell of pickled fish though,' said Prama with a small infectious giggle.

'I'll pass on the shoes, thanks Prama,' said Claire, infected by the giggle.

Claire looked closely at the food on her wooden geta.

'What's this?' Claire asked Prama, pointing to something that looked like tripe.

'I have no idea,' replied Prama. 'but it's probably not what you think it is.'

'Alright, in for a penny..,' said Claire, partially quoting an old proverb. 'How do I eat this?'

'Pick up the sushi from the other side with your thumb, index and middle finger like this,' said Prama, taking one of the sushi and turning it over so the rice was on top.

Claire copied her with another piece of sushi.

'Now soak the sushi in the sauce like this,'

Prama dunked the sushi until the rice was wet with soy. Claire copied, dutifully.

'Then eat it, like this,' Prama held her head back and lowered the sushi into her mouth.

'But, I'll choke!' exclaimed Claire.

'No, you won't try it!'

Claire ate her first morsel of sushi.

'What are the chop-sticks for?' asked Claire.

'Anything that's not sushi,' replied Prama succinctly.

'Oh' said Claire, none the wiser.

After a few minutes Claire had the hang of eating the sushi. With her jet lag under control, she decided to cross-examine Prama.

'I phoned Paul before we left the hotel,' said Claire, conversationally. 'He says Anil's in a better mood. Why would that be I wonder?'

Prama knew Claire was pumping her for information and she wanted to talk to her about it, but Prama would not make it too easy.

'I don't know,' said Prama. 'Perhaps he's won the lottery.'

'I don't think so,' Claire replied. 'Paul thinks it's to do with a letter he's received from a certain lady in Japan.'

'I didn't know he'd got it in him!' said Prama teasing. 'Who is she?'

'Ok,' said Claire grinning. 'Spill the beans!'

Prama, stalling, took another piece of sushi.

'I think I'm ready to come home,' she said. 'Anil has spoken to his parents. He tells me they are more tolerant than I had thought. I find it difficult to believe that his family could accept a woman of my family's faith. They have said if he loves me, then they will love me too.'

Prama had a tear in the corner of her eye. Claire felt she might join her, so she quickly moved to her next question.

'What about your dad?' asked Claire.

'It's difficult for him as well. My mother's beliefs and his were very close,' Prama replied, 'but he has travelled all over the world, admittedly as a soldier. He has seen a lot of different cultures. He has always been tolerant of good people.'

'He sounds nice,' said Claire. 'I'd like to meet him one day.'

'Yes, I think you'd like him,' she paused. 'Anyway I know that Anil has finally thought about the consequences of us becoming an item. He is not as reckless with his parent's feelings as I feared.'

'Sounds like your trip to Japan has done both of you good.' Claire remarked.

'I think you're right,' said Prama. She looked at their plate. 'We seem to have finished. Do you want any more?'

'No thanks, I'm full.'

'Sounds like the tea ceremony then,' said Prama, smiling.

'Oh no, do we have to?' said Claire in mock horror.

'Yes we do,' replied Prama and then to the Taisho, 'ah! gari!'

She made a sign of crossed index fingers to him.

'Hai,' he replied.

'What was all that about?' asked Claire.

'I said we're full and we would like some tea. It signifies the end of the meal.'

The tea arrived. They drank it. They performed another ritual to pay and returned to the hotel.

'See you tomorrow,' said Prama. 'Sleep tight.'

'Thanks, that was fun. Goodnight Prama,' said Claire, as she went to bed.

Claire had a restless night full of strange dreams about talking sushi wearing wooden shoes.

# Twenty-two

# The Old Fire Station

Paul had arrived early at the old fire station. He was keying in the security code to cancel the alarm. He walked over to the large steel lock that secured a gate in the chain-linked fence. He pulled out his key and inserted it in the keyhole. The compound was walled on three sides. The fourth side, the old exit for the fire engines, was now fenced off. Paul reckoned that a chain link fence would not have been a good idea on an operational fire station, but now it was a laboratory. The fence had been erected to make sure the local wild life did not take a liking to the equipment. Paul was not sure what the criminal fraternity would do with a gravity wave detector, but you could never be too careful. He closed the gate behind him and looked up at the brick built tower. It was a solid structure that seemed to be too well built to be demolished. He imagined fire engines surrounding the structure with their ladders extended so that rescuers could practice their life-saving skills. It is unlikely to see that kind of excitement again, he thought. One day, he may convert it into an observatory, he reflected. He would need a ladder to get to the top; it was a shame they took the fire engines away. Maybe that was a plan for later. He walked towards the two storey, rectangular shaped building in front of him. This was the main building of the old fire station, still resplendent with its red double doors. Differentiating the building from its former role were two long concrete tunnels exited through adjacent walls and running along the perimeter of the site. The old fire station was in the corner of an "L" shape formed by these tunnels. The tunnels were an extension to the ground floor laboratory. This was where the fire engines used to be garaged. The efficacy of the doors was clear when one realised that an exit designed for quick deployment of fire tenders would be equally useful when manoeuvring Paul's equipment into the building. The gravity wave detector was a substantial apparatus, with many large components including two stainless steel vacuum tubes. Each one was one hundred metres long and three quarters of a metre in diameter. A few months earlier, the tubes had been delivered in sections. These had been installed on the ground floor, extending inside the concrete tunnels. Paul unlocked a side door and moved into the ground floor of the building. The upper floor was still empty; they had all the space they needed on the ground. He looked up and saw the old fireman's pole coming down from the ceiling. Paul had decided to leave it in place, but the hole had been sealed to keep the area clear of dust. He was standing in the control room that was positioned in one corner of the building. He looked around at the array of computer terminals and monitoring equipment. Everything seemed to be up and running, he thought. Paul gazed through the toughened glass screen that separated the control room from the equipment room. This was where the detector was located. He put on clean white overalls and moved through the reinforced door that connected the two rooms. He scanned the room. Running parallel to the wall on his right was one of the shiny stainless steel vacuum tubes. At ninety degrees along an adjacent wall, was the second vacuum tube. Each of the tubes contained equipment that was mechanically isolated from the day to day vibrations that are ever-present on Earth. The objective was to filter out any noise that might swamp gravity waves readings. In the same vein the tubes that contained the detectors were positioned on special rubber foundations built to reduce vibrations from a passing lorry or train. Paul walked over to one of the tubes to inspect a plate bolted to its surface. He took a spanner and tested the tightness of a few bolts. In between experiments, the team needed to work inside the tubes, so there were a series of inspection holes in each tube to allow access. Each aperture was covered with a steel plate. Some of these plates had toughened glass panels in them so that one could see inside. The plates were designed to fit so that they made a perfect seal. Everything had to be scrupulously clean. This was important because inside, the tubes were completely devoid of air, or any other gas. To maintain this vacuum there were a series of pumps. Two of these pumps required supplies of liquid helium to keep them cool. As is often the way, they required a lot of complex, expensive equipment to prove a simple idea: do large, distant moving objects cause ripples in space? Paul liked the question; perhaps it would have it inscribed above the door. He had another thought there was a subsidiary question.

'And are these ripples affected by the materials they travel through?' he mumbled, to himself.

Paul was in a good mood and excited. This would be his first chance to see whether his new laboratory worked. So far everything was theory only. Today they would see if the equipment was good enough for the job.

****

Claire awoke in good time before the first presentation for the day. She was feeling the effects of jet lag and her mind seemed to be slightly disconnected from her body. So this is what an out of body experience is like; who needs existential meditation? All you have to do is travel on a long haul flight, she thought.

'Morning, Claire,' said Prama's voice, as if from another dimension, 'sleep well?'

'Sort of,' said Claire. 'I kept having the weirdest dreams about sushi.'

Prama laughed. Claire smiled.

'You need some breakfast,' said Prama. 'That will make you feel better.'

Claire and Prama loaded their plates at the breakfast bar, collected some drinks and sat down together at one of the tables. Amused, Prama noticed Claire had avoided anything that resembled fish. Claire took a pull at her coffee and bit into a slice of bread. She instantly felt better.

'You're right,' said Claire. 'Eating helps.'

'You'll be ok for your presentation?' asked Prama, concerned for her friend. 'I could ask them to swap yours and mine around if you like. That would give you a bit more time to get your body-clock right.'

Claire was due present later that morning. Prama's presentation was immediately after lunch the day after.

'That's really kind of you Prama but no thanks. I'll be ok,' said Claire. 'Anyway, this way round I can listen to your presentation without the butterflies in my stomach.'

'Ok, it was only a wheeze to get out of the "graveyard" slot,' joked Prama. 'You saw right through me.'

Claire laughed.

'That's better,' said Prama, 'you seem to be coming back to life.'

Prama and Claire finished their breakfasts and made their way to the conference registration desk. They took their badges and milled about with the rest of the delegates in the anteroom. Claire was surprised that there were so many delegates. She was becoming nervous about standing up in front of an audience of three hundred people, some of them being experts in the subject she was to present. The "butterflies" were starting to collect in her stomach. Prama was walking towards Claire with a Japanese delegate. The name on his conference badge said, "Mr Aoki, TAG". Mr Aoki was a slight man in his mid thirties. He was slightly shorter than Claire. He wore wire-rimmed spectacles that seemed to complement his friendly expression.

'Hi Claire, let me introduce Aoki san. He is from Tokyo Academy of Geosciences. He is an expert in seismology. He mentioned that he had read your Yakawa paper and was interested in the results.'

Aoki San bowed. Following Prama's earlier advice, Claire did the same but not too deeply. She held out her hand and said, 'Pleased to meet you.'

'Pleased to meet you too Doctor Powell,' said Aoki San, in faultless English.

Claire had published her paper under her maiden name. She was no longer a "Powell" but she felt it was too complicated to correct him.

'Oh please call me Claire,' she said, hoping she had not broken another protocol.

Much to Claire's relief, he said, 'I am honoured. Then you can call me Hideo.'

Hideo had many western friends and colleagues. He knew something of western protocols, better than Claire knew his culture. He was a polite and tolerant man.

'Then I would like you to call me Prama,' said Prama, addressing Hideo.

'Of course,' said Hideo, bowing and shaking her hand as if renewing an old acquaintance.

In fact Prama and Hideo had known each other for some time. As they worked in different universities, they had remained on formal terms. Prama was more familiar with Japanese culture than Claire, but she would struggle with a three way English conversation where they all addressed each other differently. They were all on first name terms. This was a level pitch and she could handle it.

'I'm intrigued that you are interested in my paper on Bee DNA, given that your discipline is seismology,' said Claire.

'I am interested in many facets of science and in particular results from the Yakawa mission,' said Hideo. 'I would be very honoured if I could speak to both of you after your presentations. It is possible that our subjects overlap more than you think.'

Claire and Prama looked at each other. There was silent agreement.

'We'd be delighted,' said Prama.

They arranged to meet the morning after Prama had given her talk and then continued to mingle with other delegates.

\*\*\*\*

When Claire stood up to talk she suspected that this particular audience wanted her to talk about DNA that had come from outer space. Unfortunately her talk was essentially the reverse. Claire explained that she could prove that DNA found in space was from Earth. She expected this to be a big let down. In fact she had not expected many people to come. To her amazement the room was packed out and she had many constructive questions. She enjoyed performing so much and she was disappointed when it was over.

The day after Prama had similar feelings about her presentation. She expected the audience to be cynical about Paul's crazy ideas on gasers and outraged by her even crazier idea about Gravitational Pliers. She was especially worried because they had only one example of the phenomenon. The delegates asked a number of questions about how a gaser could be detected and she mentioned Paul's search for gravitum. She was surprised that no body groaned; perhaps they were just being polite. Then Hideo asked a revealing question.

'We have been investigating the link between celestial gravitational forces and seismological events. Do you believe that gravity waves could influence tectonic plates?'

Prama replied, 'That's a fascinating idea and potentially a fruitful area for research. Personally, I am not aware of any studies covering this,' she paused, 'but I'd be very interested in any phenomenon that might be explained by a gaser beam.'

Prama was starting to get an inkling of what Hideo wanted to talk to them about. Interesting, she mused.

\*\*\*\*

It was now mid morning in the old fire station. The rest of the team had arrived and were busy verifying that the equipment still worked after the journey from its previous home. Paul had just finished a call from Claire. He had taken his mobile outside so he could talk to her in private. Her words were still going around in his head. Paul and Claire had had another of their long, wide ranging conversations. Amongst other things she told him about the visit to the sushi bar with Prama. It was great fun. Claire had told him about her presentation. It had gone better than she had expected. Claire wished he had been there. Paul wished that too. Paul came back to the present. He was in the control room that over looked the gravity wave detector equipment. Unusually, everything seemed to be going according to plan. It was time to find out whether his impressions were right.

Paul collected his small team together and he was explaining the sequence of experiments that he had agreed with Dieter. Paul's audience included two PhD students and Anil; a team with their first success under their belt.

'Well done,' said Paul. 'You've done really well. Despite moving our gadget ten miles, we haven't broken anything. What's more amazing is that it still works!'

'How do you know?' asked Darren, one of the students. 'Given it has never detected a single graviton.'

'Well it still doesn't detect them, so that's a start. I would be quite worried if it had,' said Paul smiling.

They all laughed. There had been a great deal of tension leading up to the recommissioning of the detector. It was pleasant to see the team more relaxed. Although there was a "snag list" of minor problems, Paul was confident they would fix them in the afternoon. He had decided that they were now ready to look forward to the next stage.

'Alright folks, I know we have a few things to finish off. In the meantime, do you want to know about our programme of experiments?' asked Paul.

Nods all round. He would have continued even if they were not interested.

'Our objective is to find materials that respond to gravity waves in a different way to other materials,' said Paul. 'We have a theory that there is a material, we'll call it gravitum, that absorbs and traps gravity energy,' said Paul.

'Was that the theory developed to explain the Yakawa DNA results?' asked Ayala, the other PhD student.

'Yes,' replied Paul. 'From the work we have been doing with Jacques' team we believe that gravitum will have an important property; the speed of gravity waves within the material will be much slower than the speed of light.'

'How do you come to that conclusion?' asked Darren, with a slight Australian intonation.

'May I?' asked Anil looking at Paul for permission to answer Darren.

Paul nodded.

'In the vacuum of space both light and gravity travel at the same speed; about three hundred million metres per second. But in other materials like glass light travels slower. Prama developed a theory that gravitum has a similar effect on gravity waves; it slows them down,' said Anil.

Paul continued, 'If we are right, then a number of things would happen. For example, imagine a gravity wave travelling through space, hits a cube of gravitum crystal. When the wave crosses through the surface of the gravitum the gravity wave will bend. The gravity wave then crossed the inside cube, travelling much more slowly. When it meets the opposite side of the gravitum cube, the beam will be bent again, but in the opposite direction. So it traces a zigzag across the cube.'

'This is refraction, like a block of glass bends a light beam,' said Ayala, perceptively.

'Yes,' said Paul. 'Except we think gravitum has a far more drastic effect on a gravity wave than glass affects light.'

Anil interrupted enthusiastically, 'We believe that gravitum slows gravity waves down to about one kilometre per second. This means that the bending and reflecting effect is extreme. If the gravitum is shaped correctly, the wave may be trapped inside the gravitum crystal, bouncing off the inside walls until it hits a critical angle.'

'What happens then?' asked Ayala.

'When the gravity wave reaches the critical angle, it breaks through the surface of the gravitum and escapes,' replied Anil.

'If it escaped, what difference has the gravitum made to the gravity wave?' asked Darren.

'It's more the other way round,' said Anil. 'You should have asked: what did the gravity wave do to the gravitum?'

'Ok,' said Darren, playing along. 'What did the wave do to the gravitum?' Darren amused by the idea of a scientific riddle. He would think of a better answer later.

'The gravity wave interacted with the crystal far more strongly than any other material,' said Anil, starting to explain.

'Because it was trapped, bouncing around inside the gravitum crystal?' asked Ayala.

'Yes,' said Anil, 'and because it spends so long inside the crystal, it can absorb much more of the gravity wave's energy.'

'Then it is this energy that we can detect,' suggested Ayala.

Paul was pleased that Anil had got his enthusiasm back. He had been concerned that Anil had gone to pieces when Prama left. Perhaps Prama and Anil were communicating again.

Paul continued, 'I've been talking with Jacques' team to decide what crystals are most likely to behave like gravitum. 'He picked up a pile of paper from the edge of the table. 'These are lists of the candidates we have found so far.' Paul handed each of them a sheet of paper. 'I want us to start by testing as many of these crystals as we can, to see if they are affected by gravity waves,'

They were all looking blankly the list he had given them. He waited for any questions. Predictably Ayala spoke up.

'How do we get the gravity wave detector to respond to these crystals?' she asked.

'We have to modify one of the detector arms. I've done a drawing showing the changes we must make to our equipment,' Paul replied. He had laid out a large sheet of paper on a table at the side of the room. They moved over to it. 'And we have to make the modification in two days,' he said.

'Why two days?' asked Ayala.

'Because that's the next time the gaser beams will intersect in this position,' said Anil.

'We've got a lot to do then?' said Darren.

'We, most definitely have,' said Anil, smiling.

The team broke up to finish their outstanding tasks. Darren and Ayala had gone into the equipment room. Paul and Anil were alone in the control room.

'You look more cheerful. Have you spoken to Prama?' subtlety was never one of Paul's strong points.

'Yes, she's written to me; an old fashioned letter,' he said. 'She's well and looking forward to seeing Claire.'

'I spoke to Claire this morning,' said Paul. 'She had dinner with Prama last night in a sushi bar.'

'How did that go?' asked Anil, clearly still keeping his cards close to his chest.

'Well, I think. Prama seemed on good form,' said Paul, then wondering whether he should mention it, 'She liked your letter apparently.'

'That's good,' said Anil.

Paul was getting in deeper than he wanted. He was not going to get any more out of Anil. Anil looked ok and that was the main thing.

'Great,' he said, wishing Claire was here. She was far better at interrogation than Paul was.

# Ni-jyu-san

# Earth Moves

Claire and Prama met Hideo in one of the hotel lounges. He had arrived before them and politely stood up as they came over they join him. They went through a short bowing routine and sat down.

They talked a little about their backgrounds and how long Claire and Prama would be in Japan. Then Hideo started to explain what was on his mind.

'Do you know much about seismology?' he asked.

Both Prama and Claire replied that it was an unknown subject to them. He asked if he could explain some of the basics, as it would make the rest of the discussion more straightforward. They agreed. He started to explain.

'You are probably aware that Japan is in the middle of a highly active volcanic area.'

Prama and Claire nodded.

Hideo continued, 'That is the main reason why most of the population lives near the coast and the interior is relatively unpopulated. You may not be aware that Japan is situated at the conjunction of four tectonic plates.'

'Is that bad?' asked Claire.

'It means that earthquakes are very common and if you go back through the records there have been many instances where the coastline has been inundated by tsunamis caused by underground quakes,' replied Hideo.

'It sound quite dangerous,' said Claire nervously.

'It can be but we have many strategies to live in this environment and one of them is to refine our tools to detect them. Part of my job is to improve those techniques.'

'And you suspect that gravitational effects may be an indicator of future seismic activity?' asked Prama, interpreting Hideo's question after her lecture.

'Yes,' said Hideo, 'Back as far as nineteen seventy six we knew that cycles of earthquakes were linked to abnormal gravitational forces arising from variations in the Earth's movement.'

'Do you mean the Earth's wobble,' asked Claire, vaguely remembering a conversation some time ago.

'Yes Chandler's wobble is an example. Because the Earth is not a perfect sphere, its rotation wobbles slightly on its axis. It's moving within the gravitational field of the Sun. We suspect this may trigger some seismic activity,' said Hideo. 'I am very interested in the triggers that cause low frequency earthquakes.'

'Is this a special category of earthquake?' asked Prama.

'It's a fairly new category that we have been investigating since 2000. To give you an example; to the south of Kyusu, near the Ryukyu Islands, there is a fault where the Philippine Sea plate is pushing against the Amur plate that extends into Asia. The plates are sliding over each other. The movement is slow and steady because the frictional forces are constant and predictable.'

'Determined by the co-efficient of friction,' prompted Prama.

'Mu,' said Claire remembering Paul's favourite joke about cats.

Prama wasn't sure whether Claire was commenting on friction or making a farmyard noise. She concluded it was the latter.

'Yes, you are both right, I am impressed with your knowledge.' Hideo continued, 'If there is a vibration then mu changes and the slip may speed up. This increases the displacement of the tectonic plates along the fault line. Occasionally there may be a blockage where the frictional forces are much higher, or the plates are welded together. As the displacement increases stresses can build up at these points. They do this until they snap!'

'Then you get an earthquake?' asked Claire.

'Yes,' said Hideo. 'We regularly send robotic submarines along the fault next to Ryukyu Islands. In the past, there have been a number of underwater quakes here. We search for places where the fault line is locked. Last week we found something different. We found a blue, glowing rock near the fault. We have no idea if it had anything to do with earthquakes, but I am investigating. The rock is in my laboratory. We have analysed its chemical structure.'

'What did you find?' asked Claire.

'We found it has virtually the same chemical structure as you describe in you paper on the analysis of Yakawa,' he said

'What the DNA?' asked Claire, confused.

'No, the other analysis that you did on the isotope content,' he paused. 'We believe the rock could have come from Yakawa!'

'Now that is very interesting,' said Prama. 'How would you like us to help?'

****

Paul had fixed all of the faults on his part of the "snag list". He was sitting in the control room looking through the observation window. He was watching Darren and Ayala doing their final checks on the equipment. Anil was next to him checking the computer systems. Ayala seemed to have finished. She came into the control room.

'Hi ya,' she said.

'Hello,' Paul replied. 'How are you doing?'

'I've finished my bit,' said Ayala.

'Great,' said Paul. 'Well done.'

'Paul,' she said. 'Can I ask you a question?'

'As long as it's not too difficult,' he replied smiling. 'Go on fire away.'

'You mentioned that Jacques' team had helped you select which crystals to test for gravitum.'

'Yes, I did,' Paul confirmed.

'I've looked at the lists and I can't see what they have in common,' said Ayala, with a quizzical expression on her face.

Paul thought for a moment about how to give her an answer without making it too heavy. Darren came over to join them. He had finished also.

Paul began, 'Jacques thinks that gravitum should have another characteristic; a characteristic that will improve our chances of detecting gravity waves.'

'What's this characteristic?' asked Darren.

'I'm getting to that,' said Paul, a little tartly. Darren was starting to irritate him. 'Jacques has a theory that gravitum will have a way of converting gravity waves into other types of energy, for example into light or sound.'

'You mean you can convert gravity waves into photons and phonons?' asked Darren, not in the least perturbed by Paul's earlier comment.

'That's the theory,' said Paul. 'A number of materials have this property. I'll call them "Transducing materials".'

Paul was quite surprised that Darren was keeping up. He did not seem to be the sharpest knife in the box and this subject was quite complicated.

'Have you any idea of the kind of material we may be looking for?' asked Paul, hoping he was wrong about Darren.

Darren returned a blank stare.

'What about a material like quartz?' asked Ayala, stealing Darren's opportunity to show he had some brain cells.

'Could be,' said Paul enigmatically. 'Why do you suggest quartz?'

'Because it's has piezoelectric properties,' suggested Darren.

Now Paul was becoming really confused about Darren. Perhaps he only looked dumb.

'Absolutely right,' said Paul. 'Quartz crystals are a good example. They are used in lots of devices from wristwatches to radios to gas fire lighters. The material has the amazing property that if you change its shape, it will generate an electrical current'

'And if you do the opposite; apply an electric current to the quartz, the crystal will distort. This means you can make earphones and miniature loudspeakers,' added Anil, joining the conversation. He must have finished his preparations as well.

'Another property of quartz is that if you cut it to the right shape and size, it will respond to very specific vibrations. When you give it a kick it resonates like a bell and produces an electrical output at the same pitch,' said Paul, thinking he had joined a music hall double-act with Anil.

'And if you give the same quartz crystal an electric shock at the right pitch, the vibrations will be much larger than any other note,' said Anil, confirming Paul's music hall idea.

'So back to our gravitum,' started Ayala, 'if we get a crystal of the right size and shape, our results will be much bigger.'

'Yes, it will resonate like a bell,' said Anil. 'But the first thing to do is to look for likely candidates for gravitum.'

'Quartz is not the only substance that has these properties. We know of several others. The ones we know about are on the list I gave you,' concluded Paul.

\*\*\*\*

'What do you make of Hideo then?' asked Claire.

'I think he's a worried man,' Prama replied. 'He thinks that their rock is made of gravitum.'

Claire and Prama were sitting in the hotel bar comparing notes. Hideo had left just a few moments earlier. Claire was not surprised that the Japanese rock had the same chemical components as the Yakawa comet as the combination was not that unusual. However the isotopic composition was a different matter. That was odd.

'I think that, just because the Japanese rock came from the Yakawa comet, it does not mean it is made of gravitum.' said Claire.

'If he is right then there could be a problem. Did you know that gravity waves vibrate in a range between ten to ten thousand times per second. Can you guess what the range for seismic stress waves is?'

'I suspect the way you asked me the question means that it's the same,' said Claire, by now she had got to know Prama quite well.'

'Yes it is. That means gravity waves and whatever generates seismic waves could resonate,' said Prama. 'Are you going to mention it to Paul?'

'I probably should,' Claire replied, 'Mind you I don't want to get him too excited.'

She paused, 'Not while I'm in Japan any way; it would be such a waste.'

They started to laugh.

****

On the morning of the day the gaser beams were due, Paul was looking over a checklist of actions for the experiment they were about to perform. Paul had already briefed the team on the day's schedule but he wanted to be sure he had covered every angle. The plan was to suspend a range of crystals, one at a time, inside one of the gravity wave detector's arms. The team would wait for the gaser beams to go overhead and take their readings. If the sample was gravitum sample, it would trap and focus gravity waves. This would cause a distortion of space and time in one of the arms of the detector. The other arm would be unaffected.

Darren came into the control room, breaking Paul's train of thought by dropping his backpack noisily in the corner.

'Hi Paul,' he called, 'what gives?'

'Hello Darren,' said Paul, somewhat irritated by the interruption.

Paul knew that all the team, including Darren, had worked hard to prepare for their first important experiment. But Darren remained an enigma to Paul. He was not sure whether Darren had grasped the complexities of the plan. Paul did not want a simple misunderstanding to screw things up. He was wondering whether Darren was an unconventional, bright student with a street-wise shell or was he just shallow? Paul had a couple of minutes. He decided to check whether Darren understood what they were trying to achieve.

'Could you check the laser alignment for me please Darren,' said Paul, suspecting that Darren did not know how. It would not matter if Darren made a mess of it because Paul intended to recheck them later anyway.

'No probs,' said Darren, heading towards the equipment room. He stopped before going through the door and turned towards Paul with a puzzled look on his face.

'I'm not sure I know how to do that,' he said, in a "matter of fact" manner.

Good, thought Paul. He's passed the first test. He's decided not to blag his way through.

'Ok,' said Paul, 'Let's have a chat about the role of lasers in a gravity wave detector.'

'That would be good,' said Darren, somewhat relieved.

'If you remember the gravity wave detector is based on a well-proven design. The method was originally developed to see if light would travel faster if it were transmitted off the front of a moving object.'

'Yes the Michelson Interferometer. The idea was to split a light beam in half and sent the two resulting beams at right angles to each other. Then, using mirrors, they were brought together so that the beams were recombined,' said Darren, surprising himself about being so eloquent and continuing, 'A pattern of interference would show whether one of the beams had travelled faster than the other.'

'That's right,' said Paul, also surprised, 'and the whole device was positioned so that one half of the split light beam travelled in the same direction as the Earth travels in space.'

'and the other at ninety degrees,' interrupted Darren, 'so that only one beam would be affected by the Earth's movement. If you add the Earth's speed in space to just one of the beam's speed, the two beams would have taken different times to get back to the recombination point.'

Paul continued, 'So when the light beams rejoined each other, they would not recombine in the same way as they started, before they were split, and you would get a shift in the interference pattern.'

'Except, when they did the experiment, there was no shift,' said Darren.

'Meaning?' queried Paul.

'It meant that the speed of light beams had not been affected by the motion of the Earth and that meant that the speed of light is constant from whichever standpoint you take,' concluded Darren.

'Spot on,' said Paul, starting to think Darren had hidden depths.

He went on, 'Our gravity wave detector works on the same principle. It uses a laser as a light source, which we split it into two halves. Each half is sent down one of the two detector arms that are at right angles to each other.'

'Except the device next door,' said Darren, looking though the window into the equipment room, 'is a lot more complicated. It has a huge vacuum system, many more mirrors, masses of electronics and special ways of viewing the results. It's like comparing the first aeroplane to the space shuttle!'

'Yes,' said Paul, 'it's more complicated, but it still works on the same principle.' He continued, 'We are looking for signs of bending of space and time. We hope to detect tiny differences in flight times between two halves of the laser beam. The further these beams travel, the more likely we are to detect something. So our detector is designed to lengthen the routes of the beams using extra mirrors.'

'So that's what the multiple mirrors are for?' said Darren, the penny dropping.

'Yes,' replied Paul, 'each beam is reflected many times. Then if there is a small change in space-time, the beam will encounter it many times. The down side is that if one of our mirrors is slightly out of position, then all our readings will be wrong.'

'So that's why I need to check the laser alignment,' said Darren.

'That's right,' said Paul. 'We'll have false results, if the mirrors in two arms do not reflect the laser light correctly. Under normal conditions this detector gives a normal interference pattern.'

'Because it has never detected gravity waves?' asked Darren, rhetorically.

'Yes,' said Paul, 'so it is quite easy to align the lasers. I'm hoping that when we put gravitum in the flight path, we'll get a reading. That would be a scientific first.' He paused, 'Come on I'll show you how to make the adjustments.'

'Great,' said Darren, with enthusiasm.

By five o'clock that evening, Paul's team had aligned the detector and tested most of the compounds on his list. The gravity wave detector remained stubbornly still. There was no evidence that gaser beams existed at all. In fact nothing of note happened. The team were disappointed. They would have to wait for two more days to test the remaining samples. Paul decided to use the time to check through his methods. He phoned Dieter for some advice.

'Hello Paul, how did it go?' asked Dieter.

'We've detected nothing, I'm afraid,' Paul replied, despondently.

Paul gave him a brief resume of their progress, or lack of it.

'I am surprised the team had got so far so quickly' remarked Dieter. Paul was surprised that Dieter was surprised. 'You can't expect to get a result on your first try,' Dieter continued, encouraging him.

'I know, but I had expected to detect something, even if it was a tiny indication of a gravity wave. It's beginning to look like I've invented another null experiment,' said Paul referring to an earlier conversation.

'Just keep going,' said Dieter. 'There must be many more candidate materials you have not yet tried. You must widen your search for gravitum!'

'Perhaps I should see if Jacques has had any new ideas about potential materials for gravitum,' said Paul sounding a little desperate. 'I'm worried if we don't have a breakthrough soon, the money will dry up.'

'My God,' exclaimed Dieter, with a smile in his voice. 'I'm shocked. It's the first time I've heard you worry about money!'

'I'm trying to turn over a new leaf,' said Paul, seeing the irony.

'Look, you let me worry about the money,' said Dieter. 'I'm impressed by the efficient way you have built the new laboratory and I'm impressed that you have created a motivated team.'

Normally, it was difficult to impress Dieter. Paul thought of asking Dieter to repeat his last sentence, just to make sure he'd heard it right. He decided not to; Paul thought that would be pushing his luck so he thanked him and rang off.

Reflecting on Dieter's comments, he arranged to meet with Jacques. Paul wanted to make sure he was not missing anything obvious. Jacques was a good sounding board. Paul decided to travel up to see him on the following day.

# Twenty-four

# Rocking Blues

Paul and Jacques yet again were sitting in Jacques' office. It was tidier than normal.

'You know Jacques,' said Paul, observing the orderliness around him. 'You need a new project to get you fired up.'

'D'accord, I miss the challenges of Claire's bumblebee,' Jacques said smiling.

'And Prama?' asked Paul, sympathetically.

'Oui, and Prama too. She has some crazy ideas, but they keep me entertained, 'replied Jacques with a chuckle.

'Ok, then you'll be happy to apply your mind to help me understand why my experiment hasn't detected anything,' said Paul leading to the reason for his visit.

'Bonne idée, I have thought so much about candidates for gravitum that my brain is starting to ache. We must have overlooked something, but I don't know what,' Jacques paused to think for a moment. 'Perhaps we should try a different approach.'

'Like what?' asked Paul, encouraged by a possible new line of enquiry.

'I have no idée,' Jacques replied, dejectedly.

They had a long, involved conversation about transducing crystals. They became quite animated. The conversation seemed to be energising both of them. However the fact remained that they talked for over an hour and resolved nothing. They slipped into silence, trying to think of the other way of looking at their problem.

'Has Prama told you about the Japanese blue rock?' asked Paul.

'No.'

'Claire and Prama met a Japanese guy from the Tokyo Academy of Geosciences,' said Paul, then elaborating. 'Apparently they found the rock in the ocean to the south of Japan. Hideo, said that it started to vibrate when they raised it from the seabed.'

'Who's Hideo?'

'Oh a the seismologist they were talking to,' Paul replied.

'How did they know it was vibrating?'

'According to Claire, they monitored it on s-wave detectors positioned in drill holes around the coast,' replied Paul.

'Sounds like a tremor to me. Not a gravity wave phenomenon,' said Jacques, dismissively.

'You're probably right,' said Paul, closing the subject.

Paul stood up and started pacing up and down. He found it was sometimes easier to think when he was standing. Jacques was also deep in thought. Paul moved over to Jacques' array of books and scanned the titles for inspiration. He found none. Distractedly he picked up the egg shaped stone that had been acting as a bookend in Jacques' office for years.

'What is this?' asked Paul, letting his mind float abstractedly.

'What?' asked Jacques, only half listening.

'Oh, that,' said Jacques, in an off hand manner.' It's just an old stone I analysed some years ago. I have a paper about it somewhere.'

'It's got some oriental writing on it,' said Paul turning it over in his hand.

'Yes,' said Jacques. 'Prama told me what it meant once, but I've forgotten.'

'Oh,' said Paul, losing interest in the rock and putting it down. 'Well, we have no choice. We must continue with the experiments as planned,' he said, returning to their original subject.

'To be sure, I too have no more ideas,' said Jacques, then in desperation. 'I wish Prama was here!'

Paul and Jacques said their goodbyes and parted both still deep in thought. It was early afternoon. Paul was thinking that perhaps there was something wrong with the configuration of his experiment. He would check again. If he hurried, Paul could return to the laboratory before everyone had left for the evening.

****

Soon after he had arrived in the gravity detector laboratory, Paul's additional checks were complete. Outside, it was dark and the rest of the team had gone home. He was churning things over in his mind. What am I missing? He asked himself. Paul's phone rang.

'Allo, Paul?'

'Blimey, I only spoke to you four hours ago,' said Paul. 'Have you no home to go to?'

Jacques was too excited to give Paul a witty repost.

'I believe I have another compound for you to test, mon ami,' said Jacques. 'You told me that you had read a journal article about a transducing compound containing crystallised lead and titanium oxide.'

'Yes, I did,' confirmed Paul.

'I looked back over a paper I wrote five years ago about a sample that was believed to have come from a meteorite over a century ago.'

'I'm listening,' said Paul. 'What did it say?'

He knew Jacques well enough to keep asking him questions. Jacques would come to the point in his own time.

'The sample occasionally fluoresced with a blue glow. However unlike other fluorescent compounds, it was not radioactive, there was no evidence of chemical fuel and light rays did not excite it. In fact no conventional electromagnetic radiation made any difference to it.'

'But it still glowed?' asked Paul, getting interested.

'Yes, but very faintly,' replied Jacques. 'I have never been able to find out why. I considered lending it to the Large Hadron Collider team. I thought I'd let them bombard it with anything they could but I guessed they were too busy making Higgs bosons.'

Ignoring Jacques' last point Paul asked, 'Did you find out the source of energy that made the sample glow?'

'No, I didn't,' replied Jacques, still holding information back to maintain the suspense.

'So the source could be gravity waves,' said Paul thinking aloud. 'Are you saying your meteorite contains transducing crystals?' he asked.

'Yes,' Jacques replied. 'So your compound should be on my list,' said Paul. 'How can I get hold of a sample?'

'That's easy,' said Jacques, 'It's in my office.'

'What?'

'It's my blue egg stone,' said Jacques.

'Good grief, that's been right under our noses for years!' exclaimed Paul.

'By the way..,' Jacques paused.

'What?' said Paul, expectantly.

'My analysis of the stone showed that it contained platinum and chromium isotopes,' said Jacques. 'I'll e-mail you my paper.' He paused, 'Have you looked at Claire's paper recently, on the isotopic analysis of the Yakawa sample?'

'No,' said Paul, 'should I have?'

'Have a look at it,' said Jacques.

'Why?' said Paul, starting to get frustrated.

'It has the same platinum and chromium isotopes.'

'What, the comet and the blue stone are the same?' asked Paul, incredulously.

'Mais oui! The comet, the Japanese rock and my blue stone all contain the same platinum and chromium isotope profile.'

'Bugger, all three are from the same source!' said Paul.

Claire would have been impressed; Paul had strung a sentence together but sadly Claire was not there to hear it.

****

It was the day before they were due to test the remaining transducing crystals. The plan was that Jacques' blue stone was last in the queue. Anil had told Paul earlier that there was only a three-hour window to perform the experiments. The ideal time to look for gravity waves was in the middle of this timeslot. This was when the two intersecting gaser beams would be directly over the old fire station, a few kilometres away from the university. Paul knew the four members of the team had a lot to do. The only way to complete all the tests in the short time available was to plan the experiment thoroughly. Each step would have to be carefully choreographed. Paul had arranged to brief them in the department's shared team room at the university. He had commandeered a small corner and a projector from one of the lecture rooms. He was using one of the team room walls as a screen. The wall was coloured a yellowy-white. Despite sticky tape marks and chipped plaster where ancient flip chart pages had been glued, Paul had managed to display a reasonably intelligible image of his agenda. The team were congregating, waiting to be told their role in the experiment. Darren and Ayala were sitting on chairs. Anil and Dieter were perched on the edge of desks. Dieter had decided to attend so that he could see how the department's budget was being spent. The small group was chattering excitedly amongst themselves. Paul was about to start.

'Are you sitting comfortably?' said Paul parodying an ancient children's programme. 'Then I shall begin.'

Paul waited for them to stop chattering. Darren and Ayala stopped talking when they sensed the silence permeating through the room.

'Before I go into each of tomorrow's tasks, I want to explain why we have so little time to get through the schedule,' Paul paused. 'In a minute I'm going to ask Anil to explain the gaser beam prediction software. I'm sure you all know that it is important to do the experiment whilst our detector is being exposed to the gaser beams.' Paul was not "sure" at all, but the turn of phrase seemed appropriate, 'This is why our experiment is different to all the others that are searching for gravity waves.'

He waited a second for it to sink in. His audience were still paying attention so he continued, 'Gravity wave beams are invisible. They travel through most materials undetected. So if we have any chance of detecting them we have got to handle each crystal really carefully. If we position the test crystals incorrectly in the detector, we will probably see no response at all.'

They all looked discouraged.

Darren asked, 'Has anyone detected the gaser beams since the Yakawa Bee samples were taken?'

'No,' replied Paul, 'the gasers have been detected only once and we worked out that the gasers existed because of the work on the bee DNA.'

Dieter asked, 'Has anybody else been looking for the gaser beams?'

'I suspect from what Claire has told me that the Japanese are looking. But, to my knowledge, nobody has detected anything since Yakawa.' He paused, changing tack. 'When we do our tests tomorrow, we may detect nothing. This could be because the crystals don't contain gravitum. There is another reason why we might fail. Has anyone any idea what that could be?'

'The gaser beams may not have gone overhead at all,' suggested Ayala, 'because we may be taking our measurements at the wrong time, in the wrong place.'

Paul was pleased he had asked the question because it confirmed that Ayala was keeping up. Over the past year Paul's experience as a lecturer had changed his approach to explaining things. In the past he did not particularly mind whether his audience were following him or not. Recently Paul had developed a habit of checking whether his audience had understood. This was a great way to teach students. However he knew the approach could get on the nerves of people who were not under his tuition. This time he had a mixed audience, so it was appropriate.

'You're dead right, Ayala,' confirmed Paul.

Ayala looked pleased with herself. Darren was fiddling with the arm of his chair.

Paul continued, 'That's why I want us all to understand what Anil's software does and what are its limitations.'

He looked at Anil. 'Over to you,' he said, inviting Anil to speak.

Anil stood up and moved in front of the screen. Paul clicked his laptop computer to step to the next slide of the presentation. It was an animated video clip repeating every few seconds. It showed the gaser beams exit from two points in space and scan the Earth. Anil addressed Paul, 'Can you stop it there Paul.'

Paul clicked his computer and the video froze.

'The sources of the gaser beams are these two binary stars,' said Anil pointing to the wall near a hole in the plaster. 'When I first developed the gravity wave prediction program or GWaPP for short, Zihang gave me general information about stars and Jacques gave me rough distances for the two binary stars. I put the data into the earliest versions of the program. We could predict the positions of the gasers to within fifty kilometres on the Earth's surface. The timing of the intersection was typically for a three hour slot that could fall anywhere within a month.'

'So you had little chance of detecting anything, because you'd never be at the right place at the right time,' said Darren, with a pessimistic tone in his voice.

'Almost true,' said Anil. 'We had measurements showing that the binary stars were bending time and space because we saw the gravitational lensing effect. This has helped us refine the software. With Prama's help, there were a number of things I did to correct the theory used in the software.'

'Like what?' asked Darren.

'Well, I started to collect information about the movements of objects that Zihang's data base did not contain.'

'For example?' asked Ayala.

'Comets, records of meteor showers; in fact anything that may lie in the path of the gaser beams. I also corrected for the fact that the Earth is not a perfect sphere.'

'Has this improved the accuracy of your prediction?' asked Dieter.

Dieter's question gave the team a bit of a surprise as most of them had forgotten he was there.

'Yes significantly, Dieter,' replied Anil, addressing him directly, 'for example the software predicts that the gaser beams will intersect over the detector for five hours tomorrow at two o'clock plus or minus one hour.'

'That's why we have three hours to do our experiments,' said Paul, supporting Anil's explanation.

'Will we have another three hours the day after?' asked Ayala.

'Unfortunately no, it's not that simple,' Anil replied.

Darren mumbled under his breath, 'Why is nothing simple?'

Ayala gave him a chastising look.

Anil continued, oblivious to the exchange, 'There will be another opportunity in a few days, but it will only last for thirty minutes. After that, the beams will trace a great circle route over the North Pole continuing on to the East China Sea.' said Anil.

His mind was distracted for a moment as he thought of Prama on an island nearby. He went on, 'At first sight, the gaser beams appear to scan the Earth in a random pattern across the landscape. The beams scan in some locations frequently, but in other places never at all. At the most frequent sites, we can wait a few hours for the beams to cross at other times it could be months.'

'How do you know that the beams will intersect tomorrow?' asked Darren, looking doubtful about the whole venture.

'I have found that the track of the beams creates a repeating pattern every one hundred and thirty seven days. I managed to confirm this by checking the information we had got from gravitational lensing measurements,' Anil paused, wondering if he should go into more depth, or had he done enough damage already.

He decided to plough on, 'There is another cycle of about one hundred and eighty five years. This cycle affects the strength of the gaser signals.'

'Where are we in this long cycle now?' asked Ayala, still alert and enthusiastic. This was in contrast to Darren who was absentmindedly fiddling with the arm of his chair again.

'We will be at the maximum intensity in one week's time, so this is a good time to do the experiment. In other words, if it doesn't work now it never will!' said Anil, with finality.

'That means that the last time there was a peak was the beginning of the nineteenth century?' queried Dieter.

'Yes that's right; in the eighteen twenties,' Anil replied. 'Opportunities like this do not come along very often.'

At that point Paul decided Anil had given them far too much to absorb. However Anil had achieved Paul's objective. Paul wanted the team to understand that this was the chance of a lifetime to do the experiment. He was determined not to mess it up. After Anil finished, Paul displayed the next slide. It was an incredibly complicated chart showing all of the things they would have to do the day after. He looked at the image on the wall. Although parts of his chart had disappeared into dark holes left by missing plaster, he was confident the details could be understood by even the slowest of his audience. He looked at Darren. Paul decided to explain the details over the next hour, during which Dieter drifted away.

Some time later Paul said, 'Ok do you all know what you've got to do?'

A mumbled reply came from the group. Paul decided to make absolutely sure.

'Anil, you will be in the control room monitoring the data capture,' said Paul.

'Confirmed,' said Anil.

'Ayala, you are responsible for loading the canisters containing the crystals.'

'Confirmed,' said Ayala.

'Darren, you are responsible for getting the vacuum chambers pumped down.'

'Yep,' said Darren, succinctly.

'I'll be in the control room with Anil tuning the sensors,' said Paul.

Paul looked at his watch. It was getting late.

'Ok team, that's enough for now. I'll see you at nine tomorrow in the detector laboratory.'

# Ni-jyu-go

## Waves and Quakes

Prama and Claire had a gap in the schedule of the presentations that interested them. Hideo invited them to tour his department. It was a fifteen-minute walk across the city to Academy of Geosciences. Hideo made it more pleasant by explaining his role in the department. He was responsible for monitoring the output of detectors located in bore holes in the Izu-Ogasawara Trench to the south of Japan, and Japan Trench to the east. His equipment monitored pressure, or "p" waves and stress, "s" waves.

'It's the s-waves that are the most dangerous,' Hideo explained, as the three of them entered the building. 'They are responsible for most earthquakes. If they get too big, they can cause the Earth's crust to tear. We monitor them both because the relationship between s-waves and p-waves is an indication of seismic activity.'

Hideo got security passes for them and led them to his room upstairs.

'Please take a seat,' said Hideo, indicating two chairs in his immaculately tidy office.

Prama and Claire thanked him and sat down.

'You mentioned that your submarine had found a blue rock on the seabed to the south of Japan. Why does it interest you?' asked Claire.

'At the time the submarine first picked it up, I was here in Tokyo monitoring seismic activity in the region. I noticed a peak of p-waves and s-waves in the vicinity of the submarine, so I sent an urgent communication to the submarine's control room to ask if they had detected anything unusual.'

'Had they?' asked Prama, curiously.

'They had detected low frequency vibrations. It coincided with the rock being captured by the robotic arm of the submarine. They had found the rock on a ledge near to the Izu-Ogasawara Trench. The vibrations were so large they were worried that the submarine would be shaken apart,' explained Hideo.

'What happened?' asked Claire, intrigued.

'They were so worried they brought the submarine quickly to the surface,' he said. 'The hydraulics of the arm had failed and the rock was still gripped in its jaws.'

'Was the submarine damaged?' asked Claire.

'Only the hydraulics, and by the time the submarine had reached the surface the vibrations had stopped,' Hideo replied.

'Did you manage to find out what caused the vibrations?' asked Prama, also becoming intrigued.

'No, we have not managed to determine their cause. My colleagues have analysed the stone and found nothing strange. They believe the vibrations were due to a tremor, but I still wonder whether it had something to do with the rock.'

Hideo paused to construct the next sentence. 'I performed some of my own research and I found your articles on the Yakawa comet. I realised that you had found a similar chemical composition in your analysis. I also read the other papers about gravity waves.'

'So you are wondering whether the rock was responsible for the tremors?' asked Prama.

Continuing, he said, 'Yes those are my thoughts. I shared my ideas with my boss, Hitzubishi san. He became very excited and told me not to worry about the stone. He has decided to take personal charge of the research from now on. He believes there is a way of using the rock to make free energy. A large energy company gives us funding. Hitzubishi san has a theory that they like. He believes he can build a machine that exploits the special properties of the rock to produce energy from space. He is planning to use the samples to do this.'

'Please excuse me if this sounds impertinent,' said Prama tentatively, 'but if he has taken over, why are you still investigating the rock?'

Claire was puzzled by Prama's question. Why should he not carry on his research? He was a scientist after all. However Claire did not have Prama's insight into the workings of a Japanese management structure.

'Ah, you wonder why I am not following my bosses wishes,' said Hideo, smiling. 'If the submarine vibrations had nothing to do with the rock then I would immediately have stopped my research as Hitzubishi san has instructed.'

He paused to assemble the right words, 'If my detectors simply picked up vibrations generated by the rock, then it may be interesting but again it is not worth further research. This is what Hitzubishi san has argued.'

'So what are you worried about?' asked Claire.

'If the rock's properties caused the Earth's tectonic plates to move and that movement was the cause of the readings in my detectors, then I am very worried. We may have found a very dangerous mineral.'

'Why dangerous?' asked Claire.

'We are sitting in one of the most seismically active places on Earth. It is not a good place to keep a rock that stimulates earthquakes.'

Claire looked at Prama and said 'That doesn't sound good, does it?'

\*\*\*\*

After Claire and Prama had left, Hideo decided to tell his boss about his meeting with them.

'You told them about my experiment!' he shouted, incredulously.

'They have expertise in this field. I thought they could help,' Hideo replied, somewhat lamely.

'I am amazed at your naivety and incompetence,' said Hitubishi san. 'Do you realise how valuable my research is to our competitors? There are foreign companies out there who would pay billions for our ideas and you just discuss them as if they were worthless.'

Hideo was speechless. He had never seen his boss so angry.

Hitubishi san continued his tirade, 'I was always unsure about your loyalty, but now I am convinced that you have been promoted far above your level of expertise.' His face was getting red with anger. 'I am instructing you to release the blue rock immediately from your control and place the samples in my laboratory. I will then consider your future.'

'But,' stammered Hideo, 'I have been doing my job. Which is to investigate the causes and effects of earthquakes and it seems to me that research into this rock is critically important.'

'"It seems to me"…"It seems to me".,' mimicked Hitubishi san. 'Who the hell do you think you are? You will do as you are told.'

Hideo protested, his courage returning, 'The role of the Tokyo Academy of Geosciences is to research seismology, not to ….,'

'You dare to tell **me** about the Academy's role! You are insolent as well as stupid,' interrupted Hitzubishi san, almost shouting. The red colour had started to move down his neck. It looked as though he was about to explode.

He continued, his voice becoming quiet and cold, 'I will explain to you simply. If you release any further information to these people you will be in serious trouble. I will see you out of your beloved Academy for ever. Do you understand?'

'Hai,' said Hideo, meekly.

What more could he say? His boss was completely intransigent. However, Hideo remained very angry, worried and uncharacteristically defiant. Why was his boss behaving like this? He did not work for the electricity generation industry. Both Hitubishi san and Hideo were employed by an academic institution involved in geological research. Something is wrong, he thought. It seems my boss has his own agenda; not one related to what he is paid for, he thought.

Hideo knew that in this culture this thought was almost treason. He had never seen himself as a mutineer; perhaps he had worked with too many foreigners.

✳✳✳✳

It was early evening when Claire phoned Paul. She had hoped to catch him before he headed for the old fire station. The phone rang just as he was going through the front door. He doubled back and picked up the receiver.

'Hello gorgeous. When's my sexy girl coming home?' asked Paul.

'Soon, I'm missing you and your silly jokes,' she said, speaking quietly to keep their words between them.

'I miss you too,' he said, softly, 'I love keeping you entertained; I'll get my boys' book of jokes out before you get on the plane home.'

'Are you on your way out?' she asked.

'Yes, I'd just got to the door. I'm on my way to get the next round of crystals testing.'

Claire told him about the meeting with Hideo.

'That's interesting,' he said. 'Did he confirm that the minerals matched our comet?' he asked.

'Yes,' she said. 'It had the same chromium and platinum isotope signature.'

'Do you remember that old, egg shaped rock in Jacques' office?' Paul asked.

'Vaguely,' said Claire, thinking about being next to him and not on a phone line.

'It has the same signature as well!' he said.

'That's odd,' she said. 'Are you going to test the blue stone today?'

'Yes,' said Paul, continuing conspiratorially, 'I've asked Anil to call Prama about entanglement.'

'That sounds like fun,' Claire said, with a smile in her voice. 'I'll tell her. Talking of entanglement, I think Prama wants to come home. She is missing Anil very much.'

'Does Anil know?' asked Paul.

'No and don't you tell him,' said Claire, with a threat in her voice.

'Yes maam,' he said.

Claire chuckled.

They said their goodbyes. Paul headed for the laboratory and Claire headed for the shower to prepare for another adventurous meal with Prama.

****

Paul had arrived ahead of the rest of the team. He keyed in his security code and let himself in through the gate in the chain-link fence. He stopped briefly to look up at the fire station's brick training tower. It looked pristine. He would not let the structure go to waste. Maybe a radio telescope would be better than an optical telescope. He could operate that remotely and save on ladders. It would be something to do after they had proven gravitum exists, he thought. He made his way into the equipment room and looked around. He remembered how, only a few days ago, he was so excited about trying out the new laboratory. He was still excited. Paul wondered whether he would still be as enthusiastic in a month's time if they had not detected anything. Well that will be then and this is now, he thought, his brain unusually allowing him close to a philosophical idea. He forced his mind back to the day's plan. Paul had devised an ingenious modification to the system; Ayala could insert the various samples into the detector without letting air in. This meant she could change the samples very quickly. Paul was proud of his laboratory. He hoped it would detect something useful. He heard a noise in the control room. Anil had arrived through the back door. Ayala and Darren followed him shortly afterwards.

The team took a few moments to discuss the plan of action. Including the blue rock, they had four crystals to test. It was time to get down to work. Ayala' job was to load the crystals. She placed the first sample into the container. Darren's role was to operate the vacuum. He started the pumps and checked the vacuum system to ensure there were no leaks. Paul was rechecking that each of the laser ranging devices was properly aligned. He compared his measurements to those monitored by Anil who was sitting in the control room on the other side of a toughened glass window. Paul was not sure why he had protected the control room in this way. Nothing dramatic had ever happened in the twenty-year history of this detector, so looking at it now, it seemed to be overkill. They were almost ready for the gaser beams to go overhead. The final checks on the detector were almost complete, when Dieter arrived.

'Good morning everyone,' he said, 'is everything ready?'

Paul was surprised by Dieter's appearance, but he was pleased he was interested.

'Hi Dieter,' replied Paul. 'I didn't expect you to come over today.'

'I have to admit I'm quite fascinated to see how Jacques' blue stone performs,' he said. 'When are you due to load it into the detector?'

'In about four hours,' said Paul, looking at his watch.

Dieter was quiet for a few moments watching the team making various adjustments.

'Why do the detector arms have to be in a vacuum?' he asked.

Paul replied, 'We're trying to measure tiny movements in the detector arms. The air would cause all our readings to be swamped with background effects such as local heating and sound waves.'

'If I could do the experiment without the vacuum system I would,' he went on, pointing at one of the stainless steel tubes. 'It's the most cumbersome part of the apparatus. You can imagine how difficult it is to keep a system of that size air tight!'

'I guess it could be dangerous too,' said Dieter looking at the toughened glass screen between them and the detector room.

Paul knew how much the control room had cost, so he did not want to express his earlier thoughts to Dieter.

'Yes,' said Paul. 'Vacuum systems have been known to implode violently. If a weakness forms in the vacuum chambers' structure, air rushes in with all the force of the Earth's atmosphere. It can be very dangerous.'

Paul did not want to over do it so he added, 'Mind you this set up is pretty robust.'

'Good,' said Dieter, feeling happy to be on the safer side of the reinforced glass.

By noon they had finished their final checks. They had a break together in the control room. Darren had fetched some pizzas. Dieter paid for them. Paul was glad Dieter had visited. Then the magic hour arrived. They were ready to test the first sample.

Nothing happened.

Then the second; nothing happened.

In fact nothing happened for all the samples until they came to Jacques' blue stone.

Ayala loaded the capsule containing the Jacques' stone on to the bracket on the detector arm. Darren pumped out the small amount of air that had entered the chamber. He opened the air lock around the arm holding Jacques' rock. There was the sound of the air pumps working harder. When all of the extraneous noise had settled down, they gathered around Anil as he stared at his two computer screens. He clicked a button to start the experiment. There were streams of numbers scrolling down the left hand screen. Everybody's attention was focussed on the second screen. It had several panels with graphs and waveforms.

However they were all focused on the simplest display. It showed two concentric circles in orange and green. The orange circle formed a tightly fitting frame around the green circle.

'It moved,' said Darren excitedly.

'I didn't see anything,' said Dieter.

'I'm sure it did,' said Darren emphatically.

'Ok,' said Anil, sliding on his chair over to another computer monitor. 'I'll scan back through that data.'

Anil was quiet for a few moments. Darren was looking over his shoulder, whist the rest of the team were continuing to look at the concentric circles.

'Good God,' exclaimed Anil, using a phrase he rarely used. 'Darren's right. It's a tiny deflection, but it's there alright!'

There was a moment of stunned silence. Then the team exploded into excitement. Paul punched the air. Forgetting herself, Ayala hugged Dieter, then embarrassed, hugged Darren. For the rest of the afternoon they checked and crosschecked their results. They had achieved a scientific breakthrough; they had successfully detected gravity waves from the gasers one hundred and eighty light years away!

The local pub was a bit closer, just over a hundred metres away. It had not had seen any new customers for years. One by one the companies in the industrial estate had moved to better, more modern locations. Their employees had moved with them. The fire station was closed because there was nothing of value, except the pub, to catch fire. The publican was pleased when a small group of strangers with money, walked into his bar; even if they were an odd looking bunch of scientists.

'They must be from the disused fire station,' he said to his wife.

Their spirits were still high when they arrived in the bar. It was not clear what the locals thought. However they watched tolerantly as the boffins from the old fire station were having a lot of fun and drinking too much. It was Paul's round.

'Three pints of bitter, a cola and a gin and tonic please,' he said with a slight slur.

'You celebrating?' asked the publican's wife with an amused smile. She had decided this lot looked harmless but it was always sensible to get empathy, just in case.

'We most definitely are,' Paul replied, amazed that his diction seemed to improve when he'd had a couple. The publican's wife was not so sure. Paul continued, 'We've got a result from a gadget that's been silent for over twenty years. It's brilliant!'

The publican's wife put the last drink on Paul's tray.

'That's nice,' she said smiling and taking Paul's money. Funny way to make a living, she thought, watching Paul return with the tray to his friends. They stayed there until throwing-out time. Dieter conscientiously paid for a taxi to make sure Ayala got home safely. The rest of them went their separate ways.

Paul had sobered up during the walk from the bus stop to the flat. He was reflecting on the phone conversation he had had with Jacques when Paul told him about their success.

'Jacques, it works!' Paul had said, almost screaming into the phone. 'The blue stone is gravitum!'

'Calm down, mon ami,' said Jacques. He could hear the noise of excitement in the background. 'Tell me what happened.'

Paul having difficulty with his composure explained what they had seen. Jacques asked Paul about the details and some of the measurements.

'Alors, this is tremendous news,' said Jacques, in a calm voice. 'You realise don't you, that the readings are too small to explain our Yakawa results?'

Paul thought for a second, the noise continuing around him.

'Because they are not strong enough to trigger teleportation?' he said reflectively. 'I guess you're right. There must be something else we've forgotten.'

Jacques' heard the background noise get louder.

'C'mon, Paul it's your round!' said a voice.

'I think you're needed, let's talk tomorrow morning,' said Jacques.

Paul slept badly that night. The next morning he made his usual call to Claire. He asked her when she was coming home, even though he knew the answer. She made a yearning noise and they talked intimately for a while. Then she told him about a conversation Prama and she had had with Hideo. Her account of how the Japanese rock had been found beneath one thousand meters of water unsettled him. There was something important inside that story that he was missing. He could not put his finger on it. They said their goodbyes. He was sitting in the kitchen drinking his morning coffee when the penny dropped.

'That's it!' he said out load. 'It's the ocean!'

\*\*\*\*

As a non-drinker Anil had slept well. He arrived at the university early. Anil wanted to call Prama when no one else was around. With all the work leading to the experiment and the time zone difference, it had not been easy to choose a time when they would both be near a phone. Anil wanted to speak to her so very much. Since Prama had gone, Anil had an ache that would not go away. If he did not know before, he knew now that he loved her. Over the last six months they had written, but he had not spoken to her. You can express so much in a letter, he thought, but he would love to hear her voice. Even so, Anil was worried that he may say something wrong. He did not want to break the spell. He assembled his last reserves of courage to make the call. He had delayed too long. He dialled the number. It seemed to ring for an eternity.

'Hello, Prama speaking.'

He was startled by her voice. It was wonderful to be this close again. He was tongue-tied.

'It's you Anil, isn't it?' she said gently. 'Oh how I've missed you.'

'Yes, it's me,' he said, quietly.

Then it all came flooding out. Prama was energised by the call; their conversation flowed backward and forwards. Time ticked by. Dieter would have been worried about the phone bill, but Anil did not care. Anil would have talked to her for the rest of the day except Paul had arrived.

'Paul's just walked in,' said Anil.

'Oh,' said Prama, mischievously, 'shall we talk about sex then.' She could picture Anil blushing at this point.

'That's fine,' he said. 'I'll just listen.'

'That's no good,' she said, 'it's only half the fun.'

'We'll have to talk about work then,' said Anil, knowing Paul was in earshot. 'Paul said you need to tell me about entanglement.'

'I thought that's what I was doing,' said Prama, teasing. Then sensing more people had arrived in the team room, 'All right, what do you want me to tell you about entanglement?'

Paul caught Anil's eye and mouthed the word 'Prama?' to him. Anil nodded. Paul grinned and discreetly left to make a cup of coffee.

'What has entanglement to do with our gasers?' asked Anil, trying to be professional.

'Like me and you the two binary stars are a long way away from each other; sad isn't it?' said Prama.

'Very,' he replied, softly.

'But somehow they have managed to send two beams of coherent radiation towards Earth. In other words, they are exactly in harmony; like you and me,' she said enjoying the analogy.

'They are working together like we are now. So they must have some link between them like our telephones,' said Anil, also starting to enjoy the game.

'Yes but our conversation is sexier,' she said. Then returning to the theme, she continued, 'The thing is that if we tried to have this conversation one hundred and fifty years ago, we couldn't, because no one had built the telephone system. So our beautiful intimate letters would have taken days, maybe months to arrive.'

'But they're worth the wait,' remarked Anil, conspiratorially.

'Letters are nice aren't they,' she said. 'Are you going to write me another one?'

'Maybe, if you're a good girl and you finish the story of entanglement.'

'Oh yes,' Prama said distractedly. 'Entanglement; well, if one of our two binary stars sent a letter to the other one, the mail could go no faster than the speed of light. As the stars are over two hundred light years apart, it would be a long wait. In fact the wait would be so long that they could not keep in harmony.'

'They would drift out of love,' said Anil, lost in the simile.

'I love you when you're romantic,' she said. 'Anyway, we've seen that the two stars work together. So there must be something that links them at a very high speed.'

'Like a telephone link?' asked Anil, rhetorically.

'Yes, but faster and the "link" must have been put in place earlier,' said Prama. 'This is where entanglement comes in. Something must have laid down the connection between our two star-crossed lovers many years ago. I think this was done by creating two halves of a message and sending one half to each binary star. The two half-messages would have travelled no faster than the speed of light. So they were created hundreds of years ago, but once in place communication is very fast.'

'So these half messages could be packets of light, photons?'

'They could,' replied Prama, 'and I suspect there were billions of entangled photons created in a place equidistant from the two stars.'

'So that makes Earth a possible source,' said Anil.

'That's what Paul thinks,' Prama confirmed.

'According to Jacques, the binary stars are between one sixty and two hundred light years away from Earth,' said Anil.

'So if Paul's right then something caused the gasers to intersect on Earth around one hundred and eighty years ago,' said Prama 'Now back to our entanglement,' she said, suggestively. 'When would you like that to be?'

Anil blushed and coughed.

'Don't worry, I won't seduce you any more,' said Prama sighing. 'You can write me another letter though, if you like.'

Anil promised he would.

# Twenty-six

# Energy for Nothing

Paul had returned with his cup of coffee. He nodded to Anil who was still on the phone. Anil seemed too preoccupied to notice him. Paul was pleased to see Anil back to his old self. Paul wanted to read an article he had seen about piezoelectric materials. At the back of his mind was a memory of skimming the article in either Science or Nature. Paul could search through both journals on his computer. He looked across at Anil, still talking quietly and engrossed in the conversation. On the floor above, there was a small departmental library and it had back copies of both journals. He thought for Anil's sake and his own embarrassment, he would leave the lovebirds alone. He would find the article the old-fashioned way and look for it on the bookshelves upstairs.

A few moments later Paul was inside the library searching through the indices. To call it a library was probably an overstatement. It was a large seminar room with the walls lined with books. Most of these were bound copies of journals going back twenty years or so. The administrator protected the volumes like a she-tiger. Paul knew she would appear in a few seconds to make sure he did not steal anything. Sure enough she appeared. At first glance she looked harmless but looks can be deceiving.

'Are you looking for anything in particular Paul?' she asked, with a charming smile, that Paul interpreted as a warning snarl.

'Hello, Anne,' he said, avoiding her question. 'You look radiant today. Have you done something to your hair?' Paul knew it was cynical but he found she was more tolerant if he complimented her.

She smiled coyly.

'No I haven't changed anything,' she said, cocking her head to one side.

'Well, your hair looks very nice,' Paul said, continuing with his strategy to disarm the tiger.

'Well, thank you,' she said. Then completely forgetting why she had come in, Anne said, 'I'll leave you to it.' She turned towards the door and left in a flutter.

That was close, thought Paul. He went back to the open index in front of him.

'There it is,' he exclaimed out loud.

He looked around to make sure he had not woken the jungle animal again. No, the coast was clear. He walked toward the shelf and pulled out one volume of last year's issue of Nature. He placed the book on a desk and sat down with the journal opened in front of him. Paul started to read the paper somewhat more thoroughly than he did last time. For a while, he read quietly but something had attracted his attention. If he had been Archimedes, this would have been a Eureka moment, and even though Paul was in a library and not in a bath, he could not contain his emotions.

'Pressure you fool, Paul! Pressurise it!' he said, much louder then he intended. 'The damn thing had a thousand metres of water on top of it!'

Paul had to tell someone he quickly stood up and headed for the door. He must find Anil immediately. Paul met Anne on her way back to the library. He had woken the she-tiger. Paul did not know why, but he felt grateful to her for letting him read the books.

'You're brilliant!' he said excitedly. He took her head and kissed her. He would have kissed Dieter if he'd been there.

'Sorry,' he said, embarrassed, 'got carried away.'

He headed for the stairs, leaving Anne bemused by the door. She had a strange smile on her face.

****

Back at the Tokyo Academy of Geosciences, Hitzubishi san had made the same connection. He had realised that the crystals in the Japanese blue stone, became more sensitive when they were under pressure. That was why the crystals stopped vibrating as they came to the surface. But Hitzubishi san was not interested in detecting gravity waves; what was the profit in that? He was interested in generating energy, free electricity. This would make billions for the corporation and he would become a highly revered man. He had built his prototype device some weeks ago. In the core was a spherical steel container. He had pumped oil into it to a high pressure. This would simulate the water pressure under the ocean. His apparatus would then convert the energy given out by the vibrations to electricity. Hitzubishi san was a genius; well that is what he thought. His only problem was that he could not predict when the gravity waves were overhead. Hitzubishi san had read Anil's paper, but it did not include the latest refinements to the software. Hitzubishi san decided that he would tell the weakling Aoki san, to get more information.

****

When Paul arrived back in the team room, Anil was no longer on the phone and he was humming to himself.

'Anil,' said Paul, excitedly and fortunately without kissing him, 'when's the next window. We've got to put it under pressure.'

'What?'

'When's the next window?'

'Slow down Paul,' said Anil, as if trying to humour a lunatic, 'what's happened?'

'The Japanese rock absorbed gravity waves, because its crystal structure was under water,' said Paul, as if what he was saying was obvious.

'So?' said Anil.

'The water pressure must compress the crystal structure so that it becomes sensitive. I've just read an article in Nature where this happens with a similar piezoelectric compound.'

'Oh, I see,' said Anil, catching on. 'The next window is this afternoon.'

'I must call Jacques,' said Paul, finding it difficult to contain his enthusiasm.

He picked up the phone and dialled.

'Morning Jacques,' he said, before Jacques had time to respond. 'I know what we have missed!'

'Quoi?' said Jacques, deciding to keep his responses succinct.

Paul explained about the article he had just read and the need to pressurise the sample.

'That will be a challenge,' said Jacques, 'pressurising a rock that's held in a vacuum. Let me calculate the pressure gradient..,' Jacques paused whilst he worked out the sea water pressure where the Japanese rock had been found. He had his answer; 'I make it about one hundred times the pressure on the surface air pressure.'

'That's no problem then,' said Paul, relieved. 'I designed a special steel cylinder to hold the crystals that we test. The cylinder is made to isolate the crystals from the vacuum of the detector. This allows Ayala to change samples without letting air into the detector. The cylinder should take pressures up to four hundred atmospheres.'

'Mon Dieu, Paul,' Jacques exclaimed. 'Does Dieter know you over-engineer in this way?'

'I never told him,' said Paul. 'I just gave him the bill.'

Paul was quiet for a moment he had thought of a snag.

'I need to work out how to pressurize the cylinder after the blue stone has been loaded. Have you any ideas Jacques?' he asked.

Jacques thought for a couple of seconds than came up with his suggestion. 'Perhaps you could pump it with hydraulic oil. The pumps are easy to obtain and the oil will pressurise the stone.'

'Great,' replied Paul, enthusiastically. 'I'll have to make sure the hydraulic systems are robust. If they break then we will have a hundred atmosphere bomb explode inside a vacuum chamber.'

'That would be very dangerous,' agreed Jacques. 'Be careful.'

After the conversation with Jacques, Paul's mood had become more sober. His attention was now focussed on the practical problems of getting ready for the next experiment. He needed to know how much time they had to make the modifications. Anil still had not answered his earlier question about the next scan of the gaser beams.

'Anil,' Paul said, attracting his attention.

'Yes?' said Anil looking up from his computer screen.

'You didn't answer my question about the next gaser beam intersection.'

'I'm just running the simulation now,' said Anil. He clicked the mouse. 'That's it,' he said, 'You've got twenty three hours.'

'Thanks,' said Paul. 'We'd better hurry then.'

'Yes you had,' confirmed Anil. 'Is it alright if I don't go to the lab for this one? You can upload the data to me here.'

'Why?' said Paul. 'What are you working on?'

'I'm following up on my conversation with Prama.' Anil was talking about the scientific part of the conversation. 'She thinks something triggered the entanglement between one hundred and sixty and two hundred years ago. I have started to collect data on events covering that period. I'd like to work on that, if you don't mind.'

'Of course,' said Paul. 'I can call you if I need help?'

'No problem,' replied Anil.

Paul went back to his thoughts. Twenty-three hours; that was two days before Claire would board the plane home. He realised that they were about to solve the question that had brought Paul and Claire together. Paul was sad that Claire would not be able to share the moment with him. Paul looked at his watch; it would be early evening in Tokyo. If he phoned now, he might catch her before she and Prama went out for another adventurous dinner. At least he could share his discovery with her.

****

On the instructions of Hitzubishi san, Hideo had arranged a meeting with Prama. Hideo's integrity was important to him. He had grown to respect Prama and her friend Claire. He would not deceive either of them, even if by doing so, it would help his academy's sponsor create a fortune in royalties. When Hitzubishi san had instructed him to arrange a follow up meeting with Prama, Hideo had refused. He did not believe the reasons were honourable. As in his last encounter with his boss, Hitzubishi san had become angry and threatened to fire Hideo. Hideo had acquiesced, even though his conscience told him it was wrong. Was he weak? Certainly Hitzubishi san thought he was. Hideo may be weak, but he was not dishonourable. He would do everything he could to share what he knew without being explicit. Prama was an intelligent woman. She would work it out. He wondered whether he was a little in love with her.

Prama arrived as arranged in the late afternoon. Claire was attending an esoteric lecture on biochemistry so Prama thought this was a good time to schedule Hideo's requested meeting. As usual Hideo was politeness itself. He was waiting in the foyer of the Academy as she came through the door. He bowed and they shook hands.

'I am honoured that you accepted my invitation,' said Hideo smiling. 'Let me show you to the meeting room. My boss, Hitzubishi san will be joining us for part of the meeting.'

They made their way into a small room with space for four or five seats around a small table. There was a white board screwed on the wall with a hand drawn diagram of some kind of apparatus. Each of the components was labelled in Japanese. Hitzubishi san made an entrance into the room. He waited for Hideo to introduce them. Hitzubishi's bow was barely perceptible. Prama mirrored with a small nod. Prama could see that this was a man who considered himself to be important. She was not about to be intimidated by a "stuffed shirt". As they had been introduced in English, Prama realised that Hitzubishi san did not know she spoke Japanese. He rudely told Hideo to get on with the meeting. Hideo was embarrassed. Switching to English, Hitzubishi san, through his thin lips, gave Prama a cold smile. He said that he must leave for another meeting in five minutes. During the five minutes he asked many questions but he gave Prama no reasons for his curiosity. She was happy to share her knowledge, but this seemed to be one-way traffic. Finally, Hitzubishi san stood up abruptly and told Hideo in Japanese, to find out what Hitzubishi san needed to know. Again Hideo was embarrassed. Prama was amused and intrigued.

'I am sorry for my boss' rudeness,' said Hideo apologetically after Hitzubishi san had left. 'My boss is driven by the need for commercial security and he will not let me talk to you about the details of his project. I have explained that your interest is only academic, but he is still adamant.'

Hideo unexpectedly changed the subject.

He said, 'This room is used for discussions about his experiment. Hitzubishi san gives presentations about his project using the white board. He sometimes forgets to clean it. Of course he writes in Japanese so our foreign visitors could not understand it. Would you like some refreshment, some tea for example?'

'Yes, thank you Hideo. That would be very kind,' replied Prama, amused by the whole situation.

Hideo left the room in search of refreshments. He was pleased with his choice of meeting room. It was not his fault that Hitzubishi san did not clean the whiteboard. Whilst he was away Prama examined the diagram and the kanji notes around it. It was clear that the device would apply hydraulic pressure to the blue rock. Hitzubishi san must believe that this would somehow trigger the rock's properties. Hideo returned with a pot of tea and two small cups.

'If you have already guessed at the kind experiments that are being performed here, our conversation would be easier,' said Hideo with an innocent expression.

'I believe I have guessed,' said Prama, also with an innocent expression.

'Good,' said Hideo. 'Then I would like your advice about some of my concerns.'

Hideo reiterated his earlier worry about the rock generating seismic activity. He was interested about the progress made by Prama's friends. At that point Prama was only aware that Paul's team had detected gravity waves but the response had been very weak. Prama told Hideo that she believed that Paul's team had tested a similar rock to the one found by the submarine, but the experiment was done at atmospheric pressure.

'Do you think it would make any difference if the rock was pressurised?' asked Hideo.

Prama thought for a moment. 'I have heard that the properties of certain crystals will change when they are stressed, but I have never heard of the kind of dramatic change you are worried about.'

'But you believe it is possible?'

'It's beyond my experience, Hideo,' Prama replied. 'One of my colleagues may be able to answer your question. I'll ask him to contact you.'

Prama had decided to phone Jacques the following morning. She did not know about the follow-on experiment that Paul was about to plan.

'Your information helps to put my mind at rest,' said Hideo. 'For me, a weak response to the gravity waves is good.'

'I'm not sure my friends would agree, Hideo,' replied Prama smiling, 'but the rock seems to be less dangerous than you may think.'

They chatted for a few minutes longer. Prama agreed to speak to Hideo after she had spoken to Jacques.

Prama made her way back to her hotel. She had a lot to tell Claire about her visit to the Tokyo Academy of Geosciences. Claire was waiting in the foyer of the hotel as Prama collected her key.

'I've just been speaking to Paul,' said Claire, grinning.

'You lucky thing,' said Prama, indulgently.

'He believes that if you put the blue stone under pressure, its response to gravity waves will increase.'

'Does he indeed?' said Prama, thoughtfully, 'although he'd deny it, Hideo told me that they've come to the same conclusion. Let's talk about this over dinner.'

\*\*\*\*

Whilst Claire was sleeping in Tokyo, Paul, Ayala and Darren were working hard to be ready for the next experiment. Like Jacques, Paul was worried that the high pressure cylinder inside the detector's vacuum could be dangerous. So Paul had decided to take extra precautions. He was working on the design of a mechanism that allowed Ayala to load the sample without manual intervention. Paul's modification would let her control the whole process from within the control room. Likewise Paul wanted to automate other tasks so that Darren could work from behind the glass screen as well. Unfortunately one of Darren's jobs had to be done manually. This involved pouring liquid helium from large flasks into the vacuum pumps. Darren would be able to do this job before the experiment started in earnest so Paul thought it would be safe enough. Was Paul being over cautious? The thought had certainly crossed his mind. It would be sometime later when Darren and Ayala would have cause to thank Paul for his tendency to over-engineer. On the other side of the world Hitzubishi san had no such reservations. This he would live to regret.

Anil was working on his software ten miles away in the team room. All the data from the old fire station would be sent to him over a network link, so he could process the results at his desk. At that moment Anil was working on something else. He had built a database of natural events going back over two hundred years. It had taken a long time to load the data. There were many events to be recorded, but he was satisfied. All that remained was for him to complete the modifications to his software. That would take him the rest of the day. He would then run the program on a spare computer. With luck he would get the results just before the team started the next test of the blue stone. He had a nagging feeling that the results of this computer run would be very important.

# Twenty-seven

## Sky

The twelve hours had gone quickly. They had three and a half hours to complete Paul's modifications and get ready for the next exposure of gaser radiation. Paul was in the equipment room of the old fire station. He was working on the detector with Darren. Both Paul and Darren were wearing clean white overalls, so that they would not contaminate the space inside the apparatus. There was a constant background noise from the mechanical vacuum pumps. These were extracting air from system. They would soon reduce the pressure sufficiently for the next stage of pumping. At this point, Darren would start the diffusion and cryogenic pumps. These would create a vacuum as empty as a vacuum one would find in outer space. Ayala was in the control room operating controls to Paul's instructions. She could see them though the reinforced glass screen but she was out of earshot. They were communicating over an intercom system.

'Ayala, click the "Lock" button please,' shouted Paul, over the hum of the vacuum pumps.

Ayala was sitting in front of a computer monitor in the control room. She moved the mouse so that the pointer was over the appropriate button. She clicked.

'Done,' she said.

Paul peered through a glass panel in the detector. Something was not quite right.

'Ayala, is the airlock closed?' Paul shouted.

Ayala clicked another button and confirmed that it was.

'Can you click "Unlock" please,' he shouted.

Ayala did as instructed. Paul opened the small door and reached inside.

'It's not sealing properly,' said Paul, speaking to Darren. 'Is the replacement cylinder handy?'

'Here,' said Darren handing Paul a shiny stainless steel tube.

'Ok let's try this one and see if it's any better,' said Paul, inserting the new cylinder through the orifice in the detector.

'Now let's connect the pressure hoses and the servos,' grunted Paul as he strained with his arm inside the apparatus.

Darren moved round to the other side of the section that Paul was working on.

'Can I help?' he asked.

'Yes please,' said Paul. 'Can you open the cover on your side and hold a spanner on the locking bolt?'

'No problemo,' said Darren.

He started to undo a second panel in the apparatus.

'Be careful with the seal,' said Paul. 'We don't want a gas leak.'

'Ok,' said Darren.

They worked together like this for a few minutes as Ayala watched them through the reinforced glass screen.

'That's it,' said Paul, finally. 'Ok let's put the inspection covers back on and test it again. I hope it works this time. We've only got ninety minutes left.'

They sealed the apertures up and went back to view the mechanism though the small window in the detector.

'Ok, Ayala,' shouted Paul. 'Click the "Lock" button again.'

'Aye aye captain,' came the reply over the speaker as she operated the mouse.

Paul and Darren peered though the little window as the robotic system operated.

'Eureka!' said Darren. He liked the sound of the word.

Paul smiled.

'We're ready,' he said.

The phone rang in the control room. Ayala answered it.

'It's for you Paul,' she said over the intercom. 'Jacques is on the phone.'

Paul made his way into the control room and picked up the receiver. Darren worked in the equipment room on another part of the apparatus. He topped up the diffusion pumps with liquid helium and checked the pressure readings on the mechanical pumps. He followed Paul into the control room and sat in front of the computer screen next to Ayala.

'Hello Jacques,' said Paul, cheerfully.

'Allo, Paul,' replied Jacques 'You sound as though all is well.'

'Yes, we're nearly ready,' said Paul. 'The servo systems work, the blue stone is ready to be loaded. In ninety minutes or so we will have the vacuum down to an acceptable level.'

'Good work,' said Jacques. 'Are all the team back in the control room?'

'Yes, I've managed to automate everything. The only manual process involves keeping the liquid helium topped up. Darren's just done that, so we only need to go into the equipment room once more.'

'How will you pressurize the sample?' asked Jacques.

'I built a self contained hydraulic system that has its own oil reservoir joined to the steel container that holds the crystal sample. We can operate it by a wireless network signal.'

'You don't think the radio signals will affect the detector's readings?'

'No it only sends pulses when we ask it to. I've also fitted a camera inside the cylinder, so that we can watch your rock as we pressurise it,' said Paul.

'I am impressed, mon ami' said Jacques. 'I know why Prama called you the "Engineer" now!'

Paul was surprised. He did not know Jacques knew about that.

Darren interrupted, 'Can I start the diffusion pumps?'

'Go for it,' said Paul with his hand over the phone's mouthpiece.

'We're just about to start the diffusion pumps. Can I call you back in about forty five minutes?' said Paul.

'Of course,' said Jacques. 'But before you go, I remembered the meaning of the oriental ideogram on the blue stone.'

'Oh, what does it mean?'

'"Sky",' said Jacques, enigmatically. 'It's Chinese.'

'Does that help us?' asked Paul.

'No,' replied Jacques.

'Ok,' said Paul, retaining his reputation as a man of little words.

They rang off.

****

Just as Paul and Anil had agreed, Anil was working in the team room on his computer program. It had been running for most of the day. He was starting to wonder whether it was stuck in a loop. He decided to look at the data base log. He keyed a few commands into his keyboard, then slid his chair over to another terminal and keyed some commands followed by a click on the mouse.

'It's still running,' he said out loud. 'I wonder which records it's reading.'

His latest program was designed to match a gaser beam intersection with an historical event. If it found a match, the system would drill into more and more detailed information. He was guessing that the software had found something. He slid his chair back to his original terminal and keyed another command. This would tell him what part of the database the software was searching that in turn would tell him what latitude and longitude the program was interested in. He could wait for the program to finish, but he was getting impatient.

'Nansei shoio,' he mumbled, reading the message on the screen. 'I wonder where that is?'

Non-the-wiser, he headed off to the tearoom to make himself a tea without milk.

****

Paul, Ayala and Darren were ready and watching the clock. Paul promised to call Jacques, so he dialled his number.

'Allo, c'est Jacques,' said the voice at the other end.

'Hi, it's Paul. We're about to pressurise the sample. Do want to listen on the conference phone? You can hear how we're getting on.'

'Magnificent,' said Jacques. 'Thank you, that would be good.'

Paul switched the phone to loudspeaker mode and checked Jacques could hear everybody in the room.

'Ok team, let's start. Darren is the vacuum ready?' asked Paul.

Darren looked at his screen and read the vacuum pressure. 'Yes, it's ready,' he said.

'Ayala can you start the hydraulic pump and pressurise "Sky",' said Paul. He had started to call the blue rock by its Chinese name. It sounded friendlier somehow.

Ayala moved the mouse to the button marked "Stress crystal" and clicked. Her instruction was processed by the computer and converted into a message that was transmitted to the steel cylinder containing "Sky". A small, but powerful hydraulic pump started to pump oil into the cylinder. The pressure reading inside the cylinder started to increase. Whilst the pressure outside the cylinder was virtually zero. The force on the walls of the cylinder was massive.

****

Anil arrived back to his desk with his cup of tea. Just as he sat down the screen in front of him started to fill with information.

It has finally finished, he thought. He scanned the text. He read the word 'Tsunami' then 'undersea earthquake'. He stopped the text scrolling and started to read in more detail.

'Oh my God!' he said.

****

Ayala was continuing to watch the pressure inside the cylinder increase.

'We're up to ten atmospheres,' she said.

'Ninety to go,' said Paul, hoping he had made its steel walls thick enough. 'How's it going at your end Darren?' he asked.

Darren examined the various panels on his screen. 'Everything is stable,' he replied.

Paul glanced through the window at the detector.

'The gasers will be overhead in about ten minutes,' he said.

Paul moved to a spare computer terminal and started to scan through a series of screens. 'The crystal is starting to generate electrical discharges in the oil,' he said.

'The piezoelectric effect in action,' commented Jacques, clearly not surprised.

'That's interesting,' said Paul, as he changed to another screen. 'The crystal is emitting ultraviolet light; it's behaving like a laser crystal!'

Ayala and Darren looked over Paul's shoulder at the screen.

'What a beautiful blue glow,' said Ayala.

'Weird,' said Darren.

As Darren turned back to his screen, he noticed something.

'The liquid helium level is low on the second pump. I need to top it up,' he said, addressing Paul.

'Ok, but be quick,' said Paul.

Darren put on his insulated gloves. Whilst he headed for the liquid helium flask, Paul turned back to the screen. He then saw the deflection of the detector arms. The reading was growing rapidly.

'Jacques, are you there?' asked Paul.

'Oui,' said Jacques, but his voice had a different pitch.

'The readings are increasing,' said Paul. 'They are already ten times the value of our last test.'

'I could not understand you,' said a voice, quite unlike Jacques'.

Ayala exclaimed, 'Paul, look at this!'

Paul came over to her and looked at her computer screen. She was looking at the view of "Sky" though the camera fitted inside the cylinder.

'Good grief,' said Paul. 'It's shaking.'

The rock, still with its blue glow and surrounded by electrical discharges like a full-scale lightning storm was vibrating violently.

\*\*\*\*

Anil continued to read his computer monitor.

The screen said:

## Matched records:

### *Historical database*

**1826 Tsunami estimated over twenty seven thousand Japanese dead.**

**Epicentre Chinese Loo Choo islands – Now Japanese Ryukyu Islands.**

## *Current research papers*

**Meteoric rock found near Okinawa by seismic research submarine.**

## *Gaser Simulation*

**Intersection of gaser beams tracking Ryukyu archipelago. Ten events July to December 1826.**

He looked at the screen that was monitoring the output from the old fire station. The concentric circles were moving rapidly apart.

A feeling of horror started to form in the pit of Anil's stomach.

'We're going to cause an earthquake!' he screamed but no one could hear him.

He dived for his phone.

'I must stop them!' he said, sweat forming on his brow.

He dialled the control room number. It was engaged.

He dialled Paul's mobile phone. No reply.

He tried Darren's, Ayala's the same problem.

He was sure he felt the building shake.

Please, please no, not a tremor! he thought.

Anil knew panic was taking hold. He must stop and think.

Got it, he leapt towards one of his computer terminals

'I'll shut them down from here,' he said out load.

But he did not know how to get into Paul's access codes.

He started keying like a maniac.

\*\*\*\*

The vibration from "Sky" was becoming more intense. The vibration was causing pulses of pressure inside the steel cylinder that held Sky. This was above their target hundred atmospheres. The peak pressure was up to three hundred. Paul knew he had only designed the cylinder to take four hundred atmospheres. The noise of Sky's incessant vibration was louder than the background of the vacuum pumps.

'The equipment would not stand the stress much longer,' shouted Paul above the commotion. 'Ayala, depressurise the cylinder!' he instructed, 'We've got to shut it down.'

'I can't,' said Ayala, with panic in her voice. 'The control system must have been damaged. It's not responding'

The pressure inside the cylinder had climbed above four hundred atmospheres.

Paul remembered that Darren had gone into the detector room. Paul picked up the intercom mike.

'Darren, get out!' he shouted.

Just as Darren looked up the steel vacuum tube around the detector arm started to shake.

'Get out,' he shouted again. 'It's going to blow.'

Darren looked through one of the inspection panels in the arm containing the sample. He could see the steel cylinder shaking. One of the control wires had broken free. Parts of the cylinder were starting to glow red with heat. Air would cool it.

'Kill the vacuum,' shouted Darren in reply.

Paul shouted again, 'Get out damn you!'

Ayala clicked the mouse to let air into the system as had Darren demanded. There was a hiss as air started to enter the tubes. The steel tubes were shaking violently. Letting air in had made no difference to the violence of the shaking, but it had cooled the outer casing of the cylinder. One of the arms had now come away from the concrete floor and was swinging violently.

Paul shouted, 'Darren, if you don't come out I'm going to get you!'

Darren paused, picked up a spanner and leapt at to the section holding the blue rock. He smashed the glass observation window. It cracked. He hit it again. The crack got bigger. Then the panel imploded as air rushed into the remaining vacuum. There were shards of glass around the periphery of the hole he had made. The whole assembly was still shaking. He climbed on top of the large steel tube holding the detector arm. Darren was moving with it. He was wearing the insulated gloves to protect him from the cold liquid helium. He needed them as he reached inside through the hole edged with jagged glass.

By now Paul was next to him.

'What the hell are you doing?' screamed Paul. 'Get out of here!'

'The control wire is disconnected,' said Darren. 'I just need to reach….. Got it!'

Darren withdrew from the hole. The glove had protected him from the hot steel, but not the glass. His arm was cut badly and blood was streaming down his arm. He looked at the red blood and became giddy. Paul lifted him across his shoulders and staggered unsteadily across the shaking floor towards the control room. One of the steel tubes containing a detector arm had broken free from its rubber mounting. It swung violently towards the reinforced glass window. Darren came to. They managed to get inside the control room just as a ton of steel smashed against the toughened glass window. Ayala screamed. She ran to help Paul who had lost his balance and fallen with Darren in a heap in the doorway. Just as Ayala knelt down, the detector arm made another swing at the window. In an arch like a huge sledgehammer, it crashed into the window with a merciless blow. The glass shattered into thousands of pieces and scattered over their heads. The arm continued and missed Ayala's head by inches.

'We must get out of the building,' shouted Paul above the din of breaking glass and the constant thudding.

The steel tube was making another swing at the control room. It smashed into a computer monitor that disintegrated with the impact. Pieces of metal and computer equipment were scattered all over the floor. They started to pick their way across the floor that was littered with obstacles. Darren, blood running down his arm, was still faint and Paul and Ayala struggled to keep him moving.

The concrete floor was rippling. They could not stand. They had to crawl to get to the door at the back of the control room. Paul and Ayala dragged Darren through the doorway. Paul went back in to grab the first aid kit. Another swing of the steel tube just missed him as he dived through the open door on to the concrete outside. He landed heavily, bruising his arm. The whole ground was shaking slowly, rhythmically and very violently. Paul looked at Darren's wound. It was serious; he was losing a lot of blood. He told Ayala to apply pressure to the wound. Paul opened the first aid kit and took out a wad of dressing. He held it to the bleeding wound. Ayala, now with her hands free, reached for her mobile phone. There was only a weak signal. She dialled 999; she could not get through. She tried again and again; still the relentless vibration. The phone did not work.

She looked up the fire station tower was swaying. It was going to fall.

'Paul, look up!' she screamed. 'The tower, it's going to fall!'

Paul and Ayala dragged Darren away from the building, just as the tower fell across it. There was a huge bang and a cloud of dust, but still the vibration relentlessly continued.

And then it stopped; Anil had hacked Paul's codes.

****

Jacques phone connection had been cut off before Sky had reached its destructive peak, but he had heard enough to know that things had gone badly. He immediately phoned Dieter, who was away from his desk lecturing. He called Anil, who did not answer his phone. Ok, he thought, this is serious. He called the fire brigade and, just to make sure, the ambulance service.

****

Anil did not know for sure that his program had shut the experiment down, but the signs were good. The tremors had stopped. He headed down the stairs and saw Dieter in the corridor.

'Dieter,' he said. 'Am I pleased to see you!'

'Hello Anil,' replied Dieter. 'Did you feel that vibration? What was it a tremor or a lorry?'

'It was the experiment,' said Anil, and before Dieter could reply, and we'd better get over there quickly!'

Dieter could see the anxiety in Anil's face. He knew something was wrong.

'I have my car outside. Let's go,' said Dieter with urgency. 'You can explain on the way.'

****

Thanks to Jacques the ambulance pulled up in time, before Darren had lost too much blood. One of the crew was treating his arm.

'It looks like your first aid saved his arm,' said the paramedic.

'Well I think he saved our lives,' said Paul, still puzzled why the vibration had stopped so suddenly.

Dieter's car drove through the open gate just as Darren was being treated on a stretcher. Anil and Dieter looked through the windscreen at a scene of utter devastation. There were two fire engines with their blue lights flashing and firemen surveying what looked like a bombsite. The dust still had not settled after the tower had collapsed. Through the rubble and dust Dieter could make out sections of mangled steel reflecting in the evening sunlight. Anil looked across and to his horror saw the ambulance and somebody on a stretcher.

'Oh no!' he exclaimed, in horror. 'I was too late!'

Dieter looked across and saw Paul and Ayala bending over a stretcher.

'It looks like Darren is hurt,' said Dieter.

Anil jumped out of the car and ran over to them. Darren looked up at Anil and smiled.

'How are you?' asked Anil.

'All in a day's work.' said Darren, bravely.

'I did not switch you off in time!' said Anil apologetically.

'God in heaven!' said Dieter, gently to Anil. 'Stop blaming yourself you did the right thing!'

'Ah,' said Paul. 'That explains it.' He paused and looked at Anil, 'So you killed the experiment remotely?'

'Yes,' said Anil.

'Well, if you hadn't, there is no telling how much havoc that stone would have caused,' said Paul gratefully, 'You and Darren saved us.'

'You don't think this is havoc?' said Dieter, incredulously.

'Yes, but the stone was still increasing in ferocity, when we escaped,' said Paul, looking around at the remains of his laboratory, 'I seem to have destroyed the old fire station. Sorry!'

'Well I suppose it was due for demolition anyway,' replied Dieter, tolerantly.

'We haven't lost any of the data have we?' asked Darren, from the stretcher.

Dieter and Paul looked at each other in amazement. Darren had nearly been killed but he was still worried about the success of the experiment. Darren seemed to read their faces.

'I never knew physics could be so exciting,' he said. 'It's been the most fun I've had for years. So I repeat my question: Have we saved the results?'

'Yes we have,' replied Anil, smiling. 'All the data was sent online back to the university and I've backed it up on my machine. We can start analysing it when you're better.'

The crew were loading Darren into the ambulance.

'Can I travel with him to the hospital?' asked Ayala.

'No problem,' said the paramedic who had treated Darren.

The ambulance pulled away.

Anil wandered over to the rubble. He had something on his mind. He found a section of wreckage that looked like the detector arm. He could see the hole still wet around the edge with Darren's blood.

'Paul,' he called. 'We need to get this rock out.'

'Not now, Anil,' said Paul wearily, 'perhaps tomorrow.'

'No, it must be now,' said Anil, contradicting him.

'What's on your mind,' asked Paul, seeing the concern on Anil's face.

'Prama and Claire are in danger,' said Anil, emotionally. 'We must get them out of Tokyo now! The rock is evidence.'

# Ni-jyu-hachi

## Tokyo Troubles

Dieter was aghast. He had seen the devastation around him. He could not understand what that had to do with a conference in Tokyo.

'Anil, you make no sense,' he said. 'What is the problem in Tokyo?'

'I have created a computer model that predicts where the gasers intersect. I have modified it to look into the past. The path of the gaser beams repeats over a long cycle and a short cycle.'

'Ok,' said Dieter. 'What has that got to do with Japan?'

Anil replied, 'The event we have just seen also happened in 1826, except there was no blue stone to trigger the gravity wave absorption.'

'Was there an event somewhere else?' asked Paul, becoming very concerned.

'Yes, the gasers reached their maximum intensity as they passed over the Arctic Circle, past Kamchatka then along the east cost of Japan to the Ryukyu Archipelago,' said Anil.

Paul went pale. He seemed to have worked out the implications.

'We have just experienced a devastating experiment that we were able to abort remotely,' Anil continued. 'Prama and Claire are right under the path of the gasers. The Japanese have a larger more powerful crystal in Tokyo.'

'What?' said Paul, alarmed.

'I believe their rock was responsible for an underwater earthquake that in 1826, created a tsunami that killed over twenty six thousand people.' He paused, 'We must stop the Japanese experiment before there is a bigger more dangerous disaster!'

'More dangerous than here?' asked Dieter, unsure which disaster Anil was talking about.

'No, more dangerous than 1826,' Anil paused again, his emotions almost getting the better of him. 'This time the earthquake will not be centred in the ocean. It will be centred in Tokyo!'

Paul was frozen. A feeling of terror for Claire had gone through the very roots of his being.

'How long have we got?' asked Paul, more calmly than he felt.

'Twenty three hours,' replied Anil.

****

It was four o'clock in the morning when Claire's phone rang in Tokyo.

Still half asleep she answered the phone.

'Hello darling,' she said, sleepily 'I knew you'd call but not in the middle of the night.'

'Claire, we've had an emergency here. I need you to listen to what I say.'

Claire became alert quickly. There was intensity in Paul's voice that worried her.

Paul continued, 'Anil is speaking to Prama as I am speaking to you.'

'Paul, you're getting me worried,' she said, waking up. 'What's happened?'

'Our lab is wrecked, the blue stone absorbed gravity wave energy more effectively than we could have imagined,' he said, developing the story as gently as he could.

'Are you alright, you're not hurt are you?' she asked, with fear in her voice.

'No I'm fine but Darren has hurt his arm,' he said, trying not to panic her.

'So why are you calling now,' Claire asked worried. 'There's something else isn't there?'

'Yes there is,' Paul replied, carefully. 'Anil believes that the Academy's blue stone was responsible for a Japanese tsunami in eighteen twenty-six. He also believes that the eighteen twenty six sequence of gaser intersections will repeat in the next twenty three hours.' He paused, waiting for a reaction.

Claire was now wide-awake. She was absorbing the implications.

'You want me and Prama to come home don't you?' she said, thinking aloud.

'Yes,' said Paul, succinctly. 'I want you to warn Hideo and come home. It's too dangerous there.'

'But Paul, there are twelve million people in this city,' she said in despair. 'We can't leave them to their fate!'

Paul was worried she would say this. He was frightened for her.

'Claire, I love you,' said Paul, with a crack in his voice. 'I can't lose you. Please come home. We'll do all we can to help from here!'

Claire had heard the love in his voice, but she was torn. 'Let me get dressed and get Prama. I'll call you back in fifteen minutes,' she said.

There was a knock at the door. It was Prama. 'She's here now,' said Claire.

'Ok,' said Paul. 'I'll call you in fifteen minutes.'

****

Paul and Anil had called from Dieter's car. It was seven o'clock in the evening as they walked through the door of the university.

'Ok,' said Dieter. 'Let's get Jacques on conference call. We're going to use the fifteen minutes effectively.'

They called Jacques. He was relieved to hear they were safe. Paul, Dieter and Anil then updated him on the situation in Japan. When they had finished the fifteen minutes was up. They called Claire in her hotel room. Prama had joined her. They now had all of them on the conference line. Dieter took charge so that everybody did not talk at once.

'Prama, Claire what are your thoughts?' asked Dieter.

'We want to avert the problem by working in Tokyo,' said Prama. 'It is Saturday morning here, most of the employees of the Academy will be at home over week-end. You need us here to persuade them to abort the experiment.'

'You both agree with this?' asked Dieter.

'Yes,' they said, in unison.

Oh shit, thought Paul and Anil.

Claire continued, 'But if they won't listen to us, we will get the first flight out.'

'Jacques and I will book your flights anyway and have the tickets waiting at Narita,' said Dieter.

'Agreed,' said Jacques.

Paul signalled to Dieter that he wanted to speak. Dieter nodded.

'This is Paul,' he said. 'What time is it in Tokyo now?'

'Four twenty in the morning,' said Prama.

'Do you have Hideo's mobile number?' he asked, doubtfully.

'No,' Prama replied, understanding the point. 'But I know he'll be at his desk in about three hours. He said that he had to catch up with some work. We could speak to him then.'

'Ok, we have three hours to prepare our arguments and get the evidence to Hideo,' said Dieter. 'How much influence does Hideo have?' he added.

'Not as much as we'd like,' said Prama. 'His boss Hitzubishi san is a bit of a megalomaniac and distrustful of any non-Japanese. This may be a problem.'

'I see,' said Dieter, thoughtfully. 'Let me think if there is another way to apply pressure on the Academy.'

He paused realising he had made an accidental pun.

'Perhaps "pressure" is the wrong word,' he continued, 'Jacques, do you know any academics in Tokyo?'

'One or two,' replied Jacques. 'Perhaps I could pull their tails.'

'Good,' said Dieter, then moving on, 'I'd like to make sure we all understand the position. So I'll start with you Anil; can you explain the findings from your software.'

Anil explained his predictions. Dieter asked each of them in turn to add their perspective and suggestions about the next steps. The conclusion was that they would analyse the data from the experiment at the old fire station and put it into a form that Prama and Claire could present to Hideo and Hitzubishi san. If Hitzubishi san had any sense then the disaster would be averted. As a backup, Jacques and Dieter would do all they could to find another way to stop the Japanese experiment.

'Anything else?' asked Dieter.

'Yes,' said Jacques, 'there is something.'

'Go on', said Dieter, prompting him.

'When I was on the phone during the experiment, I heard your voices change. Eventually I lost contact all together. Paul did you notice the same phenomenon.'

'Yes, I did,' said Paul. 'The pitch of your voice seemed to go up.'

'As I thought,' said Jacques, pensively. 'From my perspective, the pitch of your voices went down.'

'Why would that happen?' asked Anil.

'Time dilation,' said Jacques, enigmatically, 'the clocks in the fire station were going more slowly than mine.'

'Did your mobile phones still work?' asked Jacques.

'I don't know,' said Paul, we never tried them. 'Oh yes, we tried to call an ambulance but couldn't get through.'

'I tried to call you several times to warn you to abort,' said Anil. 'I couldn't get through.'

'That was because the mobile phones in the fire station, became tuned differently to the phone network. The gravity waves had changed the rate of time passing. This altered the radio frequencies that the phones normally use,' said Jacques.

'Would that happen in Tokyo if their rock is excited by gravity wave energy?' asked Dieter.

'Yes,' said Jacques.

'So our mobiles won't work and the land lines will sound funny,' remarked Prama.

'That is correct,' said Jacques. 'So let's assume if you are anywhere near the rock when it's vibrating, then you cannot communicate electronically.'

'Oh bugger,' said Paul.

Claire smiled and thought about "her Paul" and his limited vocabulary. She wished he were there with her.

\*\*\*\*

Ayala was sitting next to Darren's bed talking to him when her mobile rang.

'Can I answer it?' she asked the nurse.

'As long as you're quick,' came the reply.

'It's Paul,' said a voice, 'how is he?'

'He's fine,' said Ayala, 'being his normal, irritating self.'

'Well tell him thanks,' said Paul, with a chuckle. 'We have another emergency, so I won't be able to visit him tonight.'

'I'll tell him,' said Ayala. 'Can I help?'

'Probably,' replied Paul, 'but not now. Let's talk tomorrow.'

He wished Darren a get-well-soon and said goodnight. Paul felt guilty that he could not visit his sick hero.

\*\*\*\*

Hitzubishi san may have been a "megalomaniac", but he was no idiot. His apparatus that had a different purpose to Paul's, was well designed and documented. Hideo was at his desk looking over Hitzubishi's technical schematics. Hideo was a seismologist, not an engineer and the design had much that he did not understand. He could not understand why there were three active crystals not one. He was about to turn to the next diagram when the phone rang. It was Prama.

'Hello Prama, what causes you to call me on a Saturday morning?' he asked.

'We have a problem with the crystal,' said Prama. 'We urgently need to see you and Hitzubishi san.'

'I am available any time Prama, but Hitzubishi san is a different matter. He will be away from the academy all weekend.'

Hideo paused, thinking that the documents in front of him were completely incomprehensible. He was getting no where on his own and he needed all the help he could get.

'Why do you not come over now? We can meet in my office.'

'Yes,' said Prama. 'Claire and I will leave straight away.'

A few minutes later Prama and Claire were outside the Academy waiting for Hideo to let them in. As it as Saturday, the main door was locked and the security man was doing his rounds elsewhere in the building. Hideo arrived, unlocked the door and let them in.

'I quite often work on Saturday morning,' he said, locking the door behind them. 'I have a master key that opens most of the doors.'

He escorted them upstairs into his office. The plans of Hitzubishi's device were laid out across Hideo's desk.

'We have had some bad news from the experiment with the blue crystal,' Prama started, seriously.

'What is the problem?' asked Hideo with a worried look on his face. 'I hope my concerns have not come true!'

'I'm afraid they have,' said Prama. 'During the experiment, the laboratory at the old fire station was destroyed.'

'Oh that is terrible!' exclaimed Hideo. 'Was anyone hurt?'

'Yes,' said Claire. 'A PhD student, but he is ok now. They were lucky; they managed to abort the experiment.'

'What happened?' asked Hideo.

'The stone absorbed energy from the gaser and the vibration started earth tremors,' replied Prama. 'The team managed to depressurise the crystal before the earth tremors became violent enough to damage the surrounding suburbs.'

'But their laboratory is not in an earthquake zone. Imagine what would happen if such an event occurred here!' he exclaimed, with a slight note of panic in his voice.

'That's why we came to see you,' said Claire. 'You must persuade Hitzubishi san to abort the project before tomorrow morning. We have all the experimental proof you need.'

Hideo was silent for a moment. The enormity of the potential disaster was sinking in.

'I cannot do it!' he said softly, with fear in his eyes.

'You can't do what?' asked Prama incredulously.

'I cannot persuade Hitzubishi san to abort the project,' he said, desperately.

'Why not?' asked Claire with exasperation in her voice.

'Hitzubishi san is not here. He is on holiday and I do not know where he is. Hitzubishi san has set the experiment to work automatically. The apparatus is prepared and ready to respond to the next gaser beam intersection. All the measurements will be controlled by computer.'

'There must be a way of turning it off!' said Prama. She looked at the papers on his desk.

'There may be,' said Hideo, 'but I don't know how to do it. I do not understand these diagrams. We need an expert. Hitzubishi san works alone. He is the only one who knows what his device does.'

They were silent for a moment. Hideo seemed to have resigned himself to their fate. Claire and Prama were thinking hard. Prama moved to the papers. They were patent documents; in English and Japanese. She scanned a page and realised that it would take her days to understand them.

'Paul,' said Claire suddenly.

'Excuse me?' said Hideo confused by the outburst.

'Paul,' she repeated. 'He will understand the documents. Can we fax them to him?'

'Of course we can,' said Prama with excitement on her face. 'Hideo where is your fax machine?'

'Will he understand,? They are very complex.' he said, Prama's question passing him by.

'If he can't, nobody can,' said Claire, 'besides he's our only hope.'

'We will do it,' said Hideo springing into action.

'Will you give me his number please,' he said, addressing Claire.

Claire gave him the details and keyed Paul's telephone number into her mobile. She explained their plan and what they wanted him to do. Prama and Hideo would remain on-hand, in case there was any information that needed translation. They would be in Hideo's office waiting for Paul's call.

# Ni-jyu-kyu

## Saturday Night Blues

It was one o'clock in the morning in the team room. Jacques had boarded the last train and was expected to join them any minute. Dieter, Anil and Paul were standing next to the fax machine as two hundred pages of technical information came through. Anil took the first one hundred pages and started to make three extra copies. It was going to take all night to understand the Japanese apparatus, so they had decided that each of them would read the entire document. The three of them planned to pool their understanding after the last person had finished. They had asked Claire and Prama to read the documents, so that when they fed back their ideas, the two women would provide a crosscheck. All agreed that Paul was the best qualified to lead the process.

The dawn sunshine was breaking through the window of the team room when Paul wearily put down the documents. The rest of the team followed one by one. Jacques was last, because he had started after everybody else. Paul went to make everybody a drink whilst they were waiting for Jacques to finish. Even Anil asked for a strong black coffee; for once he needed the caffeine. Paul handed Jacques the cup just as he finished the last page.

'I'll get Claire, Prama and Hideo on the phone,' said Paul, keying the number.

When they were all able to hear, Paul started the discussion.

'At the moment, I cannot see how to abort this device without access to Hitzubishi's computer system,' said Paul a little despondently. 'So firstly I'd like to explain how I think it works. Maybe that will give us some ideas.'

The group in the team room nodded in agreement. Prama had become spokesperson for the Japanese team. She confirmed their agreement.

'Hitzubishi's design is very innovative,' Paul started. 'It appears that he has cut the Japanese rock into four equal crystals. Each one is about four times the size of "Sky".'

'I make it four times the diameter,' interrupted Jacques, 'so that is sixty four times the mass.'

'Or sixty four times the energy absorbed?' said Prama over the phone link.

'Yes that's right,' said Paul, frowning. 'So this system is likely to generate two hundred and fifty six times more damage than Sky.'

'Four crystals, each sixty four times more dangerous than Sky,' said Dieter, also frowning.

Hideo was listening intently. He could feel panic starting in his stomach.

Paul continued, 'Hitzubishi san has arranged the crystals in a tetrahedron. Radiation from one excited crystal is transferred to the other two crystals. These will in turn transmit energy to their neighbours. The effect is that the gravity wave energy will be trapped until it reaches a maximum.'

'That is my understanding,' said Jacques.

'He has arranged the geometry of the crystals so that when the maximum is reached the energy is channelled on to the fourth crystal. This is used to convert the energy into electricity.' Paul paused checking to see if he had interpreted it correctly.

Paul went on, 'Like our experiment in the old fire station, he has pressurised the crystals using oil. The main difference is that he is applying four times the pressure.'

'Isn't that the weak point,' said Anil. 'Can't we kill the pressure in the same way that we did on our gravity wave detector.'

'I don't think so,' said Paul. 'Hitzubishi san has designed the device to use gravity wave energy not to measure it. His system has no vacuum and his crystals are sealed tightly inside a pre-pressurised steel chamber. The only way to get at them would be to completely dismantle the whole apparatus. This could take days.' He paused, 'Days that we don't have.'

'Could we extract the whole assembly that holds the crystals,' asked Prama.

'We could, but the assembly would still be under pressure and more dangerous if it was outside the apparatus,' Paul replied, then continuing, 'Hitzubishi san has built an elaborate system of hydraulic dampers to absorb and dissipate vibrations.'

'Yes, I noticed that,' said Jacques. 'It appears the designer knew that there would be violent shaking. It would absorb much of the energy.'

'Maybe Hitzubishi san has a better understanding of the crystals than we do. Perhaps the device is designed to vibrate and not transmit the effects to the environment around it.'

Hideo knew Hitzubishi san. He was aware that Hitzubishi san was ruthless and would ignore safety in the interests of profit. Hideo did not want to take the risk with twelve million lives.

'What if we removed the cylinder and carried it away from the fault line in the tectonic plates?' asked Hideo.

'That would save Tokyo, but it would be suicide for the person who did it,' said Paul, becoming fearful about where the conversation was going. There must be another way, he thought.

The team needed time to think. But time was short.

'I will dismantle the apparatus and take the cylinder to a safe place,' said Hideo, with tears rolling down his cheeks. 'I cannot allow Hitzubishi's stupidity to destroy this city.'

Claire looked at him in despair. They knew they had to help.

'There is another way,' said Paul, realising what would happen if he did nothing. 'Do not take the cylinder. Take the whole apparatus. The dampers and the outside shell will give you some protection.'

'But it's bolted to the concrete on the seventh floor of the building!' said Anil.

'Yes,' said Paul. 'But you can unbolt it and if you strip off all the cables and wires, it will be as difficult, or as easy, to move as a domestic washing machine.'

'This is what I will do,' said Hideo.

There was silence. The whole group realised the enormity of what Hideo was planning to do.

'Hideo, Prama, Claire, keep your mobiles on,' said Dieter. 'We will call you every fifteen minutes to check on progress.'

'Hideo,' said Jacques, 'remember dump the device in a remote place and run like hell!'

'I will,' said Hideo.

'Good luck Hideo,' said Paul, 'Claire, Prama please, please get on that plane.'

'We will,' said Prama. 'But we will help Hideo steal the device first.'

Paul and Anil did not believe her.

****

After they had disconnected from the call, the three of them felt alone and frightened. Hideo opened his desk drawer and took out his keys.

'Let us begin,' he said, as he led the way towards the lab holding the apparatus.

Hideo tried the key to the door. It did not turn. He tried another. It did not turn either.

'This is a special lock,' he said peering through the wire-grilled window. Claire looked at her watch. There were only ten hours left, to get the apparatus out of the city. Claire looked around her. She saw a fire extinguisher.

'Hideo, why don't you use this?' she said.

Hideo looked aghast. He had always been a person who behaved himself. Prama could see what he was thinking.

'Hideo, we're going to steal the equipment,' she said. 'You don't think a broken lock is going to matter when we're arrested!'

Hideo unhooked the fire extinguisher from the wall. He took a wild swing and hit the door. It did not budge. The echo resounded around the empty building. He hit it again and the wood around the lock splintered. He dropped the extinguisher. It landed with a clatter on the floor.

'There it is,' said Hideo. 'The equipment is in the corner.'

It was a magnificent shiny cylinder of steel. There were pipes and wires attached all over it that went off in various directions like the arms of a hydra.

Hideo took a spanner from a toolbox in the corner of the laboratory. He started to undo the bolts holding it to the floor.

'Please start cutting the wires,' said Hideo addressing Prama.

She took a pair of wire cutters and cut the first wire. An alarm sounded on the other side of the room. Quickly she put the two ends of the wire back together and the alarm stopped.

'How are we going to do this without attracting the attention of the security man?' she asked.

'You are right he will stop us,' Hideo replied. 'We leave the wires until last. Claire, can you find out which ones will trigger the alarm. In the meantime you can help me with the bolts.'

Claire phoned Paul and asked him to look at the diagram. He should be able to tell them which wires they could cut. He would phone them back.

'I'll go and look for a trolley,' said Claire. 'We will never be able to carry that machine without one.'

Hideo and Prama struggled unsuccessfully with the bolts for nearly forty-five minutes. In the meantime Claire had arrived with a large trolley that she had found in the post room. As promised, Paul had called every quarter of an hour. He had given them advice about which wires they could cut without setting off the alarm. They had eight hours left, the traffic would be building up outside. According to Hideo, the security man would be doing his rounds in an hour. Then Claire realised that she could hear his steps echoing through the corridor outside. He was doing his rounds early.

'Hideo, the door,' she whispered, urgently. 'If the guard see it's broken, he will raise the alarm. You had better intercept him. I'll try to tidy it up.'

Hideo stopped work and rushed into the corridor. He caught up with the guard just before he turned towards the laboratory door. Hideo started talking to him. Claire had already placed the dented fire extinguisher back on its hook. She pushed the splintered wood back into place as best she could, went inside the lab and pulled the door closed. She placed her index finger vertically to her lips making a "shushing" sign to Prama. They waited for a few minutes until the voices subsided. Prama and Claire were very tense and nearly jumped out of their skins when Hideo walked through the door.

'It is Okay,' said Hideo. 'The guard is gone. How are we doing?'

The equipment has been cut free. Claire's phone rang. It was Paul.

'Hello luv,' he said, 'has Hideo left yet?'

'No,' said Claire, 'we're just about to cut the alarmed wires.'

'You must get out now,' he said with anxiety in his voice.

'We are worried about the alarm. It may bring the security guard back,' said Claire.

'Just do it and go!' Paul snapped, losing his patience, 'He's the least of your worries.' The stress was getting too much for him.

Hideo cut the remaining wires, while Claire called the lift. The alarm went off. Paul was still on the phone. Prama and Hideo manoeuvred the apparatus on to the trolley and they wheeled it rapidly to the waiting lift.

Claire touched the body of the steel chamber in front of her. 'I think it's started vibrating,' she whispered.

Then the lift doors closed and the phone connection to Paul was gone.

****

Paul was sure he heard Claire say that the vibrations had started. That must be wrong. It was too early. He desperately hoped it was wrong. He had been using the conference phone, so he was not the only one who heard it.

'Did anyone hear what Claire said before we got cut off?' Paul asked hoarsely. He was starting to go into a cold sweat.

'She said it was vibrating,' whispered Anil, in despair. 'It's too soon! They'll never make the airport.'

There was stunned silence. They felt helpless. Paul phoned hoping they had got out of the lift. Anil phoned Prama, and Dieter dialled Hideo. None of them could get through.

'What the hell is happening?' said Paul, helplessly.

Paul became pale with anxiety. He had no idea what to do next. 'Think damn you, think,' he whispered to himself.

'Hideo's phone is ringing!' shouted Dieter.

They all waited. It rang. They waited.

'It's Prama,' came a voice. 'Hideo is driving; the equipment is on the back seat. It's shaking the whole car!'

'Where are you?' asked Dieter with a tremor in his voice.

'We're just leaving the city,' said Prama. 'The vibrations are getting worse. Can I talk to Anil please?'

Dieter handed Anil the phone.

'Tell Paul we left Claire at the Academy. She was annoyed but the machine was too big to go in the boot,' she paused. 'I love you Anil.'

He could hear a break in her voice.

'I love you too Prama,' he said. 'Don't leave me.' A tear rolled down his cheek. He could hear a shuddering noise as the vibrations became more violent. The line went dead.

Paul's phone rang. It was Claire. He could hear she was crying.

'They have gone Paul, they've gone.'

'I know,' he said softly. 'Prama has just spoken to Anil.'

'What are their chances?' she asked.

'Not good, I'm afraid. We can't contact them.'

Claire's pent up emotions boiled over.

'I can't do anything. I feel so helpless,' cried Claire.

'You must get outside into the open, away from buildings. They left you so you could live. I love you so much; please be safe,' he said, his eyes filling.

'I love you darling, I'm coming home.'

'Where are you now? He asked.

'I'm on a park bench,' she said. 'Prama was a lovely person wasn't she?'

'Yes she was,' said Paul, with a lump forming in his throat and realising they were talking in the past tense.

He could hear a loud rumble, people shouting.

'It's starting isn't it?' he said.

'Yes,' said Claire calmly, with a vision of Prama in her mind.

'How is Anil?' she asked quietly.

'He's devastated,' said Paul.

'You know she loved him very much don't you?'

'Yes, I know.'

'Does he know?' asked Claire, holding back a sob. There was another huge rumble.

'Yes, he knows.'

'That's good,' she said. 'Prama would not have wanted him to think otherwise. My battery is going flat.'

'Ok you'd better save the power. Stay where you are and you'll be safe.'

'I will,' she said. The connection died.

Paul looked around the room. There was a mixture of grief and bewilderment. He looked across at Anil. There was a forlorn expression frozen on his face. How could he console him? Paul felt guilty that Claire was safe. Paul walked over to Anil. They said nothing. Paul just sat next to him and put an arm round his shoulder. Anil started to sob. The rest of the team were silent; all deep in their private thoughts and memories.

A phone rang. Nobody wanted to answer it. The whole team was bereft of hope. Jacques moved slowly across to pick up the handset.

'Allo,' he said. He listened for a moment. He looked worried. Then he started to smile. He became animated. His smile turned into a grin! The team watched him transfixed. 'Quoi?' he listened. 'He dumped you in the countryside!' he shouted. 'You damn crazy woman. Don't you ever do that to me again!'

He looked at Anil, 'It's for you I think,' he said gently, passing him the receiver.

# Matter of Perspective

## David C. Fletcher

What happened to Hideo? What was Hitzubishi san trying to achieve? Jacques realises that the objective of the Tokyo experiment was quite different from Paul's. He decides to apply his mind to this Japanese enigma. As he digs he uncovers a fascinating story about a clandestine search for uses of Paul's theory, far beyond the esoteric detection of gravity waves. At least one of these could be of great value to mankind, so why are they kept secret?

Jacques does not know that the seeds of the Tokyo Project were germinating in the East long before Jacques was born. They were planted by a group of Korean monks and nurtured by an ancient Japanese sect. When he tries to publish his ideas, Jacques comes up against some powerful commercial interests. What is their problem? Why are his and his family's lives in danger?

A Wise Grey Owl Publication

www.ingramcontent.com/pod-product-compliance
Ingram Content Group UK Ltd.
Pitfield, Milton Keynes, MK11 3LW, UK
UKHW021317180426
11947UKWH00015B/1292